PRAISE FOR

THE NOVELS OF JASON F. WRIGHT

"Plenty of uplift and tradition-affirming sentiment."
—*PUBLISHERS WEEKLY*

"Beautifully written. I believe the *Christmas Jars*
tradition will change lives."
—RICHARD PAUL EVANS, #1 *New York Times* bestselling
author of *The Christmas Box* and *The Christmas List*

"Just like *It's a Wonderful Life, Christmas Jars*
is American storytelling at its best. Jason Wright has
written the next Christmas classic."
—GLENN BECK, talk radio host,
#1 *New York Times* bestselling author

"Sharp prose, clever characterizations,
thought-provoking insights . . . fresh and spiritual."
—DON PIPER, *New York Times* bestselling author of
90 Minutes in Heaven and *Heaven Is Real*

"In the tradition of Catherine Ryan Hyde's
Pay It Forward, Wright's holiday novel could inspire
others to Christmas generosity."
—*LIBRARY JOURNAL*

The
Wedding
Letters

The

Wedding
Letters

A Novel by

JASON F. WRIGHT

SHADOW
MOUNTAIN

Visit us at ShadowMountain.com

Library of Congress Cataloging-in-Publication Data
Wright, Jason F. author.
   The wedding letters / Jason F. Wright.
       pages cm
   Sequel to: The Wednesday letters.
   Summary: Noah is preparing to marry Rachel. However, when a dark secret from Rachel's past surfaces, Noah and his parents, Malcolm and Rain, must find a way to heal Rachel's heart as well as save the wedding. Perhaps a scrapbook of wedding letters filled with good wishes and marriage advice will hold the key the couple needs to find love and happiness.
   ISBN 978-1-60908-057-0 (hardbound : alk. paper)
   1. Family secrets—Fiction.   2. Betrothal—Fiction.   3. Domestic fiction.
I. Title.
   PS3623.R539W43 2011
   813'.6—dc22   2011009992

Printed in the United States of America
Publishers Printing, Salt Lake City, UT

10   9   8   7   6   5   4   3   2   1

For Kodi
Thanks for saying yes

Acknowledgments

Dear Reader,

It's been four years since the first hardcover printing of *The Wednesday Letters.* Little did I know how the book would change my life forever. Not only did it become my first *New York Times* and *USA Today* bestseller, it inspired thousands of you to send me your own Wednesday Letters and share your personal, inspirational stories of how a single letter altered the course of your life.

I'm humbled by how many of you have reconnected with the long lost art of the handwritten letter!

Are you ready for more? In *The Wedding Letters,* I will introduce you to a new tradition. It is the simple concept of gathering letters full of encouragement, advice, and personal anecdotes relating to marriage and relationships. Those letters from friends and family are compiled into a book or binder and presented to someone you love at their wedding. Who wouldn't cherish such a collection of letters forever?

This novel would not have been possible without the support of Sheri Dew, Chris Schoebinger, Heidi Taylor, Lisa Mangum, and many others at Shadow Mountain. Thanks, also, to the loyal readers who slogged through early drafts. They are, in order of ice cream preference: Cherie Call Anderson, Matt Birch, Laurie Paisley, Angie Godfrey, and Michael Armstrong. Kudos to my Editor-for-a-Day contest winner, Shelbie Ross. Her input on the very first draft was invaluable.

Jeff Wright, older brother extraordinaire, gets his own paragraph for finding errors and holes every other eyeball missed.

Finally, thanks to my number-one fan club for keeping me grounded in mac and cheese, french fries between the seats, gummy bears, and teen angst: Kodi, Oakli, Jadi, Kason, Koleson, Pilgrim, and Surf.

Sincerely,

Jason

PS: I can't wait to hear about your own Wedding Letters project for that special someone. Visit www.jasonfwright.com or find me on Facebook at www.facebook.com/jfwbooks.

Or, write me the old-fashioned way:
PO BOX 669
Woodstock, VA 22664

CHAPTER 1

April 14, 2011

Killing him was unavoidable.

Noah saw the fat squirrel plop off the curb and lumber like a sumo wrestler across Ox Road. The animal reached the center line before doubling back into the path of Noah's gold 2006 Dodge Dakota.

"Dude!" Noah shouted above the thuds and clunks. He yanked the wheel to the right much harder than he intended. First he thumped the squirrel, then he hopped the crumbling low curb, before finally hitting a woman riding a bright green mountain bike.

He was pale and mumbling a few of his mother's replacement swear words as he jumped out of the truck. "Are you OK?"

The woman, lying some five feet from the front right corner of the truck, rolled onto her back, one foot stuck between the bike's rear tire and the chain. Her hand went to a bleeding raspberry on her left cheek. One temple of a cracked pair of Oakley sunglasses poked out from under her bike helmet.

"Are you all right? I am so sorry. I totally did *not* see you." He pulled his cell phone from his pocket and dialed 911.

The woman unhooked her helmet below her chin and tossed it to the side. "Oh, really?" she said. She struggled to remove her backpack from both shoulders.

Noah reported the accident and he thought he heard the 911 operator say she'd stay on the line until help arrived, but he hung up anyway. "Totally didn't see you." Noah dropped to one knee. "Is anything broken?"

She tried to sit up but couldn't free her foot. "You mean besides my bike?"

"Let me," Noah said. "Hold on." He pushed the chain the rest of the way off its sprocket and tried to pull her foot forward.

"That hurts, no! That hurts! *What is wrong with you?*"

"What hurts?"

"Does it matter, you idiot? The foot, the ankle—it *all* hurts." She put one hand on her forehead and the other back on the raspberry on her cheek.

"You might be in shock. Just stay down." Noah jumped up and moved to the other side of the bike's bent frame. He lifted and twisted it a few degrees until the woman could remove her foot without contact.

She sat up, braced herself with her palms flat on the sidewalk, and looked up at the sky. "Really God? Today? Really?"

Noah sat near her. "Take a deep breath. I feel so terrible. My gosh. Really terrible. The ambulance should be here soon." He stuck his hand out. "I'm sorry, I'm Noah Cooper. I didn't get your name."

"When exactly would you have gotten my name? Before or after running me down?" She rubbed her hands together, dislodging tiny pebbles, before shaking his hand. "Rachel." She held his hand firmly an extra beat before adding, "And you nearly killed me."

"Yeah, sorry, I realize that." He pointed to the lump of sumo squirrel in the road. "I was avoiding him."

"You didn't."

"Yeah, I realize that, too."

Rachel stretched her neck to the left and right, and they sat quietly until Rachel began removing her shoe.

"Can I help?"

Rachel's eyes said, *Haven't you helped enough?*

"I'll just move the truck. Be right back." Noah heard Rachel mutter something that was definitely not one of his mother's replacement swear words. He hopped in the truck, put it in reverse, rolled off the sidewalk, and backed into a parking space. An ambulance and a Fairfax County police cruiser arrived on scene just as Noah returned.

While the EMTs treated Rachel, an officer named Kusel

stood next to Noah, asking questions and filling out an accident report.

"Just look at it," Noah said, leading Kusel to the squirrel. "It's the fattest thing I've ever seen."

Kusel smiled, made a note on his report, and quipped, "You obviously haven't met my ex-wife."

The two men laughed and Noah glanced at Rachel, who was watching them as she was being strapped onto a backboard. Her look could have killed a thousand fat squirrels.

"No, we're not—" He gestured at the roadkill. "Oh, forget it."

Kusel continued scribbling his report, followed that with a quick ticket for Noah, and said he'd be trailing the ambulance to the hospital to finish his paperwork.

"Can I come too? I want to be sure she's going to be all right."

They both looked at the ambulance. With the rear door open, they could see three EMTs hovering over Rachel. One knelt at her feet, fastening a black brace to her ankle, another appeared to be checking her pulse, and the last made notes on a clipboard.

"You'll take care of the bike?" Kusel asked.

"Sure."

"Fine. Toss it in the truck and hop in with me."

The two followed the ambulance along the edge of the George Mason University campus, then on to the parkway toward Inova Fairfax Hospital. Noah explained that he'd been heading to an exam study group. He quickly sent a text to a friend with the news he'd be late.

"What are you studying?"

"I'm graduating, hopefully in a couple weeks, with a BFA."

"Fine arts?" Kusel asked.

"Yeah," Noah said, impressed.

Officer Kusel noticed. "Not all cops are idiots," he said. "No matter what the ex says."

The small talk continued. Noah explained he was from Woodstock, Virginia, about ninety miles to the west. "Ever been out on 66? Just keep going until you hit 81, then go south fifteen or twenty miles. There's Woodstock."

Kusel cocked his head. "The same one where—"

"No, not *that* Woodstock," Noah stopped him. "Not the one where people got hammered and mud-wrestled in their underwear."

"Too bad," Kusel chuckled. Moments later, he pulled up behind the ambulance parked under the Emergency Room canopy and turned off the cruiser. "Here we go."

They followed Rachel on her rolling stretcher through the ER's automatic doors and into a treatment bay. They stood aside as she was carefully transferred to a hospital gurney. Then an EMT gathered a signature, handed over a report, dropped Rachel's backpack in a chair, and disappeared.

"Everything looks fine," a nurse said to Rachel, scanning

the report. "Nothing urgent. A doctor will be right here, OK, sweetie?"

Rachel cringed.

For five minutes Noah stood just outside the curtain and listened as Officer Kusel took Rachel's colorful statement. When he finished, he said good-bye with a greasy wink, slapped Noah on the back as he passed, and strode toward the nurses' station.

Noah stepped in, closed the curtain behind him, and approached Rachel's bedside. "You hanging in there?"

"You're still here? I thought you'd be arrested by now."

"Ha-ha. Of course I'm still here."

"You really don't need to be."

"Yes, I'm pretty sure I do. Are you in pain?"

She shook her head and relaxed. "No, they gave me something on the ride over."

"What else can I do? I am *really* sorry about all this."

She contemplated. "Can you go to a meeting back on campus for me?"

"Sure," Noah answered with utter confidence. "Anything. Name it. I'm your guy."

"Great, hand me my backpack, Superman."

He did and she rifled through it, producing a folder bulging with notes. She held it out to him. "Can you defend my master's thesis?"

Noah didn't know whether to run, cry, or run away crying. "You're kidding."

"No, I'm afraid I'm not."

He sat in a chair near the bed. "I am so sorry. So totally and completely sorry."

Rachel shoved the folder back in her bag and held it out for him. He took it and set it on the floor.

"Don't worry. It's covered," she said. "I texted my advisor from the ambulance. Turns out there are not many things that get you this kind of reprieve, but being run over by a truck is one of them." She half-smiled at him, and for the first time since the accident, Noah exhaled fully and took a deep, calming breath.

Noah reeled her into playing get-to-know-you while they waited over a half hour for a doctor.

Noah told her how thrilled he was to be graduating with an art degree and about his dream of publishing children's books. "I'm the next David Wiesner."

Rachel gave him her last name. "It's Kaplan." She also mentioned her graduate degree, an MA in sociology, and her master's thesis: "Private Sector Cures to Inner-City Violence in Washington, DC."

"Does me hitting you with my truck count as inner-city violence?"

Rachel laughed, even though she really didn't want to. It wasn't much, Noah thought, but it was definitely a laugh. He nearly lost himself in the realization that her eyes were as bright and big and beautiful as he'd ever seen.

Eventually a doctor came. He checked the bruise on Rachel's cheek, applied a fresh bandage, and manipulated Rachel's ankle in every possible direction before ordering X-rays.

An hour later, the same doctor told Rachel she had a high ankle sprain, but no break. He wrapped it, advised her to apply ice and to stay off it for a few days. He gave her an extra bandage, crutches, a prescription for an anti-inflammatory drug, and sent her home.

Noah helped Rachel into a cab and surprised her by getting in the other side.

"Are you kidding me? We're sharing cabs now?"

"I've got your bike in my truck. You want it back, don't you?"

"You're insufferable!" She laughed, but was already thinking: *More like irresistible.*

They took the cab back to his truck near the GMU campus. Noah drove them to a CVS pharmacy, insisted on paying for the prescription and re-freezable ice pack, and then followed Rachel's directions to an apartment complex a few miles away.

He helped her up a flight of stairs to her front door and held it open as she hobbled inside. Without turning around or stopping her momentum, she said, "Yes, you can come in."

Noah put the ice pack in the freezer and filled a small bag of ice to use in the meantime. He also slid the coffee table close enough for her foot, and, without being asked, searched for and found a pillow to go underneath it. Though she begged him not to, he scavenged through her refrigerator and found Chinese food. "How old?" he asked.

"Three months," she called back into the kitchen.

"Ha."

"It's from last night." Again without her blessing, he warmed the food in the microwave and the two shared what was left of orange chicken and noodles.

Noah asked about roommates and learned Rachel hadn't had one since finishing her undergrad. He didn't comment, but it was clear to Noah from the unusually nice college apartment and its furnishings that Rachel didn't need a roommate to make her monthly rent.

Rachel asked about his roommates, and Noah said that with their divergent schedules he hardly knew them. "They put a check on the corkboard every month, that's about it."

Noah asked about Rachel's family.

She said very little.

Rachel asked about his, and Noah talked for ten minutes.

An hour after arriving, he left with a pledge to get the bike fixed and return it ASAP.

A week later, after twenty-two text messages from him and ten increasingly friendly messages back, Noah returned with a good-as-new bike, a pair of Oakley sunglasses, and something he'd visited six toy stores to find: a fat, plush, stuffed squirrel.

CHAPTER 2

D omus Jefferson was quiet.

There were times when Malcolm and Rain loved the silence. They often looked forward to the weekends with no guests, no late night crises, no 3:00 A.M. ding-dongs at the doorbell. On those nights they'd lie in bed and bathe in the spirit of the Inn and in the spirit and history of Thomas Jefferson, whose image and interests lined the walls and crammed the bookshelves.

Rain and Malcolm had built an entire marriage at the Inn. It wasn't just a bed-and-breakfast; it was a home. It was the only home they'd shared as a married couple.

Recently, however, what had settled in the air at the Inn just south of Woodstock, Virginia, was a sadder sort of quiet. It was the quiet only doubt knows, the quiet that portends uncertain change.

Since the bailouts, failures, presidential election, and economic collapse of 2008, business had been slower than ever.

Malcolm had been a part of *Domus Jefferson* since his parents had bought it in 1968. He had been thirteen years old then and had seen wild swings in business and occupancy rates through the years. He often reminded Rain that the ups and downs were part of the life of owning and running an inn.

They knew that every inn from Virginia to Vancouver had months when the proprietors wonder if it is really worth it anymore. But then a couple on their honeymoon, or a dying man on his last adventure before leaving the world, or a mother and daughter reconnecting after far too long, find their way to one of the many B&Bs still standing and make all of those slow patches worth it.

Domus Jefferson, situated so perfectly at the feet of the famed Skyline Drive, Luray Caverns, and all the history of the Shenandoah Valley, had sustained and outlasted, even thrived, through many economic droughts. But this one, they feared, they could not survive.

They thanked God daily that they had a security blanket: a series of inherited investments Malcolm's older brother, Matthew, had managed since their parents' deaths. It wouldn't make anyone wealthy, but it was enough to patch the occasional holes in the profit-and-loss statement. Malcolm and Matthew had not always been best-of-friend-brothers, but when it came to money, Malcolm trusted him with every last penny.

On just another of many quiet mornings, Rain made herself

comfortable in her favorite place on earth, a small garden on the south side of the Inn. A fence that few animals respected marked the twenty-by-forty-foot plot. Every time a deer or rabbit enjoyed breakfast at Rain's expense, Malcolm suggested an electric fence, but she only pretended to consider it.

Rain worked in the garden until her fingers were sore. During one of the dips in business, Rain decided the Inn could set itself apart in some small way from their competition by offering natural, locally grown foods every morning at the breakfast table. The small garden hadn't attracted much new business, but it had turned into something even more important for Rain. It was her very own temple, a spot of complete peace, a place to feel God's love and to be reminded she—and the Inn—were never alone.

If Malcolm needed her and she couldn't be found inside, there was only one other place he ever checked.

Malcolm watched her from the kitchen window. He thought it ironic he couldn't tell from where he stood whether she was weeding or praying. He sipped his orange juice and smiled at the sight.

This moment and this view, he thought. *This is what I'll miss most about* Domus Jefferson.

The two would only admit to one another that it wasn't just about the economy. Their passion for the Inn seemed to be dipping with the markets. They wondered if it was worth the stress, worth the routine of checking people in and out for twenty years. The mixture of it all had them thinking a change might be due.

Rain and their only child, Noah, frequently nudged Malcolm about the novel that everyone knew wasn't going to publish itself. Malcolm's book, set primarily in Brazil, was two decades in the making. The story advanced a chapter or two now and then, a few hundred words here, a few hundred more there, but the story he wanted to tell was still much longer than the actual manuscript.

Rain enjoyed poking him in a loving tease, "Your hundred-and-fifty-page manuscript is the longest short story in the history of literature."

Ever since Noah was a child, he'd told his parents that his dream was to take over the bed-and-breakfast. He would tell the guests as they left that they should come back someday, because when *he* was in charge, he would do things better. "Not just different," he said, "but better."

Through the years Noah had coached his parents in the art of customer service, and they took it in good-natured stride. Most of the guests enjoyed the precocious boy and rewarded him with pats on the back, firm handshakes, the occasional tip, and even a gift or two that return visitors had hauled across the country. A handful of couples had become so close to Noah that they sent Christmas and birthday cards even many years after their most recent visit.

Noah had been twelve and in the sixth grade at Peter Muhlenberg Middle School when he realized that running the Inn was no longer his dream. As is the case with many young men and young women, something happens during their teenaged years. Just as they start noticing cute boys and attractive girls, they realize how much smarter they are than their teachers, parents, and pastors, and they begin to yearn for more. They discover a desire to see the rest of the world. Many return to their homes, to familiar streets, churches, and the small-town shops that took their money and made their memories as children.

But many do not.

Noah was noncommittal on whether the Shenandoah Valley would be home again after college, but he was certain his professional future held more than just running the Inn. His constant doodling during school had uncovered an undeniable talent. There was nothing he couldn't draw, and his imagination played out impressively on whatever canvas he chose. His drawings and paintings through the years found their way into antique-looking frames, and not a single room at the Inn was decorated without at least one piece of Noah's art.

A&P Prestwich appeared in the distance through the kitchen window and Malcolm smiled. She was walking Putin, her newest cat, on the same leash she'd walked Castro, the first cat she'd adopted. There had been many world leader cats in between. As was her custom, A&P took her sweet, slow time, making her path toward Rain and the garden.

Twenty years after the funeral of Malcolm's parents, Jack and Laurel Cooper, A&P continued to live in a fabulous Southern mansion on an adjacent lot with several unused guesthouses. She'd discovered the valley, and the property, not long after her husband was killed in 1984 in a plane crash near their home in the Florida Everglades.

Not much had changed since her first stay at *Domus Jefferson.* She had continued being extraordinarily kind to Jack's brother, Joe, until his death at a nursing home in Strasburg. She even insisted on paying for his funeral and burial at the same cemetery that held Laurel and Jack.

A&P also continued leaving ridiculously generous tips every time she visited the Inn or any of the local restaurants around town. It was her way of spreading her husband's wealth, and she'd committed to leave nothing behind when she met him again in heaven. Of course she was now well aware that her tips at the Inn went to a number of charities of interest to the Coopers. Some were in the valley, some as far away as Washington, DC. But the game pleased her, and her happiness pleased Malcolm and Rain even more.

A&P also knew about and had finally embraced the fact that a small children's shelter in the city bore the name of her and her husband. She'd only been there in person once, but she knew she'd never forget sitting in her car in front of a building her husband's wealth had built and knowing that, save for an early exit from life, he would have done the same thing himself. The tears and longing for the only man she'd ever loved made it difficult to return.

Malcolm took a seat at the kitchen table. He finished his juice and looked at his watch: 8:30 A.M. He looked at the seven empty chairs pushed in carefully around the table and the seven place settings besides his. He admired the place mats Rain had purchased at a craft fair in Petersburg, West Virginia. She had purchased dozens of matching place mats and napkins through the years, forever concerned a guest might return to the Inn to the same place setting they'd used on their last visit.

Malcolm couldn't remember the last time every seat at the table had been filled at 8:15 in the morning. There had been many mornings in the Inn's history, both when his parents ran it and after he and Rain took over, that not only had every seat been filled, but someone would be lingering in the kitchen or in the doorway. Another couple might have been reading the paper in the oversized chairs in the living room, patiently waiting for seats to open up.

Those were memorable mornings. They came after nights when every room was full and when some last-minute, tired travelers had to be turned away with directions to another nearby inn or highway hotel. It had been quite some time since Malcolm had watched Rain scurry about in the morning, hair and flour flying as she readied breakfast for as many as sixteen people.

I will miss this, Malcolm thought.

But as the words passed from one side of his mind to the other, he realized he didn't know exactly what he'd miss. Was it the quiet moments, the guests, the land around them, the fulfillment of knowing that the Inn was full of good people passing through for good reasons? Was it the thank-you notes? Was it the romantic notion that guests were allowed to take a pocketful of the Inn's magic with them, leaving plenty behind for the next guests to absorb and enjoy?

I will miss it all, he thought.

CHAPTER 3

"How long has it been since we slept until 8:30?"

"Too long," Shawn said. "But enjoy it while it lasts, because a grandchild isn't going to let you sleep in past 6:00, never mind 8:30."

Samantha knew he was right, but didn't mind a sleepless wink. Her daughter, Angela, was a mother for the first time at age thirty-five and was headed for an extended stay in Woodstock. Samantha had wanted nothing more than to be there when Angela's baby had arrived in a small, suburban hospital in Florissant, Missouri. But there were simply too few officers and too many man-hours to fill in the county sheriff's office for her to escape to Missouri for the big day. With her grandbaby just two weeks old and cleared to fly, Samantha convinced herself it was nearly as good as having been there herself for the delivery.

Samantha rolled toward Shawn and pulled the covers up to her chin. "Why do I feel like I'm not really a grandma?"

"Because you slept on the warm side of the pillow?"

Samantha pulled a hand from under the comforter and gave him a thumbs-down. "It just doesn't feel real yet," she said. "Seeing Ang get married took enough adjustment. But now my baby has a baby? It's hard to digest. Suddenly I'm so, so *old*."

Shawn put his hands under his head and looked up at the ceiling. "No comment on being old. But there's no escaping that you, my dear, are indeed a grandmother. And in a few hours when Angela makes her way through that front door with her baby, you'll be no more grandmother than you were two weeks ago when she was born. And, if I might add, you'll be the cutest grandma sheriff in the state."

"You're just saying that because there's a gun on the night-stand."

"True."

Samantha admired a wedding picture of Angela and her new husband on the nightstand. "I wish Jake could be here, too. Sort of a bummer."

"Bummer indeed."

Samantha offered a few words in a silent, thankful prayer that after what felt like two dozen close calls, her daughter had finally found a man who treated her as if she wore a crown. As much as she wished Jake were coming for the visit, she knew his job in St. Louis kept food on the table and she also knew that there had been weekly rumors of layoffs. Samantha was grateful that Jake was the first man who'd told Angela if she wanted to stay home and raise children, he'd move heaven and earth—and pallets in a warehouse—to make it happen. And so far he had.

Shawn noticed Samantha lost in the photo. He, too, gazed into the memory, and his eyes settled on the thick book Angela held in her hands in the photograph.

"I wonder if she's read all the letters yet," Samantha said.

"How long have they been married? A year and a half now?"

"Uh-huh," Samantha said.

"Probably so then. Probably so."

The long, smooth quiet that came next was broken by Samantha's loud yawn. "I wish I didn't have court today."

"Me too," Shawn said and kissed her on the end of the nose.

"I could play hooky," Samantha said.

"I don't think they call it that when you're in charge. Shoot, you could probably skip work all week—isn't that one of the perks of being the sheriff?"

Another smile. "I think *you're* one of the perks of being the sheriff." Another yawn. She made a gun with her thumb and index finger. He did the same and they touched gun barrels, the tips of their fingers in the space between their two pillows in their king-size bed.

"I'd take a bullet for you," Samantha whispered.

Shawn whispered the same.

The two had met on September 12, 2001. Shawn was working in the Pentagon when American Airlines Flight 77 crashed into the west block of the building. Shawn was nowhere near the impact zone, had never been in any danger that day, but he had struggled with the memories.

Shawn was a contractor for a defense corporation based in an office in North Carolina. He was staying in a hotel near the Pentagon the week of 9/11. After the attack, he wandered the area in shock, feeling guilt that he hadn't been in the right place at the right time to do anything for anyone but himself.

He spent the evening of 9/11 at a hotel in Arlington, glued to the news coverage like millions of other people around the world. The next morning he got as close as he could to the crash site, which wasn't close at all. Later in the day he checked out of his hotel and began the trek back to North Carolina. He drove west and then picked up 81 South. He listened to nonstop coverage on WTOP radio until the static and scratches overtook the weary announcers.

When he reached Shenandoah County, he was emotionally and physically drained. He was desperate to crawl into bed—any bed—and turn off his anxiety and let the night drape his concerns about what the world would look like in the days and weeks ahead.

He exited in Woodstock and asked at a Handy Mart about local lodging. The two hotels near the freeway were booked but the young woman behind the counter gave him directions to *Domus Jefferson*. "Don't know if they've got room, but it's peaceful there."

Shawn could tell she'd been crying.

He said good-bye, easily found his way to the Inn on Route 11 between Woodstock and Edinburg, and was relieved to find they had a room for him. He set his things down and fell on the bed. Tired of being in the car and tired of being alone, he returned downstairs to the living room and introduced himself to two women, Samantha and Rain, and a young man, Noah. The three Coopers invited Shawn to join them in a game of Uno. "We needed a break from the news," Rain said as she dealt the cards.

Rain played until retiring for the evening.

Noah wandered off an hour later to the same guesthouse behind the Inn where Samantha and Malcolm had grown up.

Samantha and Shawn played until 2:00 A.M.

Later that morning, Shawn checked out, drove home to North Carolina, and thought about Samantha with every passing mile.

He returned one week later.

They married the next spring.

The couple settled into life in Woodstock and into a new home they purchased on Eagle Street. Samantha was on her second marriage; Shawn was on his first. A few years later, Samantha was elected in a tight race against Sheriff Carter. Shawn worked from home as a consultant for a new defense contractor. Twice a month he spent the day in meetings at a corporate office in Herndon.

Simple life. Simple town. Simply ideal.

CHAPTER 4

May 7, 2011

"You know I really don't have time for this, right?" Rachel pulled her long, dark chocolate brown hair behind her and tied it into a loose knot behind her head.

Noah had kidnapped Rachel Kaplan for a day-trip to the valley less than a month after sending her flying across the sidewalk in the opposite direction from the university and her appointment to defend her thesis.

"Rachel, if we wait for you to have time to meet my family, you'll be meeting them at a funeral. *Their* funeral."

"Ha," she mocked.

"Not two *ha's*?"

"Be lucky you got one."

"I'll take it." Noah merged into traffic onto 66 West. "Look, you know I've been talking a lot about you to my parents. So before they send me to a shrink for having an imaginary girlfriend,

I thought it would be nice if they actually laid eyes on the real thing."

Rachel groaned. "Please tell me you didn't actually use the word *girlfriend*."

"Is that a question?"

"Yes, that was a question—did the rise of my voice at the end not give it away?"

"Just checking. And no, not exactly, I don't think I used the word *girlfriend*. I'm pretty sure I said we were seeing each other. Yes, that's what I told them. That we're seeing each other. That's cool, right?"

Rachel grinned. "Yes. You know I just hate the word *girlfriend*. Always have. Don't really know why, it just creeps me out."

"I know, I know. Just humor me for the day, OK? Make me look cool to my folks?"

"I suppose," Rachel answered. She leaned her arm on the fat cloth armrest between them and took his hand. "It won't be easy, but I'll try."

Noah squeezed her hand back and drove them westward. "Honestly, Rach, I think this will do us good. Don't think of it as meeting my family, think of it as a mental health day for us both. My finals are over, and you're still waiting for a phone call, right?"

Rachel crossed her fingers. "I hope so. It's time to put all those *Rachel Kaplan* business cards to use."

"It'll happen," said Noah. "Come on, if the honchos at the Department of Justice don't hire you, they're insane. Plus, you can count today as an educational adventure. You wouldn't believe how many people think there's nothing west of northern Virginia."

"You mean we won't fall off the face of the earth once we clear the beltway?"

Noah set the cruise control on his truck as they passed under the Haymarket exit and traffic thinned. He'd shared with Rachel more than once the details of his deep love of the valley, and as the miles rolled by, Rachel saw Noah's face relax and a smile begin to grow.

As they drove in quiet, Rachel noticed the exits appearing farther apart. She enjoyed watching the trees become taller and the groves denser. She smiled that even the hills were taller and more distinctive. And everything, *everything*, was green. She'd always appreciated the color of the East Coast, but as they put more and more distance between themselves and the city, she felt as if they were driving into a jungle.

"Don't you just love it?" Noah said, looking out his window.

Rachel rested her left hand on his headrest and drew circles in the back of his thick hair.

Noah enjoyed the city. He loved the Washington Nationals,

despite their horrid record. He loved walking around Georgetown and eating in Adams Morgan. But there was something about the Shenandoah Valley, something about the air, the soil. There was a peace that rose from the earth through his feet and took over his soul every single time he returned home.

Rachel looked concerned when Noah took the Strasburg exit for Route 11. "This isn't right, is it?"

"No, it's the long way. But it gets us there just the same."

They drove south through downtown Strasburg and Noah eagerly pointed out landmarks.

Rachel couldn't decide what was more interesting, the scenery or Noah's reaction to being home.

They continued south and Noah gave a history of the Old Valley Pike road. They rolled through the tiny towns of Toms Brook and Maurertown. When they hit the northern end of Woodstock, Noah pulled into a shopping center parking lot. "See that? That was a Ben Franklin department store until just last year. My mother's favorite place to buy little things for the Inn. Not many of the old five-and-dimes left."

"You sound like an old crusty retiree," Rachel teased.

"Ha-ha," Noah answered with punched sarcasm.

"Just two?"

"Yes, and just for that, we're going to the Woodstock Tower first."

"Excuse me?"

Noah pulled out of the parking lot and turned toward the eastern mountain and the winding road that would lead them into the George Washington National Forest and, ultimately, to the tower the Cooper family knew very well.

They walked the path from the gravel-covered parking pull-out on the narrow road to the metal tower.

"You're going up there?" Rachel asked.

"Correction. *We.*"

With modest coaxing, Rachel followed Noah up the three flights of grated stairs and onto the platform that sat atop the mountain.

"Gorgeous," she said simply, admiring the stunning vistas on both sides.

Noah shared some of his favorite memories from the tower and pointed out the more interesting landmarks across the horizon. "I come up here sometimes to draw or paint. There's not a better place in the valley for that, there really isn't."

Rachel was energized by Noah's sincerity.

"It's such a quiet place to just reflect on life, to figure things out. I love being able to see valleys on both sides. There aren't many places where you can look forward and backward with such clarity."

Rachel took a picture of each valley with her phone.

"But even with this majestic view," Noah said, pulling her into his arms. "There's still nothing more beautiful than you."

"Wow. I am *not* the first girl you've brought here, am I, Noah Cooper?"

"Have I mentioned how beautiful you are?"

They hiked down to the truck and took the windy, switch-back road to Route 11. Noah pointed out Dellinger's Funeral Home and complimented them on how sensitively they'd handled his best friend's passing in high school. He called out other area staples: the movie theater and the next-door office of a reclusive, oddball novelist, the county courthouse, which was the oldest continuously operating courthouse west of the Blue Ridge Mountains, and Lawyer's Row, where Nathan Crescimanno, Rain's only serious boyfriend before Malcolm, had had an office before the controversy around Noah's grandparents' death landed Nathan on probation and out of the valley.

"Coming up on your left, you'll see the Chamber of Commerce office where a young Noah Cooper interned one summer for the perky, attractive executive director."

"Oh, *really?* Is she still attractive?"

"Not at all. Perky? Yes. Attractive? No, why would you say that? No, definitely not, not in the least. She's ghastly, in fact!"

"Uh-huh."

They moved on and Noah dropped nostalgia about the historic Walton and Smoot Drugstore, Woodstock Café, and Joe's Steakhouse. He spoke fondly of his dear family friend, Mrs. Lewia, who was still running the town museum with an iron fist and working to preserve the history and reputation of the town and the valley. He pointed at the Massanutten Military Academy and then a Cooper family favorite, Katie's Custard. Each spot got a point and a nugget of information Noah found fascinating. Even if Rachel didn't always agree, she played along just as he hoped she would.

They pulled into the long driveway at *Domus Jefferson* a few minutes before 11:00 A.M. Rachel popped the sun visor back into place and gazed up the hill toward the Inn. "Wow. Gorgeous," she said.

"Yes," Noah said, looking first at the Inn then pivoting toward her. "Gorgeous."

CHAPTER 5

There he is!" Rain had her arms open before Noah had shut the truck door behind him.

Noah scampered around the Dodge to open the door for Rachel, but she was already stepping out by the time he got to her.

"Come here," Rain said, stepping off *Domus Jefferson*'s wide porch steps and onto the gravel driveway. She hugged him, kissed his cheek, then hugged him again.

"Come on, Mom, it hasn't been *that* long."

"Long enough," she said. "Long enough." Then she hugged him again for good measure. When she finally let him go, she kept her arms open and reached for Rachel. "And you must be the one."

"The *one*?" Rachel answered. She placed her hands lightly on Rain's back and endured the hug.

"The one he's been talking so much about. The one he met

in the . . . well, in the most *unusual* way. You're Rachel, right?"
Rain released the tight embrace and eased back but kept her
hands on Rachel's shoulders.

"Then, yes, I'm the one." She glanced toward Noah. "Unless
there's another Rachel he's pegged with his truck lately."

Noah put his hand on his chin and looked up. "No, there
have been other accidents, but not with any Rachels."

"Boys," Rain said, looking back at Rachel. Then she hugged
her again, quicker this time, and led her up the stairs. "I am so
glad to meet you. Noah has never—and I mean *never*—talked
about a young lady as highly as he's talked about you."

"Uh-oh." Rachel looked over her shoulder at Noah as they
climbed the stairs.

"All good," Rain assured her. "It's all been good."

Rain led them into the Inn, past the rustic rolltop registration
desk, past the family photos on the wall, and into the large living
room. "Sit anywhere, dear."

Rachel dropped into an oversized, black leather recliner.

"Can I get you something to drink? Or a snack? It's a long
drive."

"I'm good for now, thank you."

Rain sat on the stone hearth, and when Noah appeared in the
doorway, she slapped the slab next to her.

Rachel breathed it in. The walls, heavy with years and memories, the country décor, the Civil War history, the knickknacks.

"This is really a lovely home, Mrs. Cooper. I don't think I've ever been in a bed-and-breakfast."

"No kidding?" Rain stood. "Would you like a tour?"

Noah smiled as his mother took Rachel by the hand and led her through the door to the kitchen. "Have fun," he said as the swinging door shut and the women disappeared. After a moment or two, he stood and stretched his arms above his head. "Is Dad around?" he said to no one.

A moment later, giggles rolled from the kitchen and Noah smiled again. Then he walked out of the living room, down the hall, and through the front door. "Dad?"

Seconds later, Malcolm appeared from the south side of the house. He wore jeans and the same leather jacket he'd owned for as long as Noah could remember.

"Hey, old man," Noah said as Malcolm walked up the steps.

Malcolm reached out to shake his hand, but Noah pulled him into a bear hug. "Has Mom taught you nothing, Dad?"

"I should know better," Malcolm answered as they separated. Then he faked a punch to his son's gut and pointed to one of the rockers on the porch. "Where's the lady?"

"Mine or yours?" Noah said.

"Yours. And if your mother hears you say that, she'll whack you."

"So would mine," Noah said. "They're taking the grand tour."

Malcolm nodded.

In the comfortable, cool spring air, father and son caught up face-to-face for the first time in more than a month. They discussed Noah's finals, his updated plans for the summer, and Malcolm's recent run-in with one of the county commissioners.

"So, you like this one."

Noah rocked his chair back a little higher. "What makes you say that?"

"Oh, please, son."

"What?"

"When's the last time you brought a girl out here?"

Noah thought for a moment. "Melissa Skinner."

"Who?"

"The drama major."

Malcolm squinted his eyes. "Oh, yeah. I liked that one."

Noah laughed. "Want her number?"

The two men could hear more girlish giggling from inside the house as Rain and Rachel climbed the stairs to the second floor.

"Who else . . ." Malcolm said to himself as the rocking resumed. "Oh, yeah, Kayla. The blonde. Remember her? Wasn't she the one with a sister who you also went with?"

Noah threw his head back. "Dad, seriously, no one has said *went with* since like the 1800s."

Malcolm stopped rocking and stared at his son, eyes focused and narrow. "Boy, don't make me do something I'll regret." He tried to sound gruff and intimidating, but he started to smile before he could finish his threat.

"Yes, Dad, I *went with* her sister, too. Cami. But she never came out here. Cami was too much a city girl for this place."

Malcolm nodded toward the Inn. "Isn't she a little bit city, too?"

"Yeah, she's all about the city, no doubt about it. But she's way more layered than that. She doesn't fit any of the molds like a lot of the girls I've liked at Mason. She's been around the world and seen some cool stuff. She always looks comfortable wherever she is, you know? Like she belongs wherever she lands. A local in any town."

Malcolm's eyes were wide and his unibrow even more uni than normal. "'A local in any town'?"

"What?" Noah asked.

"You're in deep, boy."

Noah looked away and scanned the tree line to the south.

"You are in something deep. Deep, deep, deep."

"I like her, Dad."

Malcolm began drumming on the armrests of his rocker with his thick thumbs. Without realizing it, Noah began doing the same. "Does she feel the same?" Malcolm asked.

"I think so. I mean, she's here."

Malcolm nodded. "True enough."

They continued rocking back and forth, the only noise

coming from the porch's well-worn floorboards. The two Coopers enjoyed the morning's transition to afternoon and the sun's ascent into the soft blue sky.

"Dad?"

"Yeah."

"When did you know?"

"Know what?"

"About Mom. That she was the one."

Malcolm stopped rocking and stretched back in his chair, extending his feet and crossing his arms. "I guess I just knew."

"But when? When did you first look at her and say, *She's the one.*"

Malcolm closed his eyes. "When I first looked at her."

"The first time you saw her?"

"Exactly."

Once again Noah relived the moment his truck met the tire of Rachel's mountain bike. Though weeks had passed, there on the porch, breathing in the crisp valley air, over a hundred miles away from the accident site, he could still see her sprawled across the sidewalk. He saw her backpack twisted and her hair exposed from the back of her helmet. The potentially tragic accident, particularly when Rachel retold the story, had become so slapstick that even the memory of a red raspberry on her face made Noah smile.

"You're in deep," Malcolm said again, and Noah realized his father had stood and descended the porch steps to the driveway.

Noah shrugged.

"Come walk with me."

Noah followed his father to the Inn's workshop, a small stand-alone building Malcolm had built shortly after taking over the Inn after his parents passed away. Malcolm picked up a long, freshly stained plank of wood from a table saw, removed a wrench and a cordless drill from the wall hooks, and fished several pieces of hardware from a jar.

Malcolm led them out of the workshop and around the back of the Inn to the swing that Jack and Laurel had enjoyed thousands of times during their years at *Domus Jefferson*. It was the same swing Malcolm and Rain had sat on together after his return from Brazil.

"Grab that end, would you, please?"

Noah secured one end of the swing as Malcolm struggled to loosen an orange rusted bolt. Once the bolt was free, they switched places and Malcolm worked the other side. Together they removed the fat ropes from the front and back of each side and set the swing on the ground.

"Been meaning to do this for a long time," Malcolm said. Using his drill, he removed a broken plank from the middle of the swing's seat and carefully slid the replacement into its place.

"Not quite the same color, Dad. Do you care?"

"It will be." Malcolm winked at his son.

"How long?"

"That depends on Mother Nature. But in time, they'll fit. They'll start to look alike. They always do."

Malcolm secured the new plank into the swing with screws in new holes. When it was snug in the seat, they rehung the swing one rope, one clamp, one bolt at a time. When it was secure, Malcolm gave it a shove into the air. "Perfect."

Before the swing had come to a stop, Rain and Rachel appeared through the back door, stepped off the stairs, and spotted Malcolm and Noah.

"Noah," his mother called. "Lunch here or out?"

"Here is fine," he yelled back.

Rain said something to Rachel, squeezed her arm, and walked back into the Inn alone. When Malcolm saw Rachel sauntering their way, he gathered his tools from the ground, winked at Noah, and vanished back to his workshop.

Noah slid onto the swing and kept his feet grounded long enough for Rachel to join him. Then he pushed off and sent them into motion.

"How was it?" Noah asked.

"Pretty amazing. I had no idea what a place like this really was."

"Really?"

"Well, yeah. My sort-of-stepdad had money when my mother was with him, and he was used to five-star hotels and resorts."

"B&Bs get pretty good ratings, too, you know."

Rachel slapped his thigh. "I didn't mean anything like that. I just meant that he was used to room service, a restaurant, a bar— all those luxuries." She looked back to the Inn. "But this place is lovely, really lovely."

Noah reached over and took her hand. "You don't talk much about your family. What's a *sort-of-stepdad*?"

"He and Mom never got married, but he took really good care of us. We were basically a family, just not officially. I call him my stepdad anyway."

"Do you see him often?"

Rachel took a few beats to recall his most recent visit to DC and their short meeting over Thai food in Alexandria. "What's often?" she asked.

"You tell me."

"He and my mom aren't together anymore."

"Oh. Is it recent?"

"What's recent?" she asked with a sparkle. "Just kidding. They separated when I graduated from high school and left home."

"Oh."

Rachel shrugged. "It's complicated. He found us in a bad

place and took us in. He became like a dad to me and really helped us. Still does."

It hadn't taken long for Noah to learn when it was best to switch topics, even when his boyish curiosity thirsted for more. "Play a game?" he asked.

"Sure."

"I tell you one thing, just one, that you don't know about me. Then you follow. If I say something you already knew, I have to go again and say *two* things. Same for you."

"Hmm. This sounds dangerous," Rachel said.

"I'll start." Noah pushed them into motion again and the swing creaked a bit on the tired branch above. "My middle name is Joseph."

"OK. I don't have a middle name," Rachel replied.

"I knew that." Noah smiled and pointed at her. "You owe me two."

"Why do I think getting hit by your truck again would be more fun?" When Noah didn't let her off the hook, she continued. "I've been to twenty-eight countries."

"Wow. Twenty-eight? I knew you traveled, but twenty-eight? That's impressive."

Rachel made a *how-about-that* face.

"You have to say—"

"One more—I know," she stopped him. "Patience, patience." Rachel looked around the yard as if searching for something of interest. "I broke a toe playing horseshoes when I was a kid. My dad—my real dad—threw one the wrong direction and it landed on my foot. Broke two toes, actually."

"Ouch. OK, me again. Let's see. Hmm. My grandparents, the ones who bought this place and moved my dad here from Charlottesville, they wrote letters. Actually Grandpa Jack did the writing. He wrote Grandma a letter every Wednesday of their entire marriage."

"Really?" Rachel said, her mouth dropping open slightly.

"Yep, they called them the Wednesday Letters. Lots of secrets in them. Lots of adventures. Crazy, huh?"

"I'll say."

"Top that," Noah taunted.

Rachel thought for a minute. "My mom and my real dad split up when I was seven. I haven't seen him since."

"That doesn't count, I knew they'd split up, you told me that once."

"But did you know how old I was?"

Noah tilted his head to the side. "Technicality, but I'll give it to you." He let the wind clear the moment. "You ready for this? I didn't know who my real grandfather was until I was eighteen and moving up to Mason as a freshman."

"What?"

"You heard right. Grandpa Jack wasn't my biological grandfather."

"What? Your dad's dad?"

"Uh-huh. Obviously Grandpa Jack raised my dad—and my aunt and uncle too—but he wasn't Dad's biological father." Noah hesitated to finish; he hated saying the words aloud. "Grandma Laurel was attacked."

Rachel's mouth fell the rest of the way open.

After a period of processing Noah's latest entry in the game, Rachel took his hand again and said, "Can we quit?"

"Are you OK?"

Rachel looked away.

"Rach?"

Without turning back, she said to the wind, "Let's just quit for now, OK?"

Noah stood up from the swing and faced her. He took her hands and tugged her to the edge of the swing. "I'm an idiot. I'm sorry. I didn't mean to ruin a good thing."

"You didn't." Rachel inched off the swing and hugged him. "You didn't at all."

The two walked arm-in-arm back through the yard toward the Inn. Masking a perplexed expression as best she could, Rachel wondered how she and her heart had traveled from a heap of broken bicycle pieces and a sprained ankle to this charming young man's childhood home so quickly.

Noah wondered much the same thing, but his face featured a pleasant smile he didn't bother hiding.

CHAPTER 6

"That was the best sandwich I think I've ever had." Rachel wiped her mouth and placed the green cotton napkin on the matching place mat next to her plate.

"Thanks, sweetheart."

"No, I'm serious, Mrs. Cooper, that was really delicious. Is it the bread?"

The *I told you so* look Rain launched at her husband couldn't have been any louder if she'd screamed the words through a bullhorn. "Spot on, Rachel. It's all about the bread. A ham and Swiss sandwich is a ham and Swiss sandwich. Not a great deal of mystery to that. And, of course, the vegetables are fresh and both the ham and cheese come from the valley, but the bread is what makes it a sandwich, and I make the bread right here."

Malcolm snorted, but Rain continued, undeterred. "Our neighbor on that next hill, A&P, she taught me how to make bread twenty years ago, maybe longer, and we just get better and better with every loaf."

Malcolm snorted again, much louder for effect, and Rachel raised her hands. "What am I missing here?"

"Not a thing, sweetheart. My husband here has no taste buds. None. Doesn't matter how much I insist one loaf or one recipe is different from another, he can't taste the difference between my homemade seven-grain and a loaf of Wonder Bread. My painstakingly honed baking skills are completely lost on him."

"And you?" Rachel gave Noah a playful elbow in the seat next to her.

"Not me. I must have been born with an extra batch of good taste. I can seriously taste Mom's bread before she's even baked it. Sometimes she sends me pictures of a steaming hot loaf right out of the oven. Anything to persuade me to come home, right, Mom?"

"That's my boy," Rain said, blowing him a kiss across the table.

Malcolm stood and began clearing plates. "Oh, give me a break. I may not be able to taste like Julia Child over there, or what's his name, Emeril the Chef Dog Whisperer, but I can smell like a hound dog, and it's starting to smell like you-know-what in here."

"Malcolm Cooper! We've got company."

He reached down and took Rachel's plate. "We are who we are, right, Rachel?"

"Wouldn't want to meet you any other way." She grinned.

After each enjoyed a caramel-walnut brownie and a scoop of vanilla ice cream, Malcolm again cleared the table, kissed Rain on the top of her head, and invited Noah to join him on a trip to town. "Be gone an hour. Hitting Tractor Supply, post office, Four-Star Printing."

Rain and Rachel waved approving good-byes as the front door shut. The women chatted about food, place settings, and chocolate as they did the dishes side-by-side. Fifteen minutes later they settled into the living room. Rain sat in a small chair she used for reading and Rachel sat in the oversized black recliner.

Rachel eyed a large, leather-bound binder on the coffee table. "Pictures?" she asked.

"Letters actually. Help yourself."

Rachel leaned forward, picked up the heavy book and slid back into her soft chair. "Are these the Wednesday Letters?"

"Oh." Rain didn't mean to sound as startled as she did. "He told you?"

"About the weekly letters, yes, ma'am. He said his grandfather wrote his grandmother every Wednesday while they were married."

"That he did. Quite a romantic, don't you think?"

"And then some," Rachel said, holding the book on her lap with the cover half-opened.

"Guess who else writes letters like that," Rain said.

"Mr. Cooper?"

"The very same. He's not quite as precise now. They don't always come on the same day, and he's missed weeks now and again. But I've got boxes of letters from that nutty husband of mine."

Rachel couldn't wait. "And these?" she asked as she flipped the cover over and looked at the first page. It was a letter slid into a thick plastic sheet protector.

"Those are something different. Those are my Wedding Letters."

Rachel looked up. "Wedding Letters?"

"It's a tradition that started with my wedding. Did I mention A&P, our friend next door?"

"You did."

"When Noah's dad and I finally became engaged—and that's a long story for another day—A&P contacted just about everyone we'd ever known. Friends from town, old neighbors, people who'd stayed at the Inn, a few politicians, even some celebrities, and had them write a letter to us. She was very secretive about it. She had a lot of the letters mailed to her place. Others she drove all around the valley to pick up. And if someone even breathed the word *letter* in our presence, she'd get all paranoid and change the subject."

"What a nice woman," Rachel said.

"The nicest. She's as much family as my own sister and brother-in-law."

"So when did you get the letters?"

"At our reception. Right here at the Inn. A&P said she bought the nicest binder she could find and then apologized that it was just a binder. The book was wrapped like any other gift."

Rachel looked back down at the first letter in the book. "So what are they? Letters of advice?"

"Some of them, yes. Some were just congratulatory notes. Some were funny, or clever. Definitely some advice to follow and, quite honestly, some to ignore." She laughed out the final words.

"How many did you get?"

"I never counted, believe it or not. It felt like every time I opened the book, there was another gem. There must be more than a hundred in there. Even today, when I open the binder, I swear I see letters I've never read before."

"May I?" Rachel asked as she flipped to a random letter in the middle of the book.

"Of course."

✉

Dear Rain and Malcolm,

I am so happy for you!!! I am so happy you're finally doing what we all knew was going to happen one day!!!

A&P asked for a few words of advice. Mine is really simple, kids: Find out what matters to the other, what's really important, and make it important to you.

Before Randy and I got married, I didn't know the difference between a racecar and taxicab. When Randy told me he was addicted to NASCAR, I thought it was some kind of drug or something. The first time he dragged me to a race down in North Carolina I thought I'd found evidence of aliens on this planet. I mean have you been to a NASCAR race before? WOW!!!

But listen when I say this: I learned to love racing. I love it because Randy loves it. I love it because it makes him happy. We have been married over forty years, and I know in my heart it's because I learned to love what he loved and he learned to love what I love.

We have been to races, we have been to beauty supply shows, we have hunted ducks together, we have made quilts every Christmas for each of our grandkids. We have done it together, side by side, sitting in front of some TV show I don't like or some TV show he doesn't like. But we've done it all together.

I love him. He loves me. I know it. He knows it. And people all around this valley know it!

I wish I had some advice more important sounding or better written down. But that's it.

Congrats, kids!

Love,
Nancy Nightbell

✉

To Malcolm, my second favorite brother,
and to Rain, my very best friend in the world,

Is it real? After so many years and so many disasters, are you two
really tying the knot? There are mornings I wake up and feel such
excitement for you two that I have to remind myself it's not my wedding. Insane, I know.

First, my advice for Rain: Be patient, dear. I know my brother
better than anyone alive and I know there will be days when you
want to break multiple laws and many of his bones. He will drive
you mad. He has a short fuse, which you already know. But I can
promise you that you will never be on the wrong end of it. The same
may not be said for Ping-Pong paddles, pool cues, or cereal bowls.
(Ask him about those stories sometime.)

Malcolm is a good man. A great man. He loves this town, the
Inn, his family, his writing, and Brazilian food.

But there is nothing in this world or any other that he loves
more than you. I've seen it in his eyes since you first met. I've heard
it in his voice.

I believe with all my heart he is meant for you.

And now a few pearls of wisdom for my knuckle-chops brother:

Read what I've written for your new bride. If anything I said
doesn't come true, if you say an unkind word, raise a hand, stray
from her, or break her heart with even the tiniest little crack, I will

come down on you with the full force of the law. There will not be a country far enough away for you to hide in. Got it, bro?

I love you, Malcolm. Thank you for being the only man I ever believed could make Rain happy. Thank you for being a son that Mom and Dad could love unconditionally.

I am proud of a lot in my makeshift, make-the-best-of-it life. But nothing makes me prouder than to call you my brother.

I love you both.

Sam

CHAPTER 7

R achel would have said something if she could speak at all.
"So?" Rain said.

Rachel hadn't realized that while she had been reading the
letters aloud, Rain had changed chairs and now sat right next to
her on a wooden stool topped with a heavy slice of polished tree
trunk.

"Are you all right?" Rain put her hand on Rachel's forearm.

Rachel sniffled and closed the book, gingerly setting it back
on the table in front of her. Then she swiped under her eyes with
the tips of her index fingers and sniffled a second time. "Huh,"
she said, looking to her left and making eye contact with Rain. "I
didn't see that coming."

"I'm so sorry, sweetheart. Do you want to talk about something?"

Rachel smiled. "Seriously—you Coopers do like to talk, don't
you?"

Rain smiled back. "It's the only way."

With both hands Rachel covered her face briefly, massaging her forehead with her fingertips. "I'm so embarrassed," she blurted and the volume surprised them both.

"Don't be. Many of the letters are quite touching. I cry all the time, too, and I've been married twenty-five years."

Rachel looked back down at the book. "So much honesty. I don't think my family has ever known that kind of truth. Good, bad, ugly—it doesn't matter." She took a long breath. "I hope I get letters like that some day."

When Rain was sure Rachel was done, she added with all the confidence of a mother: "You will."

The two women talked about the Shenandoah Valley, A&P, the challenges of running a B&B, local restaurants, shopping in nearby Harrisonburg, and Rachel's master's degree and future— she hoped—at the Department of Justice working on a first-year grant. "It's about encouraging corporations to invest in solutions to violence in the nation's capital. Getting government and business to work together, you know?"

Rain raised her head as if complimenting her own daughter. "I love that passion."

"I just really believe in this," Rachel said in one of her most genuine, revealing moments of the day.

They chatted about Samantha, Samantha's daughter, Angela, and Angela's new baby, Taylor. Rain told stories about Uncle

Matthew, his wife Monica, and their adopted son, Jack. "Most of us call him LJ, short for Little Jack. He was named after his grandfather before the adoption was even final." Rain added proudly that he'd become an all-American track-and-field star at Arkansas.

Rain shared anecdotes about Laurel's eccentric and thoroughly adorable sister, Allyson. "Believe it or not, Allyson wrote a *New York Times* bestselling book at the age of seventy-one. It's an autobiography, or a memoir as they are calling them now. It's hilarious and very, very Allyson."

"She lives nearby?"

"She lives—I should say *runs*—a very hoity-toity retirement facility out west in Las Vegas."

"Oh, so she's a manager?"

"No," Rain chuckled. "Just a resident, but she runs it anyway. Think of it like this. Allyson is the kind of woman that if she were, say, a junior chef at the White House, she'd be the one actually running the country and pushing all the buttons."

"Scary," Rachel said.

Rain laughed. "You have no idea."

Rain pulled a photo album from a shelf and described the night the family found Jack and Laurel's stash of letters. She shared some of the more entertaining stories and even excused herself to retrieve the Tennessee license plate still hanging on one of the bedroom walls upstairs.

She handed it to Rachel. "Read it."

Rachel turned it over and read the message on the back, written in black Sharpie that had faded little in forty-one years. "'To Laurel and Jack,'" Rachel read. "'Enjoy your last days. Elvis and Priscilla, 1970.'"

She flipped the license plate back over. "Are you kidding me with this?"

"Not. An. Ounce." Rain punched each word for effect.

Rachel handed it back to her. "That's crazy cool."

They chatted on until they heard Malcolm and Noah's voices outside and growing louder as they raced toward the house. Their arms and legs tumbled in a tangled heap as they fell through the front door.

"Bam!" Noah shouted. "My foot hit the inside first!"

"Cheater," Malcolm mumbled as he regained his balance and followed Noah down the hallway.

"My boys getting along?" Rain said when they arrived in the living room.

They took turns rattling off their self-described impressive list of accomplishments during their trip into Woodstock.

"Isn't that so like men?" Rain said, turning to Rachel. "They run a few errands all by themselves and suddenly they think they've solved gridlock in DC."

Rachel agreed with an exaggerated nod, and Noah reached down for her hand. "Shh. Don't say anything," he whispered loud enough for all three to hear. "It's a trap. Next she'll ask for your voter registration card to see if you have chosen a political party."

"Watch it, kid. I still bake the bread," Rain said.

The good-byes took longer than usual and Rain threw a thousand options at the couple to occupy more time in the valley, one of which involved taking advantage of another evening without guests and staying the night in separate rooms. "You can go home in the morning."

"We need to head back, Mom. I promised Rachel we'd get home at a decent hour, and I still want to take the Skyline Drive."

Even though Noah didn't need them, Malcolm gave his son detailed directions for entering the scenic byway off Route 33 east of Harrisonburg and exiting in Front Royal.

"Thanks, Corn Pops." Noah wrapped his arms around his father's lower back and with a grunt lifted him off the ground. Then he hugged his mother, told her he loved her and waited for Rachel to say her good-byes as well.

"I won't try to lift you," she said to Malcolm, shaking his hand firmly and flashing her broad smile and model-white teeth.

"She's a smart kid." He yanked playfully on Noah's ear. "See what a master's degree would get you?"

Rachel instinctively extended her hand to Rain as well, but Rain stepped toward her and hugged her tight. "You are a gem of a woman, Rachel. I just loved having you here today." Then she whispered in her ear, "Come back anytime. You don't even have to bring Noah."

Malcolm and Rain trailed the young couple down the hallway and outside. They called another round of good-byes from the porch as Noah beat Rachel to the door and waited for her to offer her own final wave. She stepped up and into the truck.

As he circled around to the driver's side, his mother called out once again. "Wait," she said and bounded down the porch stairs. She wrapped her thin arms around Noah's shoulders and said, "Drive safe, son."

"I always do, Mom. Love you."

Then his mother glanced at Rachel fiddling with her seatbelt and said softly in his ear, "Don't let this one go."

CHAPTER 8

Even in his deepest of daydreams, Noah couldn't have imagined how well Rachel's first trip to Woodstock would go. It had unlocked something inside her, perhaps even inspired her.

"You need to get out of the city more often," Noah joked.

Rachel raved about Noah's parents on the drive home, the next day on the tennis court, and over dinner with a group of friends the next night at a Brazilian restaurant at the crowded Fair Oaks Mall. The more time passed, the more enamored she seemed with the Coopers' warmth and sincerity.

"I love my mom, obviously," Rachel said. "She's been through a lot. But your mom was more open and kind to me in a few hours than my mother has been in years." Rachel offered a variation of those words many times and Noah nodded and smiled on each occasion. "And your dad is amazing, you know? My stepdad has been good to us. He's provided a good life, paid for school, all that, but he's never provided much else."

Noah loved observing and absorbing Rachel's thaw.

Over the next two weeks, Noah and Rachel went from dating to inseparable. They visited museums, the zoo, shared a kiss at night on the steps of the Lincoln Memorial. They saw movies Rachel loved and Noah tolerated. They listened to music Noah downloaded from iTunes that Rachel couldn't believe he actually paid for.

As Noah dropped Rachel off one night at her apartment, he wondered aloud why another magical night had to end. She said it didn't and dared him to drive them around the entire Capital Beltway, just to see how long it would take. So he did. But even then, two hours and a trip to IHOP later, he regretted having to walk her to her door when the date came to a conclusion.

As he kissed her at her apartment door he nearly said the three words he'd been rattling over and over in his head all evening, but she broke his courage when she invited him to take a DC Ducks tour with her and her roommates the next afternoon. So the words returned to his heart for another day.

Rachel was officially awarded her master's degree and Noah graduated with his undergraduate degree. They celebrated together at Komi, one of the finest restaurants in DC. Noah's parents came, as did his Aunt Samantha and her husband, Shawn. A&P joined them, too, and over the repeated objections of

Malcolm, she paid the enormous bill and tipped the handsome server $270.

Rachel had also invited one of her best friends, Tyler Clingerman, to join them for the evening. Tyler was a friend from Rachel's undergrad years at George Mason University, and they'd had a number of classes together since meeting early during their sophomore years. Noah tried to hide his jealousy when Rachel and Tyler's long embrace ended with a kiss on her cheek.

Rachel's mother, Stephanie, flew into town for the occasion and met Noah for the first time. Noah was stunned by the petite woman's appearance. Only her thin frame and eye color matched Rachel's. The skin on Mrs. Kaplan's neck and cheeks was unnaturally tight, her jawline sharp, and her forehead too smooth and unblemished for a woman who'd lived as many years and had endured as much as Rachel said she had. Her hair was blonde and her tan looked more like the leather from one of his father's tool belts than feminine, sun-kissed skin.

Rachel apologized that chairs needed to be moved to accommodate her mother. "She likes to be able to see everyone's faces," Rachel whispered. Later, she apologized that she had to escort her mother to the restroom, twice. And before the dinner was quite over, she told Noah how sorry she was for any disruptions and for leaving early. "She's not feeling well," Rachel whispered again. "I should make sure she gets settled at the hotel."

"Of course," he said.

"I'm really sorry, Noah."

Outside in front of the restaurant, Rachel's mother griped that her hired car for the evening wasn't already waiting at the curb. A minute later, the Lincoln Town Car appeared from around the corner and Stephanie cursed the driver as he held open the rear door. Rachel kissed Noah good-bye, apologized yet again, and promised to call the next morning.

The evening when Noah planned to say *I love you* for the first time ended with a wave and a forced smile. He spent the rest of the night making awkward small talk with Tyler and wishing he weren't.

One week later, Rachel received the letter she'd been waiting for. The position at the Department of Justice was hers and she'd begin work later that summer when the rest of the team and the funding were in place. Much to her delight, a phone call the very next day revealed that Tyler Clingerman would be transferring from another department to work on the same project. She was grateful that a familiar, friendly face would await her on her first day on the job.

Rachel acknowledged that the money wasn't great, but it was sufficient that she could stop relying on her mother and step-father and, at long last, pay her own way. She was grateful to not have a penny in student loans and few obligations to the world besides an apartment lease and a cell phone bill.

Noah had already decided to take a year off before considering graduate school and was experimenting with every imaginable medium in his art. He painted pictures in both oils and acrylics of Rachel asleep on the grass of the Washington Mall. He sketched her face in both charcoal and ink. Over dinner at a Chinese buffet, he accepted the challenge to finger paint her on a napkin using red and green Jell-O. The likeness was uncanny.

They returned to Woodstock to visit the Coopers. Over lunch in the back of the Café on Main Street, Noah and Rachel watched and listened as Samantha showed off new pictures of her granddaughter, Taylor. Noah had never seen such a soft side to the aunt he called Sheriff Sam.

Later in the afternoon, Samantha, Rain, and Rachel went for a hike to the Woodstock Tower while the boys helped A&P move several heavy antique pieces around her house. Then they moved it again, and again, then back to its original spot. Even Noah, who hadn't spent much time with A&P since leaving for college four years earlier, could sense what A&P needed most was company.

More than anything else that day, Noah would remember the peaceful drive home. Just as they passed the Marshall exit on 66 East, he looked at Rachel fading to sleep next to him and said, "I love you."

She looked at him, her eyes half-open. Then after the longest ten seconds of Noah's life, Rachel smiled and said, "I love you, too."

CHAPTER 9

The vibrating phone danced across Noah's dresser. "Uhhh," he groaned and ignored it. After thirty seconds, the phone vibrated again in a single, short voice mail *bzzz* and Noah tried to doze back to sleep. But before he'd flipped the pillow, the phone came to life again and he crawled out of bed to retrieve it.

The caller ID excited him: MATT CELL

"Uncle Matt! It's early—what's up with that, huh?" He fell back on his bed, one arm behind his head, one holding the phone to his ear.

"It's almost nine o'clock, slacker. That's only early if you're in California and it's actually six."

"Whatever. I'm a college kid; we sleep in. That's what we do."

"But, in fact, you're *not* a college kid anymore, are you? That's reason number one for my call. I'm really sorry I didn't make it to Mason's graduation. Things have been crazy up here."

Things are always crazy up there, Noah thought. "It's not a big deal, Uncle Matt. I got your card and puny check—it's all good."

Matthew laughed. "Good to see college life hasn't changed your sense of humor. You're still as funny as your old man. Which, as you know, isn't so funny at all."

They traded more friendly barbs until Matthew regained control of the conversation. "There's a second reason for my call—"

"You're such a bean counter. Only an accountant numbers his reasons for making a phone call."

"You want a free lunch or not?"

Noah sat up. "You're in town?"

"Got in yesterday morning. I'm staying at the JW Marriott over in Metro Center. You know it?"

"Definitely. You here long?"

"Two days," Matthew said. "I know it's bad form to call on such short notice, but this trip came together last minute."

Noah hardly heard the last part through his own laughter. "And you're probably the only Cooper who's ever used the term *bad form.*"

"You can make fun of me at lunch. I'll even pay for the abuse. Meet me here at 12:30. The buffet is fantastic."

"I'm in," Noah said, but immediately realized the conflict. "Ah, fudge goats, I'm supposed to meet my girlfriend at 1:15 at Union Station. She's getting a tour of the DOJ today and I'm tagging along."

"Noah, you know you're old enough to ditch your mother's substitute swear words, right?"

"Tell *her* that," Noah said.

"Well, listen." Matthew was serious again. "I'm only a couple stops away. Let's make lunch at noon and have her meet you here at the hotel at 12:30. I'd love to meet her anyway. Sam says she's something special."

They finished the call quickly and Noah texted the updated plan to Rachel.

> Noah: morning to you! :)
> Rachel: You too :)
> Noah: uncles in town!
> Rachel: From Hartford?
> Noah: yep
> Noah: meeting 4 lunch at marriott by metro center
> Rachel: Tour with Ty still ok at 1:15?
> Noah: yep, meet me at marriott restaurant, 1230
> Rachel: Make me late and I'll . . .
> Noah: i wont! see you at 1230 :)
> Noah: ttyl luvu

Noah arrived at the restaurant five minutes late and Matthew tapped his watch as he stood from his table near the hostess stand. "Just like your dad—always late." Matthew held out his hand and Noah slapped it away.

"Get in here, Uncle Matt." Noah squeezed him hard. "Great to see you. It's been a long time."

They separated and Matthew gestured to the buffet. "Let's see if you can still put the food away like a teenager."

The men sat and reconnected about Matthew's foray into international business, LeBron vs. Kobe, and Obama's reelection chances. Matthew showed Noah a recent photo of his son, LJ, the baby he and Monica had adopted the year Jack and Laurel died.

"Man, that kid is big. I really need to hit him up on iChat one of these days. Been way too long."

"You should," Matthew said. "He asks about you a lot."

Noah excused himself for a second trip to the buffet and when he returned asked, "How's Aunt Monica? I'm an idiot for not asking earlier."

Matthew stabbed at a black olive. "She's well . . . I guess."

"Uh-oh." Noah's fork full of pulled pork stopped midair.

Matthew scanned the restaurant as if looking for someone he knew he wouldn't find, as if looking away was the right thing to do. When he swiveled back to Noah, he said softly, "We're separated."

Noah leaned in and nearly toppled his drink. *"You're what?"*

"Since last October."

Noah set his fork down and also surveyed the restaurant to see if anyone was listening. "Are you serious?"

Matthew nodded.

"Totally none of my business, I know, but what the heck happened?"

Matthew forced a smile. "Noah, I wish I was in my twenties again with your simpler view of the world. And I don't mean that disrespectfully, I really don't. I just wish I had another turn at being your age."

Neither spoke for a few long seconds. "We haven't gotten along for a while," Matthew continued. "More than a while, really."

"I . . . I can't believe it. You guys seemed great."

"We *were* great, for a few days here and a few days there. But we were never great for that many days in a row."

Noah picked up his fork again and tipped it toward Matthew before putting it in his mouth. "That's why you didn't come for Christmas."

"That's right." Matthew conceded.

Noah took a pull on his Pepsi. "I am completely floored. When will it all happen?"

"The divorce? Later this summer, I hope. We're trying not to fight about every jot and tittle but it's tough when you're paying attorneys to do exactly that. It's funny, it takes only a few seconds to marry someone for thirty years, but it takes a lot longer to unmarry them."

Actually, Noah didn't find it funny at all.

After the restaurant manager stopped at the table to check on them, Noah asked Matthew the question he was most curious about. "Did she cheat?"

Matthew pulled his napkin from his lap, wiped at the non-existent food on his mouth, and folded and laid it across his plate. "It's complicated."

"I'm not a kid, Uncle Matt."

"That's not what I mean."

They sat quietly while a busboy cleared their plates.

"She was unfaithful, yes. But not in the way you're thinking."

"What other way is there?" Noah's voice rose.

Matthew turned the dial on an imaginary knob between them.

"She was unfaithful emotionally. Monica had this business partner she picked up ten years ago when the gym took off and they started franchising. It was a good move, and he seemed like a nice enough guy. I ran his financials, called his banks, did lots of homework, and gave her my complete blessing for the partnership. He brought the money; Monica brought the health know-how, the fitness certifications, all that. She promises me nothing ever happened, but I could tell their friendship was more than two people who worked together and got along. She told him things she'd never tell me." Matthew gave a pleasant "Thank you" to the server who stopped by and refilled his ice water.

"I realized how much we'd grown apart when we were at a grand opening for a gym north of Boston. Gorgeous building. State of the art. I was standing nearby when she introduced him to someone as her *best friend*. That's the night I realized she was being unfaithful and it was time."

"Time?" Noah posed.

"To move on. We'd been drifting a long time anyway."

After another prolonged silence, Matthew said very quietly and very simply, "So I cheated too."

Emotionally? Noah thought, but did not articulate.

"I fell in love with an investment banker. Someone who had packaged a few deals for me overseas."

"Oh," Noah said.

"Yeah. I know. It's not easy for me to say out loud. But the secrets have been killing me inside."

Noah wanted to change the subject and quickly, but before he could, Matthew let the words spill right out. "She got pregnant."

Noah felt sick. "Oh."

"Yeah."

"Are you getting married?"

Matthew shook his head. "She didn't want the baby. She didn't want me. It's over."

"I see."

"And, Noah, listen to me, I haven't told your folks yet. Let me tell them, would you? Please?"

Noah nodded. "Sure."

"I need to," Matthew added. "I need to talk to them about some other things as well."

Noah jumped back in before Matthew could rock his afternoon any further.

"So, what's LJ been up to?"

Matthew grinned, both at the abrupt change of subject and at the subject Noah had changed to. "I'm assuming you know he's a fifth-year senior at Arkansas? He's consumed right now with trying to make the US track team. He's one of the fastest kids in the country. We think he's got a real shot at this."

"Wow." But Noah didn't know whether he was commenting on his cousin's success on the track or still weighing the fact that his aunt and uncle's long marriage was over.

Before it mattered one way or another, Rachel appeared at the hostess stand, scanning the restaurant. Her hair was up, which Noah never cared for, and she wore a black business power suit and the pearls he'd given her for her first day of work.

"And there she is," Noah said both to her and to Matthew as he stood up from his chair.

She walked toward him, tugging awkwardly on her suit jacket. "I look ridiculous."

"Wrong." Noah kissed her cheek. "You look amazing."

"You must be the famous uncle," she said.

Matthew stood for her. "Matt Cooper. Or Matthew, whichever. A pleasure."

They shook hands firmly then sat all at once. Noah flagged down a server and ordered an iced tea with lemon for Rachel. "You had lunch?" he asked her.

"I ate at home. Thanks though." She adjusted the pearl strand around her neck and leaned into him. "I'm a little nervous about this tour. What in the world is wrong with me?"

Rachel talked about her first post-college job and briefly explained how she'd landed it.

Matthew was noticeably impressed.

Noah got the largest piece of carrot cake from the dessert bar and swiped a fork from another table so Rachel could try a bite. She ate more than half.

Noah told Matthew how he'd met Rachel on the side of the road after she'd been hit by a truck as she rode her bicycle to campus.

Rachel filled in the inconvenient detail that Noah had been driving the truck.

Before they could touch another topic, Rachel looked at her watch and said, "We better run, Noah. It's one o'clock."

They said good-bye; Matthew promised to keep in touch with Noah during the summer, and Noah made him promise to tell his folks the latest news as soon as possible.

Rachel enjoyed every minute of their personal, behind-the-scenes tour of the DOJ with Tyler. Unlike Rachel, he'd not pursued a graduate degree and had taken an entry-level job with the department right out of school. After a couple of years he seemed to know every nook, cranny and, at least in Noah's opinion, useless detail about the DOJ. There was nothing Tyler didn't know. *Except,* Noah thought, *how fake his tan looks.*

Noah would have preferred being almost anywhere else than trailing Rachel and Tyler around their new turf. But at least for an hour or two, his mind was on something other than his Uncle Matthew's infidelity and shattered marriage.

CHAPTER 10

News of Matthew and Monica's divorce surprised no one else quite like it had Noah. His Uncle Matthew had been a mentor and friend for as long as Noah had memories. Matthew was the Golden Boy for whom nothing went wrong. He'd been successful in business, gifted at sports—even the ones he didn't enjoy playing—and had a gorgeous, talented wife.

Noah's mind sorted memories of his aunt and uncle at Christmases, at the occasional summer reunion, at his graduation from Central High School.

Thirty years, he thought. *Thirty long years.*

Matthew extended his business trip to DC by two days and drove his rental car to Woodstock. He laid the truth and his heart on the same kitchen table where he and his siblings had poured through thirty-nine years of his father's letters. He sat in the same chair where Malcolm had learned of his mother's rape and the anguish that followed.

Samantha felt stung by the word *divorce*. Of her brothers, to her Matthew had always been the most like their father, Jack. Hearing that his marriage to Monica was over was something she couldn't have predicted in one hundred lifetimes of family meetings.

Across the room, Rain cried and admitted that, though her loyalty was always to Matthew, a man she loved more like a flesh-and-blood brother than an in-law, some of her tears were for Monica. "She wasn't here a lot, I know, but I enjoyed her so much when she was."

Malcolm did not remember the last time he had seen his older brother become so emotional. Even with his parents' death and during the intense drama of the week that followed, Matthew had been calm. He was the patriarch.

"I felt like I needed to take charge when Mom and Dad passed. Like that's what Dad would have wanted." Matthew arranged and rearranged the red, white, and blue place setting in front of him. "And you made that easy, Malcolm, you always did. You were the one with the issues. The one who needed saving time and time and time again, right?"

Malcolm looked at his brother's tired profile. "And you did a pretty amazing job, didn't you? Every tangle I got into, you got me out. Really, Matthew, you stepped out there in the fire so many times for me. I'm only here because you were there for me every time. Every. Time."

"Thanks," Matthew scratched out the word and cleared his throat. "There's something else I think you should know." Matthew took a long breath and looked down at the Kleenex in his hands.

The Inn fell into that sense of silence that worried Rain and Malcolm.

Still staring down, Matthew uttered the words he still couldn't believe himself. "I had an affair."

The response came in concert from around the table. "What?"

Samantha gasped. "You were unfaithful?" Her tone was more surprise than question.

"I was."

Rain spoke next. "How old is she?"

"She's thirty-eight."

"Does Monica know?" Rain asked.

Matthew looked down and nodded. He waited for more questions, concerns, to be judged or ridiculed, but when nothing came, he continued. "All these years," he began slowly. "Not only was I the oldest child, but I was the level-headed one . . . College. Job. Marriage. While Mal was the ladies' man, the renegade, the troublemaker. I was the dork. I handled the taxes, the investments, all of it for Mom and Dad and this place . . ." His voice cracked. "And now I'm a mess. What's happened to me?"

Malcolm stood up and walked behind his brother's chair. He

rubbed his shoulders and leaned down. "Don't worry, you're still a dork."

Matthew snort-laughed, and Samantha slid a box of Kleenex across the table.

"But none of that matters, brother. We still love you. Married, divorced—it doesn't matter. You loved me when I was broken, and we'll do the same for you."

With tears dripping from Matthew's eyes, the others joined Malcolm on their feet and surrounded their penitent brother. Embraces, kisses on the cheek from Rain and Samantha, whispered words of encouragement.

When Matthew had composed himself, he looked at Rain and his sister. "Do you think I could have a moment alone? With Mal?"

The ladies hugged him again at the same time and excused themselves to the kitchen.

Matthew gestured to the chair Malcolm had been occupying and they both sat. "This is the worst," Matthew said. "I feel like such a failure. You can't—"

"Come on, brother, have you met me? This is all stuff we can get through. If you're in a better place, if Monica is in a better place, then you'll get through this all. LJ is grown; you and Mon both have resources and careers. It's going to be all right. I've been through worse, you know."

Matthew hadn't heard any of it. He was practicing the words: "It's gone."

"What's gone, Matt?"

"My money."

Malcolm felt his stomach twist and shrink in half.

"I've lost almost everything I've made. Some of it mine and some of my clients. I got wrapped into a scheme. I don't know why. I don't know why, Malcolm. It was risky stuff, I knew that going in, but it ended up being a complete scam."

Malcolm stood up and walked to the opposite side of the table. "What about us?"

"You're all right. *Mostly* all right. And I had Mom and Dad's money someplace else, too. So that's fine. But we'd already lost quite a bit. You know, since 2005 the value has been dipping almost quarterly. It was so stagnant, Mal. I tried something. And it was bad. Not bad, *awful*."

"Are you in trouble? Legal trouble?"

"No. But others sure are. Or will be . . . But I'll never see this money again. A lot of my clients are gone, Mal. A lot of money is gone, too."

"What do you need from us, Matt?" He knew the answer but asked the question anyway.

"I just need funds, short-term, to climb back out. I've got to save the firm. There isn't a lot left, but what's there is the family's."

Malcolm gripped the edge of the kitchen table.

His brother stood and rounded the table. "I am so sorry to ask. You can't know how sorry I am. How ashamed I am to be in this position. I know it's been tight here, too, and this couldn't come at a worse time. But I'll take what we've got left, what Mom and Dad left behind, and I'll get it all back. As much as I can. I promise I will, Mal."

As a younger man, Malcolm would have replied with a profane jab about turning the tables or the mighty falling. If he were one of the unlikely clients with nothing left, he might have considered a real jab, too. Perhaps a right hook like the one that had leveled Nathan Crescimanno in a dark alley years before.

"Send me the forms," Malcolm said as he walked past Matthew.

He walked out the door, got into his car, and drove to one of his favorite places. The place where the world told him everything would be all right, even when he knew it was sometimes a lie. The Woodstock Tower.

CHAPTER 11

July 1, 2011

The month that followed Matthew's dramatic visit to *Domus Jefferson* passed in a flurry.

During the last week of June, Malcolm sent an e-mail calling for a family meeting at the Inn. He invited everyone: Samantha, Shawn, Matthew, Noah, their long-time family attorney Alex Palmer, and A&P, who'd been an integral part of both the family and the Inn. Rachel was invited, too, at Noah's discretion, if for no other reason than to meet the rest of the gang.

Matthew and Malcolm hadn't spoken much in the month since Matthew had broken the news about his shattered life and had asked to borrow the family investments in an effort to turn it around. They'd exchanged a few e-mails, and Malcolm posed important questions about the whats, whys, and hows of Matthew's ill-placed investments.

As a thank-you, and without informing his brother or sister-in-law, Matthew arranged to run two full-page ads for

Domus Jefferson in *Bed & Breakfast America,* a popular quarterly magazine. And though he knew it wasn't going to solve anyone's problems, he sent a long e-mail to his Facebook friends inviting them to become online fans of his family's historic inn. It might have been the most passionate thing he'd ever written.

Matthew also continued winding down his marriage to Monica. Their attorneys squabbled over details large and small, and the process had worn everyone out. During one of their heated settlement conferences, Monica's attorney asked if Matthew was involved in another relationship.

"You know that I am," he answered. "And so is she."

Then, acting on a hunch, the attorney asked, "Is she pregnant?"

Matthew's face drained white. "Not anymore." Monica remained poised and perfectly still, though she felt as if she were drowning. Unable to ensure another second of the brutal, awkward silence, Monica scribbled something on her attorney's legal pad. Then she gathered her things and politely excused herself.

The last words she spoke to Matthew were a broken, "I'm sorry."

Later that night Matthew wrote her a letter apologizing for not telling her himself and avoiding the embarrassing surprise.

She did not reply.

Noah and Rachel's relationship continued to grow and ripen sweeter by the day. Rachel had parted the curtains of her romantic past and confided that Noah was, by far, her most serious relationship. She had dated little in high school or since and seemed to have myriad excuses why. "There's always been something wrong with me, I guess."

Noah doubted that and couldn't understand how any boy or man would ever let her drift from his life.

Noah asked about Rachel's friend and future coworker, Tyler, and whether their friendship had ever been more. "No," she answered, "not really. I don't think he's ever liked me that way."

Noah doubted that, too.

Rachel had also shared bits and pieces about her unusual childhood and her parents' separation. "Less a divorce," Rachel said. "More like he left us."

"I'm sorry."

"Don't be. He's turned his life around. At least I think he has."

"You're in touch?"

"In a way. . . . He sends me an occasional postcard. One or two a year from somewhere in the world."

"That's cool then, yeah?"

"Yes, it is. He's slowly been putting his life together. But I still haven't seen him. Don't know if I ever will."

Noah hadn't yet met the man Rachel called her stepfather, and when he asked about him, Rachel said she wasn't sure anymore where he was most of the time. He'd done well in international business and spoke five languages fluently. He made a lot of money and lived very well, whether with the family or on the road, but hadn't been a consistent part of her mother's life for several years.

Rachel missed him. "He was on the road more and more the older I got. When he was home, he tried to be a calming influence, a provider. He made us feel safe. He took care of us."

Noah learned that Rachel received a BMW on her sixteenth birthday. She went on every extracurricular school trip. She studied in France for a semester. When a school needed new uniforms, or new instruments, or new laptops, her stepfather's checkbook was only a phone call or an e-mail away.

It was obvious to Noah that Rachel and her stepfather were not as emotionally close as Rachel would have liked. But it was also quite obvious that she was grateful to him for the safety and financial security he had provided to Rachel and her mother.

Rain prepared for the family meeting by setting out yet another new place mat and matching napkin set and making enough appetizers to feed a reception of fifty.

"Dear, we're not hosting an Amway recruiting meeting," Malcolm said. "Relax a little." But that proved much easier said than practiced and Malcolm spent the morning fiddling in his workshop and worrying about the most important family meeting they'd had since Jack and Laurel died.

Samantha and Shawn arrived first, and A&P soon followed with mutual friend and attorney, Alex Palmer. Matthew walked in half an hour later with regrets from his son, LJ. "He hates missing a Cooper family meeting, but you know college kids. It's all nonstop."

Noah and the uncomfortable but supportive Rachel arrived last. After the requisite chitchat and how-have-you-beens and thank-you-for-comings, Malcolm invited everyone to get comfortable in the living room.

Rain and Malcolm sat side by side on the hearth in front of the fireplace as the others scattered around the room, increasingly curious about the evening at hand.

"Hi, everybody. Thanks for coming. I know everyone is busy, so thanks, really, for making the trip." Malcolm produced a manila envelope from a briefcase at his feet. "First, let me say how difficult this is. If you had asked us twenty-five years ago if this day would ever come, Rain and I would have assured you that it would not. This place, this home, this business, because it is *still* a business, has been more important to us than anything else in our lives except for one another. Taking over after Mom and Dad passed has been the greatest honor of my life." Malcolm turned to Rain. "Our lives, right?"

Rain started to speak but quickly lost her voice, then her will.

Matthew sensed he knew what would come next. He looked into the faces of his siblings, at Noah, and even A&P, and wondered if they also knew.

"It's been tough for a while. I think most of you probably

understand already. Things never quite recovered since the slow-down began back in 2001, 2002. There were months when we thought we had moved out of the worst, but then a month or two, or three or four, or more reminded us that we had not."

Malcolm looked at Rain. "It is also no secret that Rain and I are getting older."

Without looking up, Rain jabbed him in the leg with her index finger. "Speak for yourself."

"It's true we've been doing this a long time. The family has been doing this a long time. We've considered a change before, and the finances are only part of that consideration. A big one, yes, but not the entire picture. There are things we want to do. You know how long I've wanted to go to a writers' conference? Or better, one of those retreats somewhere?"

Everyone in the room seemed to acknowledge the question with their eyes, but no one answered. Malcolm continued. "You guys remember our first night here at the Inn?"

Matthew nodded.

"Sam?"

"I do," she said. "I recall how scared I was sleeping out in the guesthouse, just me and you. That idea was really exciting before we actually moved in, remember? But back then I was terrified."

Shawn took her hand and interlaced his fingers with hers. Then she went on. "I remember we went to our separate tiny rooms, mine more like a closet, and I lasted five minutes—"

"If that," Malcolm corrected.

"Before I came in and tried to climb into my big, brave brother's bed."

"Aw," Rain cooed.

"And then you put your foot in my ribs and gave me one big shot to the floor, do you remember that, big, brave brother?"

Malcolm looked at their attorney and said, "I have no recollection of any such thing and do not believe any such thing occurred." Malcolm turned to his sister and continued. "I remember that first night so well because I saw something in Dad's eyes I'd never seen before. Now I don't remember Dad's job down at UVA in Charlottesville as well as Matthew probably does, but I know that it was just a job. A job that Dad left every night when he came home to his family. But that first night here I'll never forget dancing around the living room with Mom and seeing Dad sitting right over there." Malcolm pointed at a recliner across the room. "He sat there with a smile so big, so content, that it spread to his eyes, his forehead, everywhere. It said, *I am home.*"

Rachel whispered something in Noah's ear and rested her head on his shoulder.

Malcolm opened the envelope and pulled out a thick stack of papers gathered with a black binder clip. "This is it. We are selling *Domus Jefferson.*"

A&P gasped and covered her mouth with both hands.

"We have been over it and over it and over it. We met with

Alex, we prayed about it, we ran the numbers, and we simply decided that the time was right. It's time to move on."

Samantha was the first to respond. "First, I'll say that I am not completely shocked. I have heard the hints and seen a few signs living as close to you as I do." Her voice had a professional edge to it. "But why? Why isn't this a family decision? Before anything is sold, shouldn't we discuss it as a family? Shouldn't Matthew and me, and Mom and Dad's grandkids, be involved in a decision that affects us all?"

Rain folded her hands across her lap and appeared to close her eyes.

Malcolm answered. "Sam, you're right. If we were *all* living here, if we were *all* running the business, if we were *all* going to the Chamber of Commerce meetings, the Rotary meetings, answering the phone at 1:00 A.M., checking in guests at all hours of the day no matter how many times we tell them on the phone we're not a Holiday Inn. But we're not *all* doing those things together. I respect that this Inn has been a part of all of us. No question. But when Rain and I took over for Mom and Dad—and remember it wasn't our dream to do this—we jumped in feet first. We were the only option. So we raised a child here. Built a marriage here. We have lived in this home, this Inn, this town for about as long as Mom and Dad did."

Malcolm softened. "Sam, you have been a huge help to us through the years. There are not enough ways to thank you for what you've done for us. I mean that. But Sam, Matthew, this is our decision to make. It is our names on the business license, and it is our names on the tax returns. We are the ones who wake up every morning and pray for the phone to ring with reservations. I run ads for the website, I troll Facebook looking for potential customers like a desperate sixteen-year-old looking for friends." Malcolm paused and began flipping through the stack of paperwork.

"Mal," Matthew said. "I think what Sam is saying is that we want to help in any way that we can. That's it. We want to help; we have to help." Matthew looked to Samantha to reinforce his thought, but she was busy wiping her nose.

"Are you interested in running this place?" Malcolm asked him.

"Well, not really, no, because I have a life someplace else."

Malcolm turned to his sister. "Sam? Shawn?"

"You know we can't," Shawn spoke for them both.

"Son?" Malcolm said.

Noah looked at his mother and father. "There was a time, yes. But not anymore. My dream is somewhere else, something new."

Matthew took the lead. "Guys, we love this place, too. And, of course, I never lived here. This was never really my home because I was older and moving on with the rest of my life by the time we left Charlottesville." He weighed his words before pressing on. "I don't know how much you've told Sam or Noah about the family finances, but I can reverse some things if I need to, help you get your hands on some of the cash. That's all anyone is asking for. A chance to look at every option on the table before we sign or sell anything."

Malcolm stopped flipping pages and looked at his brother. "That's all in the past, Matt. We're not looking back tonight or tomorrow or at any point between now and the day we say good-bye. That is not what this meeting tonight is for." He tapped the papers. "With the help of Alex and Shirley French, whom you know, we have found a buyer."

Samantha stood, and A&P gasped even louder than she had the first time. She hid her face in her hands.

"But you haven't signed anything," Matthew said.

Malcolm held up the signed and notarized page of the contract. "We close on September 30."

Samantha scurried from the room and Rain raced after her.

Malcolm held a moment before continuing. "We will then have thirty days to train the new owners and move out whatever personal items we're keeping. Then it's over."

Matthew put his elbows on his knees and looked down at his loafers.

"We've made an offer on a little place by the river and expect the sale to go through smoothly."

Rain reappeared in the doorway with her arms crossed and her eyes red.

"I'm sorry," Malcolm finished. "The Inn is gone."

CHAPTER 12

J ust as Malcolm and Rain could have predicted, the Inn fell silent.

A&P rose to her feet and approached Rain. The two women shared a long embrace, and when A&P let go, she leaned in and said softly, "I will help however I can." She nodded good-byes to everyone in the room, refused an escort home, and showed herself out.

"Noah," Malcolm said. "Is there anything you want to say? Anything you want to ask?"

Noah shook his head and looked at Rachel. They made eye contact and Noah smiled at her. Then he looked back at his father. "I support you. You too, Mom. Home is where you guys are."

Noah turned his head again to Rachel, said something quietly, then excused himself and walked into the kitchen. Rachel watched him take something from the table and put it in his pocket. Then he stepped back into the doorway and beckoned for her to follow him. A few short steps later, the couple slipped out the back door and let the screen door slam behind them.

Matthew and Shawn spoke quietly while Malcolm straightened and reloaded the real estate and sales documents back into the envelope. When he looked up, Samantha reentered the room and sat.

"What do we know about them?" she said evenly.

"May I?" Alex said. "The buyers are a couple from northern Virginia. The husband recently retired from a civilian position at the Coast Guard. They have a very nice pension, impressive savings, and family money on his wife's side from which to draw." He sat up a little and changed gears. "They are perhaps not as warm as your mother and father were, and they are decidedly more private. But like many in their position, living where they have for so long, they want to escape. They've looked at other opportunities like this, other inns closer to the city, but they're overpriced. This one works with their budget and priorities. Mrs. French has given them several tours of the Inn and the property and has very discreetly shown them around town."

When no one spoke immediately, Alex continued. "I have discussed the financial situation with them and presented an audit. I get the strong impression that they are decent people. Of course, they are not at the level of your mother and father, or Malcolm and Rain for that matter. And they are not as young as your parents were when they came to the Inn, but they appear to be energetic and driven to turn a profit and do more than quietly retire. He, especially, is a focused, goal-driven type. He has ideas about branching into corporate training out here, maybe building one of those obstacle or ropes courses companies use for team building, that kind of thing. Admittedly I am not familiar with that kind of work or those programs, but he seems to be."

"You mentioned their financial situation?" Matthew prompted.

"They have demonstrated the resources to give what is needed, both in sale price and operating funds. And, frankly, if I might add, this is a very difficult market to sell a business like this. You may not view it that way right now, but there are other businesses in the county equally or more attractive that have sat on the market for much, much longer."

Malcolm took the natural opening. "Rain and I have talked about this and we want to share the proceeds. Obviously we have financial obligations we need to meet. But we do want to share some of the profits from what we believe is a fair sale in this market to people we believe will find a way to make it work."

Malcolm looked at both of his siblings and added, "It's the right thing to do."

Outside Noah held the swing still for Rachel to climb on. Then just as his grandfather Jack had, and with the same gusto as his father, Malcolm, with one strong push off the ground Noah sent the swing into perfectly balanced motion.

"Everything OK?" Rachel asked.

"Yes. Actually I'm pretty great. I just feel . . . It's weird—I feel like we were ready for this."

"We?"

"Sure."

"Noah, you realize how *incredibly* out of place I feel tonight. I'm very glad to be here for you, even a little honored, but I wanted to sink into those cushions and disappear."

With one finger Noah tucked long strands of hair behind Rachel's ear. "You shouldn't have. Dad said to invite you if I thought you should be there. And I did because I do. . . . I'm ready."

"Ready for what?"

"For the change. For this to end. I know that if I'd told Mom and Dad that I wanted this life for me, they would have found a way to make that happen. I'm sure they would have." Noah looked at the sky above the roofline of the Inn. The air was thick with early summer Virginia humidity, and the overcast night hid every star in the universe.

"Maybe it will hit me harder later," he continued. "I mean, I'm going to miss this place like crazy. This was my childhood home. Not many people anywhere can say they were raised in an inn, but I was. This is the only place I'd ever lived until I headed off to Mason and started doing my own thing. But this has not been my dream, my goal, for a long, long time. Plus, I know Mom and Dad have been stressing about it for a while. And who am I to tell them what will make them happy?"

Rachel had noticed him staring into the starless sky and followed his eyes upward. "This is going to sound ridiculous, but I'm surprisingly bummed out."

Noah laughed. "Bummed out? Was that in your thesis?"

"I'm serious, Noah. I've only been out here a few times, but I love it. This place feels more like home than my own home. There's just something about it." Her voice trailed off.

The swing carried them through the valley night air, and Noah could not imagine another place, another time, or another person he would rather be with at that very moment. He looked at her shadowed profile. "This isn't how I expected it would be."

"Expected what to be?"

Noah looked up again. "Not a star to be seen. Here we are in this perfect moment in time, two people in love on a swing my grandparents used in the yard I grew up in. We should be looking up and seeing a billion stars smiling down on us and marking the path to whatever comes next."

"Oh, my," Rachel said. "Am I in a Nicholas Sparks' novel?"

Noah's laugh filled the yard. "Four *ha*'s for that one," he said. "Just stick with me for a second. You know what I love about cloudy days?"

"Tell me, Nick."

"I love the assurance that even when you can't see the sun you know it's there. Even when you can't see the stars at night, like right now, you know they're right there. It's not as if God's brilliant and perfectly placed stars just go away. They are always up there whether you can see them or not."

Rachel's expression was a cocktail of confusion and worry.

"It's like a family, isn't it? I can promise you right now Aunt Sam and Uncle Matt can't see the stars in there either. But do they love Mom and Dad? And do my folks love them back? Totally."

"I suppose that's true."

"It *totally* is. We all wish we saw the stars all the time. Who doesn't feel safe when the map is clear, when there are no secrets, when there's literally nothing between us and whatever is up there beyond what our eyes or telescopes can see?"

Rachel looked up one more time before settling her focus squarely on Noah. "Well said. And you know what? That would make a lovely children's book. Maybe your first?"

Noah hadn't heard her. Instead of answering, he stepped off the swing and put his hands on the outsides of her thighs. "So yes, maybe it would be better right now if the sky were filled with stars, if we had a little breeze instead of this air that feels like I'm wearing a wet sweater. Maybe it could be more like a scene that lovers dream of. But what I see when I look up isn't an overcast sky or a forecast of rain. I see a family. I see the hope that no matter what, no matter where we are in life or where we are on the globe, the stars are still there."

Noah knelt on one knee and took her left hand with his. Then he slid something from his right front pocket and held it in the air between them.

"Is that a napkin ring?" Rachel nervously chuckled out the words.

"For now." He smiled and slipped it on two of her fingers.

Rachel's hands began to quiver.

"Rachel Kaplan. Will you marry me?"

CHAPTER 13

88 Days to the Wedding

Rachel and Noah returned inside and found Rain and Samantha in serious conversation in the kitchen. Malcolm, Matthew, and Alex Palmer were gathered around an iMac on the small registration desk by the front door. Shawn was lounging on the couch, thumbing through a photo album.

Noah put his arm around his mother's shoulder and said something in her ear. Her eyes went wide and he pulled her closer, whispered something else, and she buried her head in his chest.

She was clinging to Rachel when Noah led them into the living room. "Dad, Uncle Matt, could you come here?" Noah turned back toward the kitchen and called for Samantha, too.

It took a minute but everyone arrived in the living room. Alex came too, but he leaned against the door frame and kept his distance.

"We have an announcement to make," Noah began. "It just

seems right that with everyone here, and all this change coming to the family, that you share this." He gave Rachel a sideways hug and kissed her head.

"Oh, for heaven's sake," Rain blurted. "They're getting married!"

Everyone approached at once and Noah winked at his mother. "Yep. What she said."

One at a time everyone congratulated the engaged couple. But when the initial burst of excitement eased, the questions and commentary came in a storm.

"When?"

"Where will you have it?"

"You've got to do it at the church in Mount Jackson, right?"

"Are you going to ask her father?"

"They should get married where *she* wants to."

"Do her parents know?"

"Can I update my Facebook status, Noah?"

"Congratulations, son, but you need to ask her father. Do it the right way." Malcolm put his hand on Noah's shoulder.

"Can I text Angela and tell her?" This one came from Samantha. "She's home with the baby. Poor girls have summer colds." She'd already hit SEND before anyone could answer.

"Oh, oh, oh, show us the ring."

Rachel reached out and displayed the back of her hand as if

her finger held a diamond. Instead, two of her fingers sported a wooden napkin ring.

"Classy," Shawn said as he slapped Noah on the back.

"All right, all right." Noah held his hands out and pretended to push back the throng. "Have a seat."

Noah stepped onto the hearth and extended his hand for Rachel to join him. "Here's what we're going to do. We're going to get married right here at the Inn." He said the words more to her than the huddled crowd.

Perfect, Rachel mouthed back her reply.

"Not in a church?" Rain asked.

"We're going to get married here, Mom."

"But don't you think—"

"Mom, just think of this place *as* a church. We worship here, we sing here, strangers come almost every week. We learn about each other, we learn who we are here, right, Dad? I mean really, it might as well be a church if you think about it."

Rain started to speak again, but Malcolm tenderly stopped her.

"This is the place, guys," Noah pressed. "We've experienced everything here but a wedding. I know it's not the way the Coopers have done it in the past. But this is a special place to all of us and especially now, with Mom and Dad moving on. Let's have a wedding at the one place that brings us all together."

"Amen," Matthew said. "I agree."

"When do we have to be out?" Noah asked his dad.

"We close September 30, but we don't have to be gone until October 31."

"Noah," Rain couldn't help asking, "you're not thinking of getting married so soon, are you?"

"No, Mother, we're not thinking of it, we're *doing* it."

Samantha raised her hand. "Just wait a second, couldn't we still do it here even after we've lost it? Pay something to hold it here? Or build it into the deal somehow?"

Malcolm did not appreciate her use of the word *lost,* but given the buoyant mood chose to let it pass.

"Uh-huh." Noah raised a confident finger as if making a political stump speech. "No, we're not waiting. We're doing it while the Inn is still ours."

Rain spoke up. "What do *you* think, sweetie?"

Rachel had been fighting tears since sitting outside on the swing and now put her arms around Noah's waist. "I love him," she said, and then the dam burst and she wept openly.

Noah guided her down and held her as they sat. "See what you've done?" he teased his mother, and she joined them on the hearth, putting her arm around Rachel and comforting her the way only a mother can.

Rachel soaked it in.

"Dad, you'll be clearing things out in October, right?"

"What's left, yes. We can start packing up and storing

personal items and whatever won't convey with the business right away. There's no reason not to."

"There is now," Noah said. "Can't we wait? Can't we leave things as is until right after the wedding?"

Rain nodded agreement.

"Sure we can, son."

"So get out your calendars," Noah instructed.

Cell phones and smart phones appeared and Rain fetched a master calendar from a drawer in the registration desk.

They bounced dates back and forth, dodging business trips and heavily booked weekends. When the digital dust had settled, Noah took the floor. "So we've got it? September 27?"

Nods and thumbs up from around the room.

"Rachel will call her parents to confirm the date, but she doesn't expect any problems. We'll get them here. I'll get with Rachel's dad and make it official."

"Good move," Malcolm said.

"Mom?"

"I've already started an invite list," Rain said, making notes on a *Domus Jefferson* stationery pad. "We'll block out the dates on the website and make a list with probably five hundred other things."

"Deep breaths, sis," Samantha said. "I'm here to help."

"Dad, how about you?" Noah asked.

"I'll meet with Pastor Robinson, make sure he can do

it. Shawn can help with a few things around here. Paint, landscaping—nothing extraordinary."

"Absolutely," Shawn said.

"Aunt Sam, how about you?"

"I work for your mom now, kiddo. I'll march to her beat."

"Uncle Matt?"

Matthew chewed on his lower lip and started to speak but awkwardly caught himself and choked before anyone even understood the first word. He tried again, "I'm sorry." He ran his hands down his pant legs and rubbed his knees. "I'm just really proud of everyone right now." He looked at Malcolm. "Dad and Mom would be amazed at what's happened here tonight."

"I'm sure they are," Rain assured him.

Matthew looked at each of the three couples in the room. All in love, all in unison, each working as one. "I'll do whatever you need. I'm a long distance away, but please don't hesitate to ask. It's the least I can do." His voice cracked again. "And I'm just so sorry Monica can't be here to enjoy all this. She'd be happy for you, Noah, I know she would be."

"I'll call her," Rain said.

"I can do it," Noah offered.

"No." Matthew threw up a stop sign. "I will."

They continued planning and processing the challenges ahead. Each person balancing the news that the Inn would be leaving the family and that Rachel would be joining it.

At some point Rain jumped to her feet. "What are we thinking? I've got to tell A&P. She will want—probably *demand*—to be part of this."

"Mom, let us tell her," Noah replied and Rachel agreed.

The room went oddly reverent as Noah held out a hand and assisted Rachel to her feet. They walked hand in hand out the door, past the swing, across the spot where they planned to be married in just three months, and over the hill to their beloved neighbor's property.

Noah and Rachel were sure the others heard A&P's delight all the way back at the Inn.

CHAPTER 14

87 Days to the Wedding

Noah spent the night sleeping in the same bed and in the same cottage he'd always known. Rachel stayed there too, sleeping in Samantha's old room. The two said long good-nights through the thin wall.

Noah fell asleep fantasizing about his honeymoon and life with Rachel.

Rachel fell asleep terrified about those same things.

Matthew also stayed at the Inn but left early to catch a flight and return home. He left behind a promise to keep in touch and yet another offer of whatever assistance was needed.

Noah and Rachel ate a breakfast fit for an inn full of paying guests. As they finished, A&P knocked on the back door.

Rain unlocked it and welcomed her in. "Can you believe it?" she said, wrapping her arms around A&P's broad shoulders.

"Yes, Reindeer, I can."

Noah laughed at the nickname. "I haven't heard that in so long. I've missed you, A&P."

Noah explained to Rachel how "Rain, dear" had become "Reindeer" one Christmas about ten years earlier.

Rachel reveled in the comfort of the inside joke.

"Let's talk Wedding Letters," A&P said. "Normally they'd be a surprise, but I know Reindeer over there has already spilled her beans that we've done them. So no use messing around; there's no time to waste. You want them, right?" She looked at Rain across the table. "Of course they want them."

Rain motioned to Rachel. "It's her wedding."

Rachel placed her hand atop A&P's. "Why do you think I said yes to the proposal?"

"My Land-a-Goshen I do like this one, son. I do like this one! You finally got it right."

"Uhh, thanks?" Noah said with raised eyebrows.

"Wedding Letters." A&P put both palms flat on the table. "You want them, good. May I handle that?"

"Who else would?" Rain said. "They are your creation. Just tell me what you need. Names, addresses—whatever I can do to help."

"All right then. And Rachel, sweetheart, can you give me numbers for your parents?"

"Um, I guess, yes. Maybe I'll tell my mother about it, if you don't mind. And I have my stepdad's cell phone number, but he rarely answers it and he could be anywhere right now."

"Does he have a voice mail thing?"

"Yes," Rachel grinned. "He has a voice mail thing."

"Good. Then he'll call me back."

Rachel didn't know A&P well, but she knew enough to know that wasn't a question.

"How would you like the letters? In a loose folder? Three-ring binder? I can go as simple or elegant as you wish. Leather cover? Do you want them collected and professionally bound in a book? Engraved cover?"

"That sounds gr—"

"And a website," A&P cruised on. "I'll have that boy in town do it. What do you think? RachelandNoah.com. We'll put on my mailing address for the letters, date, menu, gift registry—everything."

Rachel didn't have time to object before they were making a mile-long list. They continued until Noah yawned and his eyes rolled back in his head. When Rachel didn't notice right away, he did it again with more flair.

"Go," she said.

He thanked her with a kiss and went hunting for his father.

When Rain heard the front door close, she leaned in and practically sang, "So, Rachel, speaking of Wedding Letters, want to read more of mine?"

Her smile said yes.

✉

Dear Mr. and Mrs. Cooper,

Congratulations on your nuptials.

When Mrs. Prestwich called and asked me to write this let-ter, Malcolm, I told her she was calling the wrong person. I mean, really, who asks for marriage advice from someone who's been mar-ried three times?

I'm sure you'll receive a lot of very valuable advice from Mrs. Prestwich's project. And maybe if she's smart, she'll change her mind and this letter will never make it into the book. If by some misfor-tune you are reading it anyway, just remember this wasn't my idea.

I've never put this in writing. Let's see if I can articulate why my three marriages failed.

My first marriage was to a woman I met in college. It ended be-cause she wouldn't follow me to graduate school. I wanted an MBA. She wanted to live closer to her parents in Harrisburg. I begged her to come with me to the West Coast for a different life. She was upset and we fought. Then we fought some more and I used words I still can't believe I ever said to a woman. I packed up my car in a huff and told her she had ten days to change her mind and meet me in California.

She did not meet me in California.

We talked on the phone a few times, and her parents tried to convince me to return to Virginia and work on an MBA at a school closer to home. But it was not to be. After a couple of months living in East LA, I finally convinced her to come meet me for a weekend.

I hoped the city would change her mind. I was sure that we would see things and experience things she'd never seen or experienced before and that she would never want to get back on the plane.

We saw and experienced some things all right—like a mugging on the street where we parked our car outside the Grauman's Chinese Theatre. It was all I could do to keep her in town two more days until her flight left. We said good-bye at the airport and that was that. We were married fourteen months. It's not easy being twenty-five and divorced.

My second marriage ended because I did things I'm not proud of on a business trip to Toronto. We'd been married nearly ten years. And to think, I was so proud of myself for surviving the seven-year itch.

A coworker and I had gotten very close, too close emotionally, in hindsight, though we'd never crossed any other lines. But on this trip we got caught up in one too many drinks and one too many flirts in a hotel neither of us had been to and neither of us would ever return to. Then it happened.

The next morning I woke up and made a commitment to tell my wife as soon as I landed in San Francisco.

When I walked in the front door, I quickly hugged my two boys and sent them outside to play. I sat by her on the couch and told her what had happened. I don't know if I expected her to be proud of me for being honest or not. She wasn't.

She did not yell at me, she did not cry, she did not slap me or scratch me or throw me out of the house in anger.

Instead she went into the backyard, gathered the boys, got into her SUV, and drove off.

A day later she returned and asked me for a divorce. What stung me most was how she looked at me. She said she would've been less hurt if I'd stabbed her with a knife. She said there were things she could forgive me of but this was not one of them. She wouldn't have me raising our children if I could not be faithful.

The third marriage ended when my money, the new house in Oakland, the apartment in Manhattan, the cabin in Park City, and the four or five trips on a leased private jet every year were no longer enough for the woman who'd once been my assistant. She left me for a younger man who made a bigger fortune than I had.

Three marriages. More mistakes than I can count.

As I write this today I am dating a woman whom I'm quite fond of. She works for Microsoft in Washington. If this woman has any sense at all she'll break it off with me.

What have I learned from these marriages? I suppose it's pretty obvious. For certain I was decent at being a boyfriend and lousy at being a husband.

Will you do it differently? Knowing your mother, I suspect you will.

Sincerely,
Drew McConnell

✉

My sweet Rain and my darling Malcolm,

Never in my life have I been so excited at the reunion of two people. OK, with the exception of my man Alan. But you get the point.

I don't know if you'll read my Wedding Letter first. I don't suppose it matters much; you are both smart kids, you'll figure it out. If you're curious, just know the inspiration for these letters came from a late night of loneliness in my study. Alan and I were not married very long, but I did receive a few cards and letters in our short love affair. I have saved them in a very special place that only I know about. I do not read them every day, or every week or even every month, but I used to. Lately I read them on the days that would've been his birthday, on my birthday, on our anniversary, and on a few other private select days he and I shared together.

As you already know, I lived alone until meeting Alan. I had a few casual relationships with men but they never went very far. I was always everyone's buddy. Whether I like it or not, I accept that my struggle with weight was one of the reasons that I always had more friends than dates. It bothered me when I was younger, but I grew up, and I grew confident, and when I met Alan, I had never been at a greater peace in my life. Perhaps we worked out so well because I was finally being me.

But this letter—my very first Wedding Letter—is about you

and your miraculous marriage. I prayed many nights when Malcolm was in Brazil that he would return and that somehow, someway, this day would occur. It is a special feeling when two people you love so much for their own unique personalities and talents come together. Just thinking of it makes me smile here at my desk.

What kind of advice can a woman married for just a few years give to a young couple with thirty or forty or fifty years of marriage ahead of them? How about just one little A&P secret?

Learn to listen. That's it. Learn to listen to one another. Whether you're happy, sad, mourning, depressed, or just need to sit and let thoughts become words and words become a conversation, listen. Always remember that what your spouse is saying to you is very likely something they couldn't or shouldn't say to any other living soul. Just you!

The more you do it the better you'll get. The better you get the more you'll love it. The more you love it the more you'll do it. So listen!

I hope you enjoy these letters as much as I have enjoyed gathering them. They are yours to share or not share. That is up to you.

Thank you for being the best friends in the best family I've ever had.

Enjoy your day!

Love,
Anna Belle Prestwich, A&P

Dear Malcolm and Rain,

The answer is: "The game show host your father Jack Cooper most wanted to meet."

The question: "Who is Alex Trebek?"

Correct! I am honored to send this note of congratulations on your marriage.

Sincerely,
Alex Trebek

✉

"Is this real?" Rachel asked.

A&P took the book from her. "Of course it's real, darling," she said as she gingerly removed the typed letter on production company letterhead. "It even has Mr. Trebek's signature right there in real life ink."

"The truth is," said Rain, "it was really a toss-up between Trebek and Jack Barry as my father-in-law's favorite game show host. But Mr. Barry had passed away before Mal and I got married, so A&P went after Trebek. It was a fun nod to Jack to have it included, and Malcolm loves to tell people the story."

A&P returned the book to Rachel and she skimmed a few more letters. "They're all so different. Unique voices, histories, perspectives. What a treasure." When Rachel reached the back of the book, she found a series of letters that didn't fit in. "Oh, I'm sorry, I don't think these are part of the same set."

"May I?" Rain reached out for the book and removed several letters in sheet protectors from the very end of the collection. "You're right. These are not part of our wedding letters. I have just kept these here for safekeeping. These are from Noah's grandpa to each of his children. Would you like to read them?"

"I'm not sure I should. They must be very personal."

"They *are* personal. He wrote them to be read after he and Noah's grandmother died. But in no time at all you're going to be one of us, a Cooper, and I know Jack wouldn't mind you reading them. Not one bit. They are part of our family history."

"Has everyone else read them?"

"Yes. Everyone in the family who has wanted to read them has read them."

Rachel took the letters from Rain and held them like they were the most fragile thing she'd ever touched.

"Sweetheart, there's nothing in those letters you don't already know."

✉

To Matthew, my oldest,

You were first for a reason, my son. Your mind and your drive are inspirational. Do you know that? Do you know how much I respect you and am awed by your talents? You were the man given the talents who chose to double them. You have made Him proud. You have made me proud. I cannot wait to see you become a father. You will be a wonder.

Matthew, love your wife. Love her like she's the only one you'll ever have. And she will be.

I love you.
Dad

✉

To Samantha, my Broadway star,

On long days, when I tired of the monotony of the University and the men that did not like to work, I thought of you. I drove home those days, wondering what scene you had prepared for me, what part you would have me play. It never mattered, as long as I could be in the same show with you.

Get back on stage. It's time. Find your light.

I have said it in the flesh dozens of times, and now again in death I say it once more: Sammie, let my beautiful granddaughter know her father. He is not a perfect father, but he is her father.

You shine, Sammie. I would share the stage with you any day.

I love you.
Dad

✉

To Malcolm, my writer, my son,

I have always wondered how angry you would be today. I have cried at night and had dreams of you. I have dreamt of your fury. I pray I'm wrong. I'll understand if I'm not.

I tell you, son, that your discovery is not about who you think your father is. That is unchanged. Since the first time I held you on my lap after your mother's revelation—the day I returned from your grandmother's in Chicago—from that day on, from that day forward, I saw my son. I saw a son who belonged to me and was part of me the same way Matthew was. I saw a gift from God bestowed on me. There was no reason for you to ever know of the night your mother's life changed.

What was true yesterday is true today. I am your father. Your mother forgave. I forgave. Your Lord forgave. So must you.

Malcolm, if you haven't already, please finish your book. Please? Then write another and another. Know that I expect to see you again. And your mother and I cannot wait to see your children. We think they'll look like Rain. You read that right, young man, we've always known what you two have not yet seen. You are meant to be one.

> *I love you.*
> *Your Father*

CHAPTER 15

67 Days to the Wedding

After weeks of waiting and worrying that her job offer at the Department of Justice had been a giant bureaucratic mistake, a certified letter arrived in Rachel's mailbox. They celebrated her start date, September 5, with lunch at Red Robin.

To keep from losing her mind in the meantime, and because she wanted to hit the ground running, Rachel spent hours every day reading and researching online. She'd already written a policy paper for her new boss and been to the DOJ twice to fill out stacks of paperwork with Tyler's eager assistance. She also began the process of getting a background check required for her low-level clearance. Her interview with the investigator was more personal than she expected and though she expected to win the clearance she needed, the discussion left her shaken.

Noah had been sleeping in and enjoying a summer of no classes, no job, and no responsibilities besides what most men do in the wedding planning process. He drew or painted every day and spent one day at the Inn alone working on a charcoal drawing of the B&B as a gift for his parents. He also had four or five children's manuscripts in the works and was committed to selecting and polishing one to begin illustrating by the end of August.

Noah and Rachel's next trip home together came three weeks after their engagement.

Noah's cousin Angela and her baby girl were returning to St. Louis soon, something his mother reminded him of regularly.

They met for lunch at Ben's Diner in Woodstock.

"When's the last time you ate at an old-fashioned diner?" Noah asked, holding the door for Rachel.

"Does today count?"

Noah spotted Angela immediately from behind and shouted, "Cuz!" He zigzagged through the tables, put his arms around her waist, and lifted her off the ground.

"Noah! I'm an old lady, put me down." Noah did, but not before planting a wet kiss on her cheek.

Angela tried her best to act offended, but the gleam in her eye was obvious. She'd missed him. "You are such a strange little cousin of mine." She gently slapped his cheek. "Are you going to introduce me to this lovely woman standing behind you?"

"Oh, her?" Noah turned and made room. "Of course I am. Angie, meet my fiancée, Rachel Kaplan."

Rachel stepped toward Angela for a hug, but Noah put out his arm and stopped her. "Better not," he mumbled.

"Oh, I'm so sorry." Her face flushed. "I'm so used to the others hugging all the time."

Noah shifted his eyes dramatically left and right between the two women. "Well, well, well. This has gotten a bit awkward, hasn't it, ladies?"

But Angela was already laughing and taking a big step forward with open arms toward Rachel. After the embrace, Rachel slugged Noah in the stomach with a strong left fist.

"Ooh," he groaned. "Well placed."

They sat and the proud new mother immediately lifted little Taylor onto the table in her car seat carrier.

"She's not ugly at all," Noah said. "Your mom said she looked a little bit like an alien."

"Hey, Noah, just checking, but does Rachel know that I changed your diapers and potty trained you when you were—"

"Aren't you such a precious angel?" He cooed and tickled the bottom of Taylor's sock-covered feet.

After ordering lunch, Noah gave both women a quick history of the Ben Franklin, their recent closure, and the decision to section off the diner and keep it operating under the name Ben's Diner. Neither woman bothered to appear interested in Noah's trivia; they were watching and enjoying the attention Taylor was receiving from nearby diners.

"How's Jake?" Noah asked Angela.

"He's good. Tired and worked up over all the rumors about layoffs. But he's good."

"Layoffs?"

"He's been trying to get into a management job for a while at the distribution warehouse. He's stuck between being too qualified to work the floor and drive the pallet thing, but too low on the ladder for a desk job. Everyone says the company is cutting people, and he could be one of them."

"That just stinks," Noah said, and his mind cataloged another family misfortune in the midst of his personally exciting summer.

After small talk, lunch, and the dishes being cleared, Angela unbuckled Taylor from her carrier and asked Rachel if she wanted to hold her.

"No. Oh no. For *sure* no. I am *so* not ready to hold a baby."

"Not ready?" Angela was curious. "Haven't you ever held a baby?"

"I'm not sure, actually. It would have been a while."

Noah was amused by the exchange and rested his chin on his hand.

"What better time than with your almost-cousin-in-law, or second-cousin-twice-removed, or whatever she'll be to you." Angela stood up and handed the baby to Rachel. "Just cradle her. You'll be fine."

Rachel's heart raced as the baby nestled into her arms. "Oh my gosh. So little. Look at her fingers. So teeny tiny. Look, Noah."

"She's really beautiful, Angie," Noah said, and he meant it. He thought the baby looked one step removed from heaven.

A plate crashing in the kitchen startled the dozing baby and she scratched her own cheek. Cries and leg wiggles followed.

"Sorry, sorry. Here she is." It was more of a plea than anything.

Angela returned Taylor to her car seat and reassured Rachel the baby was fine. "Babies do that all the time, I'm learning. I have some little gloves to protect her hands from scratching like that but I must have left them at Mom's."

The conversation turned to Angela's husband, Jake, life in St. Louis, and as they always do, right back to the baby.

"How did she get her name?" Rachel asked, and though she wouldn't be asking to hold her again anytime soon, she found she couldn't take her eyes off her.

"It's a long story. Let's just say Jake and I are both Taylor Swift fans."

"I wondered," Rachel said.

"How about you guys? Kids in the future?"

Noah and Rachel spoke at exactly the same instant.

"Definitely."

"Maybe."

"Alrighty then," Angela chirped. "That was so fast I'm not even sure who said what."

The couple looked at one another and Noah spoke first. "Yeah, we'll have kids. Maybe not right away, but we will."

"Maybe so," Rachel countered, and they continued what appeared to Angela to be a middle school cafeteria stare down.

"We've talked about this, right?" Noah turned his chair slightly. "We've discussed having children at some point?"

"Of course, but in hypothetical planning, pros and cons, not in fixed terms."

"Fixed terms?"

For a minute Angela wondered if she was auditing a sociology class.

Rachel pivoted back to Angela. "Yes, we've talked about having children. And we may well. But who knows, right? And who knows when?" She gestured at Taylor. "I mean you waited until you were older."

Angela's expression collapsed.

Rachel felt sick. "I just meant that you were a bit older when you had your first, that's all. And look how happy you both are."

Angela rearranged a pink-and-white blanket over Taylor that didn't need rearranging. She spoke to her baby. "If I could have had you ten years ago I would have. But I wanted a husband first and that proved tougher than I thought. But we're lucky now, aren't we, baby girl?"

A cart with dishes rolled by and Rachel considered climbing on it.

Noah steered them to talk about his graduation, wedding planning, the sale of the Inn, one of the manuscripts he was working on, and A&P's Wedding Letters project. When the conversation ran dry, Noah stood and headed toward the register to pay the bill.

"I'm really sorry," Rachel said. "I honestly didn't mean a thing by it. I'm just scared, as if that isn't obvious enough."

"I know," Angela said.

"So it is that obvious?"

"You look like you could have upchucked that pulled pork sandwich and slaw."

Rachel laughed and put her hand on her stomach. "I may yet." She watched as Noah stopped at a table near the register and shook hands with two elderly men. "I love him," she said to Angela but with her eyes on Noah.

"That's obvious, too," Angela said.

"I really do. Like no one else in my life." She shifted her gaze to Angela and met her eyes. "I've never known a man like him. Or like his dad."

"That's because they're good men, Rachel. They are who they are, and they are what you see."

Rachel looked again at Noah. He'd arrived at the register and had his back to them. When he turned around, they saw he'd unwrapped two mini peppermint patties, placed them over his eyes, and was squeezing them into place with his bushy eyebrows. Above his head he held two unwrapped straws like antennae.

"Like I said," Angela laughed. "They are who they are."

CHAPTER 16

Rachel fought it, but the feeling had grown from just a consideration to the undeniable truth: She needed to tell her mother in person. She tried to share the news on the telephone, but the conversation quickly morphed into her mother's complaints about the oppressive Phoenix heat.

"Mother, you knew Arizona would be hot. That was the number one item on your list of negatives about moving there."

Stephanie grumbled something unintelligible and from nowhere asked Rachel if she could research online local spas that offered a very specific type of mud bath.

"Of course, Mother."

Rachel had given up on a marriage between her mother and technology years ago. During a visit when her mother was living in San Diego, Rachel had taken her to the mall and signed her up for the most basic cell phone plan. By the end of the weekend, her mother had tossed the phone in a swimming pool. Rachel fished it out, went back to the store alone, and canceled the agreement.

They had similar experiences with e-mail, social media, and video chatting. Rachel didn't know if her mother simply wasn't capable of adapting to the technology or whether she simply didn't have enough patience to let it happen. In the end it didn't matter; Stephanie survived with a landline in whatever home she was living in at the time and the occasional handwritten letter.

Stephanie had, at times, been a frustrating force in her daughter's life. But Rachel felt tremendous loyalty toward Stephanie and her appreciation for her mother's ability to endure was undeniable. Rachel would never forget that when others came and went, when she'd been hurt and broken, her mother was always near.

How then, with the most exciting day of her life approaching, could she possibly pass the engagement news along on the phone like a weather forecast or a funny anecdote from school?

She used those words and explanations when telling Noah she needed to visit her mother in Arizona for a long weekend. He offered to come along, just as she'd expected he would. She politely declined and said she needed to go alone. He'd expected that, too.

Rachel's long flight departed from Reagan National and landed ten minutes late. Late enough, she predicted, for her mother to be annoyed. She met Rachel curbside in a red 2011 Ford Taurus SHO with a temporary tag.

"You're late," Stephanie said through the passenger's open window.

Rachel ignored her and tossed her bag in the backseat. "Mother, when did you get this?"

"Recently," her mother said.

"When?" Rachel kissed her mother's cheek and complimented her earrings.

"Thank you. And this week, I guess it was."

"A new car? Why in the world? I didn't think you were driving anymore."

"I don't very often. Not outside of my community."

Her mother hit the gas and the powerful car jolted into the steady stream of cars passing alongside the terminal. "Furthermore, I told you I wanted to pick you up myself."

"Oh, Mom, I thought that meant you'd ride along in a cab or with a friend."

Stephanie gunned it again, and they nearly rear-ended a shuttle exiting the airport access road.

"I wouldn't mind driving, you know. If you'd like." Rachel gripped the door handle and her knuckles popped.

Stephanie declined and they sped along toward her posh planned community in Mesa. Rachel asked a rapid-fire series of questions to avoid focusing on the likelihood that she would throw up in her mother's new $45,000 car.

"So you like the new place?"

"It's fine. I've lived in better but the people pretty much leave me alone, which I do enjoy."

"That's good then." Rachel leaned over and peeked at the digital odometer. "Mother, this car has over four hundred miles on it. I thought it was brand-new?"

"I didn't say it was new. You did."

"So who else has driven it?"

Her mother smiled but kept her eyes on the road. "A woman in my building needed a ride Monday and I took her."

"Watch the truck!" Rachel slammed both feet against the floor.

Stephanie swerved to avoid a semi. "Idiot," she said. "I might have given him the bird if you weren't in the car."

"I would hope not, Mother. That gets people killed."

Stephanie mumbled a moment while Rachel's heartbeat eased. "So you gave a friend a ride. Who?"

"Her name is Arianna."

"Arianna what?"

"Something."

"Should I ask where you drove her?"

"Probably not."

"Uh-oh. Where?"

"To an Indian reservation."

"Arianna is an Indian?"

Stephanie looked at her daughter and shook her head. "No, but the money she lost is definitely *all* Indian now."

Rachel's eyes flashed wide. "Gambling, Mother? Are you kidding me?"

"Relax, I am the mother, yes?"

Rachel leaned back against the headrest and let the silence change the subject. "So where did you buy this? It's a beautiful car."

"Someplace in Mesa."

"How did you find it?"

"Arianna."

"What? So you bought a—"

"Here we go." Stephanie cut her off and signaled with her finger at the exit. "I think this is it."

After a long series of turns that Rachel insisted had sent them in a gigantic loop, her mother pulled through a gate and into her private community. She steered them into a numbered space and overshot the front, stopping with the license plate holder scratched and resting on the curb. "I hate driving," she said, climbing out of the car and leaving the key in the ignition.

Rachel removed it and seriously considered whether she'd ever let her mother have it back.

Along the winding, landscaped path between the car and Stephanie's front door three elderly neighbors called out friendly *hellos*. Stephanie ignored each one.

"You don't greet people, Mother?"

Stephanie fished through her purse for a house key. "Of course I do, sometimes, when I'm not preoccupied." She kept digging and when she'd discovered the key she held it up proudly. "Now I'm not preoccupied."

Rachel was pleasantly surprised at how lived-in her mother's home looked. She immediately spotted pictures on the wall, books in a bookcase, and a high stack of DVDs in a vertical tower rack. "This looks so homey, Mom. I love it."

Her mother excused herself to freshen up, so Rachel gave herself a tour of the rest of the spacious three-bedroom condo. The kitchen was outfitted with state-of-the-art appliances, expensive pots and pans she recognized as being from Williams-Sonoma, and china she didn't recognize at all. The refrigerator held little of substance, but a stand-up magazine rack on the counter by the phone boasted at least fifty restaurant menus.

In the bedrooms Rachel found complete furniture sets and queen beds beautifully made and decorated with various sizes of matching pillows. Each room also featured a small entertainment center with flat-screen TVs and Dish Network receivers. The living room was designed around an expensive leather sectional and recliner. A large plasma television hung snug against the wall.

"You expecting company?" Rachel asked when her mother appeared in the living room.

"Just you."

Stephanie eased into the recliner, and Rachel kicked off her shoes before making herself comfortable on the couch.

"It's gorgeous, Mom. But why so big?"

She held her hands out like a real estate agent showing a million-dollar home. "I just like the roominess. It's comfortable. I've always appreciated extra space."

Rachel knew what would come next.

"And you never know about Daniel. I like to have room in case he stops by."

She resisted the urge to say what she'd said many, many times before: *He's not coming back to stay, Mother.*

Stephanie folded her arms, reclined, and closed her eyes. But just when Rachel thought she might have dozed off, her mother said peacefully, "He visited last week."

"Daniel?"

"Of course."

"How long?"

"An hour, maybe two." Stephanie's eyes remained closed.

"That was nice of him. How is he?"

Stephanie sighed long and peacefully. "He's good. Looks so healthy. . . . He was heading to Albuquerque. Yes, I believe it was Albuquerque." She pointed to a display case on the wall. "He brought me five more thimbles."

Rachel stood and admired the collection. "May I open it?"

"Of course you may. The new ones are on the bottom."

She turned the brass knob and one by one removed the five new additions. "Buffalo, Toronto, Helsinki, St. Andrews—"

"Daniel says that's a very old golf course."

"I've heard that." Rachel smiled even though her mother couldn't see it. "The last is from Tampere."

"Wasn't that sweet of your stepfather?"

Rachel returned each thimble and rotated them so the images and locations faced out, exactly like the others.

"It certainly was, Mother."

Rachel was just nine years old when Daniel Kaplan met her mother. Stephanie had been a single mother for two years, struggling to keep her little family afloat financially and emotionally. It was impossible to get help from her first husband, and Stephanie and Rachel moved from apartment to apartment as her mother became expert at taking advantage of exclusive move-in deals, free first-month promotions and other loopholes that made it difficult for landlords to say no.

Stephanie discovered she didn't mind working as a waitress, but only took jobs in diners that allowed her daughter to sit in a booth or at the counter for long stretches during her shifts. Stephanie met Daniel on such a shift one Friday afternoon when he ducked into the diner to escape a torrential rainstorm that baptized downtown Denver.

Daniel was a business nomad who'd made a fortune internationally by using his keen intellect and an ability to learn and speak languages. He craved opportunities to invest in struggling companies and revive failing ideas.

Stephanie learned that Daniel had few friends and fewer roots. He enjoyed high-rise apartments in key cities and had friendly acquaintances at luxury hotels and restaurants that he frequented.

Something about Stephanie Ryman and her young daughter captured him. He knew very little about her background except that her first husband had been emotionally uneven and that he never provided well for his family.

Within two months of meeting Stephanie and Rachel for the first time, Daniel saved them from possible eviction and moved them into a townhouse he'd leased in a safe suburb. Just four more months passed and he moved them into his home in the gated community of Castle Pines, south of Denver.

Stephanie dreamed one day they would marry, but they rarely talked about it. He was so kind to them, so loving, giving, and generous, that both Stephanie and Rachel gladly accepted the unusual family dynamic. Daniel didn't even object when Stephanie changed their last names from Ryman to Kaplan because he knew she needed distance from her troubled first marriage. More than anything he enjoyed being their anchor, even when thousands of miles away closing deals.

Rachel liked Daniel immensely but continued to miss her father as the years flipped by. The more rough and jagged memories of her early childhood had been polished into something smoother by time and innocence. She remembered her father the way she remembered everyone from her life in St. Louis. He'd been flawed, but always trying to be better.

Rachel was overjoyed when a postcard from her father found her not long after her mother moved in with Daniel. It came from Italy and promised that someday, somehow, he would become the kind of father she could be proud of. Most important, in just a few measured words, he'd written something she didn't think she'd ever heard from him before: I'm sorry.

The new family traveled extensively during the early years. Mother and daughter accompanied Daniel to markets in Peru, museums in France, and the Great Wall of China. They toured the Outback in a dune buggy. He liked the companionship and he truly loved the experiences he was able to create for Stephanie and Rachel.

The trips abroad with Daniel and the number of nights the family spent under the same roof began to decline about the time Rachel entered high school. When she graduated and left for George Mason University in northern Virginia, Daniel suggested it was time for him move on, too.

Stephanie did not agree, but Daniel moved on anyway.

CHAPTER 17

D*omus Jefferson* was everything but quiet on Saturday morning. The Inn was near full capacity with guests from up and down the East Coast filling the guest rooms. Beginning at dawn, Rain made omelets to order, scratch biscuits, and prepared a fresh berry fruit cup for each place setting.

Malcolm sat in his office off the main hallway. The energy and lively conversation coming from the kitchen and dining room lifted his otherwise monotonous work. He ran credit cards through their online terminal for the previous night's stays, he ran reports in their accounting software, he checked his schedule for the coming week.

He leaned back in his chair and listened to a familiar voice take over the morning chatter. A&P had walked in and was surveying the guests on their stay and their experience in the valley. Her frequent morning visits had become her personalized focus groups, and she took great pride in selling the benefit of the Inn.

Malcolm wondered whether she would remain a fixture in the dining room after the new owners took over.

After another quick pass through his calendar, he spun around in his chair and saw A&P standing in the doorway.

"You the owner of this establishment?" A&P said.

"I am, my lady, at least for another few fortnights. May I help you with something? Was there a problem with your breakfast?"

"There was. The proprietor was not present to enjoy it with me. Why do you think I stay in your humble B&B if not to enjoy your company?"

"Ma'am, you know I'm married, don't you?" He looked into the hallway and amplified his faux embarrassment.

They continued the harmless banter another few lines until A&P motioned for the couch. "May I sit?"

"You may, of course."

"May I also ask you a question?"

"Is this a real question, Anna Belle, or should I be prepared to fall back into character?"

A&P allowed a slight grin and studied his eyes.

"Why didn't you ask me for help?"

It was a conversation Malcolm and Rain had anticipated and he felt prepared. "You know how much you've done for us through the years."

"No more than you and your family have done for me."

"I think you know what I mean. The nights you've stayed,

the tips that are really not tips at all but are more like endowments. Even your morning infomercials where you make guests pinkie promise to return. You have done more for the Inn and for my family than we could ever repay, obviously in more ways than one."

"Now, Malcolm, I don't believe for one second that I have done anything for you or for this place that you wouldn't have done for me in the same situation."

Still on script, Malcolm thought. "I would love nothing more than to think that is true. I think Rain would agree that we would sleep better and no doubt feel better about ourselves if we sincerely thought that was the case. But the truth is, it probably isn't. I doubt we could have done for you anything near what you've done for us. That's what makes you so unique, such a gem. That is what your husband saw in you."

A&P reached deep into her handbag. Malcolm fought a feeling of instant smugness because he knew what she would soon produce: the infamous checkbook.

Instead, a tattered and discolored brochure appeared.

"What's that?" He hoped his surprise wasn't evident in his voice.

"It's the reason I'm here. . . . When my Alan died, I went through his things and, because we had been married but a few years and he had lived a very long and interesting life before me, I found out things I never knew. He was more like an onion than I thought." A&P appeared amused by the comparison.

"Malcolm, have I ever told you he had a drug problem before we met? Not a serious one and nothing that should have put him behind bars, nothing like that, but he experimented a fair bit— more than most—and he worked hard to get past it. One of the things he did to help that process was to find a hobby, something to distract him from urges and temptations that I would imagine did not quickly go away. So he did what all recovering addicts do: he became a history buff."

Malcolm chuckled. "I do remember that, in fact."

"He loved history. Loved it. Got into some Civil War reenactment, too." A&P handed him the brochure for the Civil War Reenactment Association.

"That's neat," Malcolm said.

"And that's how we found this place." She readjusted herself on the couch and removed a throw pillow from behind her lower back. "I have always thought that if Alan's plane hadn't fallen from the sky, we would have ended up here. Who knows—could be we'd have ended up in the very same house I'm in today."

"I like to think that too, Anna Belle. And why not?"

She looked past him through the window. "I do love my walks. I have walked the hill between my house and yours and along the bank of the river just about every day that I've lived here. It's where I hear him. It's where I hear both of them."

"Both?"

"The two most important men in my life. Alan and God."

Malcolm saw no tears in A&P's eyes, but he knew they were coming. He joined her on the small couch.

"I just wish I'd known. I wish I'd known you were in trouble." She took the brochure from Malcolm and returned it to her purse. "I wish you had trusted me."

The tears did not arrive in streams or buckets. She did not sob, for which Malcolm was grateful, and she remained remarkably composed. But indeed they came, tiny drops one at a time.

"We are sorry, we are. Is there anything we can do for you?"

"You could tell me that it's not too late. That this change isn't coming."

"I wish I could. But our lives are all about to change. The time feels right."

Malcolm could tell A&P's idea wheel was spinning again. "Make me a promise?" he said.

"Maybe."

"Anna Belle?"

"Fine, what?"

"You won't do something crazy? You won't spend a penny to try to undo what's happening? You won't make some mystery deposit into my bank account?"

One of the overnight guests, a woman from Palmyra, New York, appeared in the office doorway. "I'm sorry to disturb you but your wife said I could poke my head in and say good-bye. We so enjoyed our night here. We *needed* this." A horn honked from outside the Inn and the woman whispered, "I think he needed it more than I did." Then she said thank you again and left.

Malcolm put his hand on A&P's back and rubbed it tenderly. "Promise?"

"I was sure you'd forgotten," she said with a sly grin.

"Anna Belle? Promise me."

"I won't make a mystery deposit."

"You won't make some hair-brained plan? You won't try to buy the Inn, or buy the town? Or have the buyers killed?"

"I won't promise on the last one."

"Thank you. . . . Now listen to me, my friend. Haven't you ever felt like the timing was just right in your life? Almost that it's beyond your control, like it's just the way someone above has meant for things to unfold for you? That's now. The time *feels* right. Matthew's life is changing dramatically, as you probably heard. Sammy is sheriff; Noah and Rachel are getting married. I have been dusting off that manuscript. It's all happening now." He waited for A&P to respond.

She did not.

"We probably should have told you. We chose not to tell anyone—not even our own son—because we wanted this to be our decision and a final one. Our financial situation isn't what it was a year ago, and we found a buyer who wants to keep the legacy of *Domus Jefferson* alive." Malcolm cocked his head downward and sideways and tried to look into her eyes. "I know it's hard. It will be hard to leave this behind. But we're not selling our friendship. We're not running back to Brazil. We're just moving across town and selling our home."

"No, you're not." She looked at him. "You're selling *our* home."

CHAPTER 18

The time change and Rachel's body clock meant she awoke Saturday morning well before her mother. She was grateful for the quiet time and decided to enjoy it by walking one of the many pea gravel paths that snaked throughout the community. She took pictures of cacti on her phone and texted a few to Noah.

After circling her mother's section of the community, she ventured into an area that appeared older with more mature landscaping and spots of faded paint on the awnings. There she settled in an Adirondack chair and realized she was actually sweating at 7:00 A.M.

This heat really is oppressive, she thought.

She watched an elderly couple across the courtyard walking a toy poodle. They sat on a white wooden bench and, on a hand command, the poodle leaped onto the woman's lap. Rachel couldn't hear the couple's conversation, but from where she sat, it seemed as though they were taking turns asking the dog questions. In between each question, the dog would yip and yap and they'd rub its head and the man would give it a treat from his pocket.

Rachel tried to imagine Noah and her on that same bench in forty or fifty years. She also wondered what her mother and father would have looked like had life unfolded differently. It pained her that her mother would not likely have another opportunity to sit on a bench like that with a male companion.

Daniel is a good man, she thought. *A fine man, in fact.*

It was unclear to Rachel whether her mother fully accepted that the relationship had dissolved. It wasn't bitter, hateful, or prolonged. Neither Rachel nor her stepfather wanted to hurt Stephanie, and the notion he might return permanently to her side gave her stability when her mind increasingly needed it. Though he'd long ago fallen out of love with Stephanie and her quirks, Daniel didn't seem to mind that she pined for him still. He acknowledged that his feelings had gone from pity to love and back to pity again. "I care for her," he told Rachel when he left for a new home and she left for college. "But I do not love her anymore."

Rachel watched the poodle jump to the ground and begin dancing in a circle at the woman's feet. This evidently pleased her companion because he laughed in booming cackles that filled the courtyard. He gave the dog another treat and kissed the back of the woman's hand. The couple casually waved when they realized Rachel was enjoying the show. Rachel responded with a wave and a playful, petite clap for the dog. The family of three stood and continued their walk; Rachel watched them until they'd rounded the corner.

Nearly three years had passed since Rachel determined she could never tell her mother that Daniel was seriously seeing another woman. He'd offered that they had no plans to marry and that it was a relationship of traveling companionship and shared interests more than a love affair.

As long as he continued to be kind and support her mother, Rachel supported his decisions. She would have appreciated more emotional support, but that had always been the case, and she knew most men wouldn't have rescued them in the first place. Nor would they have tolerated her mother's oddities for nearly as long.

It's time he knows, Rachel thought, and she sent Noah a text promising to call Daniel and share the wedding news as soon as she returned to Virginia. The details of his participation in the wedding and necessary interactions with her mother would wait. But telling him should not. She also resolved to thank him for the visit and for his continued support.

Her mother was up and eating a snack-sized granola bar when Rachel returned.

"Where were you?" Stephanie asked.

"Just enjoying the morning. It's warm but pretty comfortable out there."

"It won't be later. Trust me."

Rachel helped herself to a bottle of Fiji water and took a long drink. "I thought I could buy you breakfast and visit, would that be all right?"

"But I'm eating now," her mother said, taking another bite.

"That's not breakfast. That's not even a snack."

Stephanie pulled a menu from the magazine rack and handed it to her daughter. "You could order something. There's a bagel shop that delivers to the main gate. We walk there and meet them all the time."

Rachel sighed and took the menu from her. "Fine. But we're going out later for a meal, my treat, deal?"

"We'll see."

Rachel called in the order and showered quickly while her mother waited.

"You're going outside like that?" Stephanie was horrified when Rachel said that with wet hair and no makeup she was ready to leave.

"Sure I am."

"Like that?"

"It's just wet hair, Mother. It's not as if I'll catch the flu. Let's go."

"Well, I never . . ." Stephanie said as if uncovering some scandal. "Only if you must."

Bagels and juice arrived on schedule. Rachel paid and tipped the delivery driver and suggested to her mother they sit outside while it was still cool enough to enjoy.

"It hasn't been cool enough to enjoy since I lived in Sacramento."

They spread out at a picnic table in another of the many common areas and Rachel enjoyed an oversized bite of a whole-grain bagel with strawberry cream cheese.

"So, Mom, I have something pretty exciting to share."

"All right." Stephanie put a leaf-thin layer of cream cheese on half a bagel.

"I wanted to see you, of course, and to see your new place here. But there's another reason this trip was important to me."

Suddenly Stephanie seemed to engage and she looked up at her daughter. "Is it about your stepfather?"

"No, Mom. No, it's not."

Stephanie's eyes returned to her bagel and she cut it into four pieces with a white plastic knife.

"But it's really amazing news, Mom. It's life-changing news."

"And?"

"Mom." Rachel reached across and took her mother's hand. "I'm getting married."

"You're what?" she said, reflexively squeezing her daughter's hands.

"I'm engaged. I met a wonderful man out at school and we're getting married in September. That's why I'm here."

Stephanie leaned down and rested her forehead on her daughter's hands.

"Are you all right, Mom?"

Stephanie nodded. When Rachel realized her mother was dripping tears on her hands, she stood and walked around the table.

"Mother?"

Stephanie's breathing calmed and she sat up. Rachel smiled when her mother opened her arms wide and the two held one another.

"You're happy about this, Mother?"

"Are *you* happy?" Stephanie said, her head resting on Rachel's shoulder.

"I am."

"Then I'm happy, too."

The women exchanged kisses, Rachel believed, for the first time since leaving home. "No ring yet?" her mother said, examining her hand.

"Not yet. Well, I did have one, but it was a napkin ring. Long story."

Her mother grinned. "You *will* get a ring though, right, dear?"

"I will. When the time is right and everything is perfect, he'll give me a ring."

Stephanie's eyes suddenly became narrow and serious. "Are you in love?"

"Of course I'm in love. Why would we get married if we weren't?"

Rachel explained how they'd met, what Noah had been studying and where he was from.

"Has he ever gotten angry with you? Does he have a temper?"

"No." Rachel was appalled. "Not ever."

"That's good, that's all. You know how I feel about that."

Rachel described the beauty of the Shenandoah Valley and the uniqueness of Noah having been raised at a full-time, year-round, bed-and-breakfast.

"Have you told Daniel?"

Rachel held up a finger and finished taking a drink of orange juice. "Not yet. I wanted you to know first."

Stephanie was moved by this and gathered herself with a drink of her own and a deliberate wipe of her mouth. "That was so kind of you, dear."

Rachel described with excitement the Wedding Letters tradition and A&P's close-knit relationship with the Coopers. "She's like another aunt, I guess. And you'll write a letter for the book, right? It wouldn't be anything without one from you."

"I will. How about Daniel?"

"A&P—she's really the one in charge of this—she'll call him after I've given him the news."

"I'll mention it too, if I see him before then."

"That would be fine." Rachel knew Daniel's visits only came

a few times a year and wasn't concerned Stephanie might tell him first. Plus, she hadn't seen her mother this alive in a long time and would do anything to keep her mother's mood so light and agreeable.

They finished breakfast and discussed Rachel's upcoming job at the Department of Justice. Stephanie said she was proud of her daughter and would like to see her office someday.

As they strolled along the path back to the building, Rachel slipped her arms inside her mother's and said, "I only wish I could tell my dad. I think he'd be happy, don't you?"

Stephanie did not answer and as they continued walking Rachel seemed to speak more to herself than to her mother.

"Last card I got was about a year ago. He was in London."

"That's nice," Stephanie said.

"I still search online now and then, more lately I guess, hoping to find something about him somewhere. But nothing."

They arrived back at the apartment and Stephanie stopped her at the door. "Rachel, dear, I am convinced he's proud of you." She put both hands on Rachel's face and rubbed her cheeks lightly. "I like to think he knows. Somehow, he knows. And it's best left at that."

Rachel hugged her mother once more and recalled the oft-repeated saying of her childhood. "I know, Mother. We're different; he's different."

Stephanie completed it. "We're better; he's better."

CHAPTER 19

R achel had the dream again on her second night in her mother's condo. She fell asleep in a comfortable bed in a safe community with her mother sleeping peacefully in the bedroom down the hall. But when she awoke, she was in an apartment with broken windows, no front door, and only one bed that fit snugly in the only bedroom of the tiny home. They were in Kansas City, Missouri. Rachel was seven.

The oversized red clock hanging above the front door had no time, just the word LATE in bold caps. Rachel's father was late getting home from work again that night. He walked in, took off a tool belt he lugged to a job site every day, and climbed onto the center of the kitchen table. From there he shouted for Rachel and Stephanie to enter for the reading of the list.

Stephanie entered first, as she always did in the dream, and shouted back at him that he was late with the list—again. Then she joined him on the round wooden table.

He ignored her, even though she faced him from just inches away. He pulled a parchment scroll from one of his pockets, and the scroll unfurled until it hit the tabletop, fell off onto the floor, and rolled out of the kitchen and down the hallway to the bedroom.

Then Rachel arrived in the room and waved secretly at her mother. She crawled on the floor under the kitchen table and sat with her legs crossed. She looked up at the underside of the table and listened as her father began reading a long list of grocery and household items. He read the list deliberately and dramatically with one arm gesturing above his head. He enunciated every word like a Shakespearean actor on stage.

"Paper towels, lightbulbs, hammer, eggs."

Stephanie stopped him and lodged a complaint about his tardiness.

He continued reading the list. "Raisins, candles, batteries, detergent."

"The list is late," Stephanie said. "You were late. You were late with the list. We do not like you to be late with the list. The list. The list."

He ignored her and continued reading. "Lotion, bananas, flat-head screwdriver—"

"The list. The list. The list—"

"Thumbtacks, dog food, milk—"

"The list—"

145

"Shut up! Shut up! Shut up!" He screamed the words, the sound starting in his feet and rising up and exploding from his mouth. The table began to vibrate and Rachel watched its legs begin to wobble beside her.

Then with one hand Rachel's father launched her mother off the table into the air and across the kitchen. She flew like a doll through the air, her hair covering her eyes. When she landed, she was lying on the bed at the end of the narrow hall.

Rachel hadn't walked there, nor had she been thrown, but somehow she was there, too, watching from the doorway. Her father pushed past her, swearing and gathering the scroll from the floor and around Rachel's feet.

Without speaking he began wrapping Stephanie on the bed in the white paper list. He turned her over and over, covering first her feet, then her legs and her yellow and pale green sundress. Last he covered her face and head, wrapping and wrapping until every strand of hair and every sliver of flesh was covered.

Then he turned, picked up Rachel in the doorway and carried her to the couch. He sat next to her. A honey sandwich appeared on a plate on his lap. He handed half to her. They watched a cartoon Rachel did not recognize. When the program ended, the picture shrunk into a dot that eventually disappeared in the middle of the screen.

Then the dream ended, too.

CHAPTER 20

48 Days to the Wedding

A&P wasn't on the schedule to speak, but with the wedding fast approaching and the Wedding Letters coming in slower than she'd expected, she decided she had little choice. "I'm going to crash Rotary Club today."

"Um, what?" Malcolm said as the two stood in the kitchen at *Domus Jefferson.*

"I'm going to Rotary Club today. They meet on Wednesdays, yes?"

"Yes, but they probably have a program already lined up. They schedule speakers weeks ahead of time."

"Don't they have some kind of time for members to speak?"

"Sure they do, but you're not a member, Anna Belle."

Rain arrived but decided to stay in the doorway and enjoy the joust.

"Will they arrest me?" A&P asked.

"They could," Malcolm teased.

"Will Samantha be there?"

"Probably, yes. As sheriff, she's a member and she makes it to most of the meetings."

"Then I feel extremely confident that my rights will be protected."

"Oh, come on." Malcolm laughed and turned to face Rain. He held his hands out and pled, "A little help here, please?"

"I don't think so, Mr. Cooper. You're on your own." She took a sip of her coffee and hid a smile behind the cup.

"Why can't I mention something for you? Save you the drive and the harassment? I'd be happy to, really."

A&P put her hands on her healthy hips and though she stood at least four inches shorter than Malcolm, she still managed to lower her eyes and look down at him. "Are you going to make me drive myself there? Are you going to do that to me? After all I've done for you, Malcolm Cooper? Are you?"

He sighed and looked at his watch. "We leave at 11:45. Meeting starts at noon."

A&P blew him a kiss and said, "I'll wear a dress."

Rotary began exactly on the hour with a catered lunch at the American Legion in Woodstock. The one-hundred-plus members ate lunch, exchanged local gossip and business cards, and socialized at long banquet tables. Malcolm sat with his usual crowd, and Samantha, dressed smartly in her Shenandoah County sheriff's uniform, sat across the table next to A&P.

A bell called the meeting to order and, after the usual business and recitals, the president asked if any of the Rotarians had visitors to introduce. Malcolm stood first.

"Good afternoon, everyone."

A chorus of friendly replies followed.

"I'm happy to have a guest with me today. This is my neighbor on the hill, Anna Belle Prestwich—A&P to her friends. Many of you know her already. She's been a friend of the Coopers since my mother and father ran *Domus Jefferson,* and she remains a dear friend today."

They greeted her in unison.

"If you're going to say something," Malcolm whispered in A&P's ear, "just stand here and say it quickly. That's how it's done."

She patted his cheek and immediately stood and began walking to the tabletop podium at the head of the room. The president stood aside when she arrived; he shrugged his shoulders at the curious members. Two other leaders at the head table began frantically whispering back and forth.

"Thank you for that introduction, Malcolm." A&P yanked the microphone down closer to her mouth. "I'd like to take just a minute to tell you all about a special project I'm working on and to chastise you for not participating."

She heard scattered laughs from around the room, the loudest coming from the sheriff.

"How many of you have heard of the Wedding Letters?"

A smattering of hands went up.

"How many of you with your hands up have submitted your letters already?"

All but three hands went down.

A&P looked at Malcolm, still standing by his chair, and pointed at them. "You see?"

Malcolm nodded, smiled big, and sat for the show.

"All right, folks. How many of you knew, or at least knew of, Jack and Laurel Cooper?"

All but a few hands shot into the air.

"Of course you did. They were anchors in this community for a long time, weren't they? Now, how many of you know Malcolm?"

Every hand was raised.

"Some of you even like him, don't you?" Even Malcolm laughed that time.

"How many of you Rotary Club members—"

"Rotarians," the president corrected from his seat right next to her.

"Excuse me, your honor. How many of you Rotacentarians know Malcolm and Rain's boy, Noah?"

Again the majority of the hands were raised.

"So it looks to me like most of you know them. And I suspect if you like his parents, you like Noah even better. He's quite the young man."

"Yes he is," someone said from the crowd.

"That young man, now a college grad in case you hadn't heard, is getting married on September 27 at the Inn to an angel of a girl he's met at school. Most of you have heard that, I'm guessing. And in a town this small, you also know all the details about the Inn being sold to some Northern Virginia carpetbaggers."

A playful "boo" came from somewhere in the middle of the room.

"So this is it. The last hurrah for this special family at a special place that's been important to this valley. What I'm asking from you—and this is the second or third time I'm having to ask some of you; yes, I'm looking at you, Steve Shaffer—is to take a few minutes and write a letter to the bride and groom. A word of encouragement, some advice. Be sweet, sentimental, funny— whatever strikes your fancy. I don't care how well you know the family, and I especially don't care if you've been married fifty years or fifty times. Share what you've learned. Or if you're lazy at least share your short congratulations and a wish for a long and healthy marriage. The letters mean a lot, I promise you. They are cherished. Isn't that right, Samantha?"

Samantha nodded and blew A&P a kiss.

"Malcolm?"

"Yes, ma'am," he said.

"Yes indeed," she continued. "By my count we have forty-eight days until the wedding. Six weeks and a bit. That's plenty of time for each and every one of you Rotaryites to get me a letter and for me to get them arranged in the album. So drop them by the Inn, mail it to me, whatever you'd like. I'll even come get it from you if I have to." She looked down at the president. "Any questions?"

He shook his head.

"Anyone else?" She saw more headshakes and heard a couple of "No, ma'ams."

"Lovely. Well then, would everyone please raise your hand if you plan on contributing to the Coopers' very special Wedding Letters?"

All but a few hands went up high and A&P stared down the holdouts. "Sheriff, step in here if you feel obliged."

The crowd laughed and the remaining hands shot up, even the three who'd already submitted letters.

"Thank you very much." A&P stepped away from the pulpit, and the president stood and shook her hand. Everyone in the room watched A&P hand him an envelope, but only those at the head table heard her say softly, "Thank you. Here's $2,500 for your Christmas coats project. God bless."

The Rotary president's mouth dropped open and he shook her hand again.

By dinnertime that evening, A&P had fourteen letters waiting for her at *Domus Jefferson*.

CHAPTER 21

45 Days to the Wedding

Noah had made the walk between his apartment and Rachel's with a pedometer five times and driven it at least twice just to calculate the distance. He couldn't avoid the truth: The halfway point was exactly in a Giant Food parking lot on Braddock Road.

After a day they'd decided to spend apart doing laundry, paying bills, and cleaning up around their respective apartments, Noah called Rachel and asked if she'd like to grocery shop with him. "I'll cook when we're done."

"Ramen?" she asked.

"Only the best for you, babe."

"Gag."

He picked her up just after dark and drove to the Giant he'd reluctantly accepted as the spot. As they walked through the automatic doors, he saw a long bank of gumball machines and an idea sprang up and slapped him. *Might as well make the best of it,* he thought.

Noah and Rachel took their time browsing the aisles and picking up the usual items. Rachel filled the cart with granola, organic bananas, soymilk, whole-grain bread, honey, and hummus. Noah added Lucky Charms, Pop-Tarts, 2% milk, Skippy, and gummy bears.

Noah took enough pictures in his mind to fill ten photo albums, careful to capture every vivid detail. While Rachel sorted through brilliant red tomatoes, Noah stood back and considered sketching that exact scene later that evening in pastels.

He admired her gorgeous tan legs and matching tan shorts, her baby-blue flip-flops, the green *Property of George Mason Athletic Department* T-shirt that used to be his. He knew she'd lament later at not being better prepared, but he also knew it couldn't happen any other way.

When they paid for their groceries Noah asked the clerk for an extra bag and five dollars back in quarters.

"Washer broken?" Rachel asked.

"No, I'm going shopping."

"Um, OK."

They walked back toward the automatic doors and Noah stopped at a twenty-five-cent machine with plastic bubbles holding an odd variety of toys. He got on both knees and inserted a quarter. Turning the silver handle and lifting the metal door yielded one plastic bubble with a Scooby-Doo tattoo. "Sweet," he said. "This is going on one of my guns." He flexed his right arm and she gave his bicep a squeeze.

"Will the tattoo even fit?" she jabbed.

Another quarter produced a slimy hand with an equally slimy string attached. Then came a glow-in-the-dark plastic ghost, stick-on earrings, a decal with an invitation to scratch-and-sniff, but with no hint as to what the sniff actually was, and a yellow smiley sticker. "Those are free at Walmart, you know," said Rachel.

Noah kept feeding quarters into the machine until an adjustable plastic gold ring with a purple stone dropped into his hand. "That's what I'm talkin' 'bout," he said, and he shoved it into his pocket. The rest of the toys he collected in the bottom of a grocery bag, which he handed off to a mother and her young son. He captured that detail in his mind too, especially the electric smile on the boy's face.

Noah loaded the groceries in the backseat of his Dakota while Rachel rolled the cart into a rack. When she returned to the truck, she noticed Noah had walked toward the back of the lot and stopped by something on the pavement. "What the heck are you doing?" she yelled.

"Come here," he answered with an accompanying over-dramatic wave.

"This boy is not right," she mumbled to herself as she by-passed the truck to join him. "Am I going to have to start holding your hand in parking lots?" she called.

As she got closer she could tell he was standing on a white *X* someone had spray painted on the asphalt. "What in the world?" she said.

Noah looked down and tapped the X with one of his feet. "This is the spot."

"Yeah." Rachel didn't bother masking her confusion. "I don't get it."

"This is exactly halfway from my place to yours."

Rachel looked left and right. "And?"

"Isn't that interesting? That this spot is in a parking lot?"

"Noah, honey, you know those paints of yours are for art, not sniffing?"

"Ha, ha, and ha."

"I got three this time!" Rachel thrust a fist in the air.

Noah would not be deterred. "This spot on the ground marks exactly halfway from me to you. It's symbolic."

"So you spray painted on the lot? Isn't that a crime? You know I could probably have someone at DOJ arrest you, right?"

"This place is important to me, Rach. It means something. It means I come to you and you come to me. We meet in the middle on everything. It's beautiful, right?"

"I get it, and it's sweet, yes."

Noah got on one knee at the center of the X and pulled the plastic ring from his pocket. "Your hand, please."

Rachel laughed. "Are you kidding me?"

"Your left hand, please."

She extended it and he slipped the twenty-five-cent ring onto her finger. "I have a very important question for you, Rachel Kaplan. Is this ring better than the last one?"

Rachel laughed even harder. "No! It certainly isn't, and I most certainly will not marry you. First a napkin ring and now this?" She took it off and dropped it back into his palm. "What kind of girl do you think I am? The wedding is off."

Noah, still on one knee, dropped his head and plunged both hands into his pockets. "I was afraid you'd say that." Then he removed both hands and said, "Give me a do-over."

He took her hand again and slipped onto her ring finger a one-carat, princess-cut, diamond solitaire engagement ring he was sure he'd be paying for until it was time for a thirtieth-anniversary upgrade. "How's that?"

Both of Rachel's hands shot up. Her right covered her mouth and her left was directly in front of her eyes. "Noah!"

"Better?"

She nodded. First slowly, then quickly, then she began to bop up and down almost as quickly as her head.

"I need your hand back for this to be legit."

She giggled-cried and put her left hand in his.

"Yes, yes, yes!" she shouted.

CHAPTER 22

39 Days to the Wedding

Rachel and Noah drove to Dulles International Airport and picked up Stephanie during the late afternoon on August 19. It was her first trip East since meeting the family at the graduation dinner and her first trip ever to the Shenandoah Valley. Noah and Rachel both insisted she ride up front, but she flatly refused, first politely, then much less so.

Noah played tour guide as they worked their way out of the city sprawl and into the quiet country. They took a pit stop for gas and a snack at a Sheetz in Gainesville.

"Just something small, Mother. We're having a family dinner at the Inn tonight."

Noah and Rachel used the restroom and Stephanie browsed the aisles until becoming fascinated by the automated ordering system. "I've never seen anything like this," she said, tapping her finger on a Made-to-Order computer touch screen. By the time she'd finished and a lengthy white receipt appeared from an attached printer, she'd ordered five chili cheese dogs, a caramel latte, two slices of deluxe pizza, and eight bags of sliced apples. "Have you ever seen such a thing?" she said to Rachel.

They resumed the peaceful drive with Noah proudly ticking off facts and anecdotes about the area's history. Rachel texted Rain with updated ETAs and in the backseat Stephanie sipped a Lo-Carb Monster Energy Drink and munched on Goldfish crackers.

Samantha, Matthew, Rain, and Malcolm were all standing on the front porch when Noah's truck pulled into the driveway. Stephanie voiced concern at the Shenandoah County Sherriff's Department SUV parked next to them.

"Didn't I tell you Noah's Aunt Sam is the county sheriff?"

"I think I'd remember something like that, Rachel."

Noah climbed out and removed one of Stephanie's bags from the backseat and two more from the bed of the truck. "Hey guys," he called to his family. "Come on down."

Rain practically skipped to Rachel. "Hello there, sweetheart, so nice to have you out here again. We have *so* much to talk about." They hugged quickly and Rain moved immediately to Stephanie. "Mrs. Kaplan, you look even more beautiful than last time. May I?" But before Stephanie could have objected, Rain swallowed her up in a hug that Stephanie feared might last all night.

Malcolm bypassed the hug and when Stephanie reached for his hand, he took it and gave it a quick kiss. "It's Malcolm—Noah's dad. It's a pleasure to finally have you out here."

"You did not just do that," Samantha laughed. "I suggested that dare as a joke!"

"Really, Dad?" Noah said, still struggling with Stephanie's bags.

Malcolm ignored his sister and son. "It's a pleasure," he repeated.

"Thank you." She offered it so quietly they could only assume that's what she'd said.

Samantha, still dressed in uniform, reintroduced herself, and Stephanie seemed even more nervous. Samantha leaned in and joked, "I won't arrest you, sheriff's honor."

Stephanie laughed awkwardly and Matthew took his turn. "I don't think we've met. I'm Matthew, or Matt. I'm the oldest and, quite clearly, the most mature."

"Oh, please." Malcolm rolled his eyes in protest and Samantha threatened to cuff him.

"How about we go inside?" Rachel asked, and the men stepped aside for the four women to walk up the steps and into the house. When they were alone, Noah tossed a bag at his father and uncle and then dropped one of his mother's spicier replacement swear words: "Shizzle! You guys are killing me here!" He added a stern look, stepped between them and began climbing the stairs. The other two followed, eyebrows raised at one another. As Noah took the last step, Malcolm goosed him with his foot.

Shawn arrived as dinner ended and apologized twice for being late. He neither hugged nor kissed Stephanie when introducing himself and her eyes seemed genuinely appreciative.

"He's the normal one," Noah said. "He's not related by blood."

Rachel watched intently as Malcolm and Matthew cleared the dinner dishes. Then before serving dessert, Rain asked Noah and Rachel to walk to A&P's and invite her down. They were back in less than fifteen minutes with A&P and her cat, Putin. Rain introduced them both and once again Stephanie found herself chest-to-chest with someone.

"I warned you, Mother. They're huggers."

After peach ice cream, Malcolm invited the men outside to inspect the gazebo he'd been building for the wedding. The women were happy for the time alone and Stephanie appeared to relax in the living room. Rachel sat by her and reminded her she could retire to her room upstairs for the evening whenever she wanted.

Rain told the requisite stories about themselves, the Inn, a few of the famous guests, and brought up their plans for their future after they surrendered the property after the wedding.

Rachel had heard most of it before, but she still enjoyed watching her mother absorb it and begin to ask questions.

At a natural segue A&P mentioned the Wedding Letters and asked how Stephanie's letter was coming along. Rachel quickly refreshed her mother's memory on the concept.

"Would you like to see some?" Rain asked Stephanie.

"Ours?" Rachel interrupted.

"No, sweetheart, *mine*," Rain said. "You have to wait to be *married* to get *yours*."

Stephanie looked sideways to Rachel for approval.

"Sure, Mom. Why don't you?"

"Fun!" A&P beamed.

✉

Dearest Malcolm and Rain Cooper,

Please accept my humble congratulations for your upcoming marriage. May you enjoy a lifetime of health, happiness, and prosperity in the Commonwealth of Virginia.

And may you cast many votes for Democrats in the years to come!

Sincerely,

Gerald L. Baliles

Virginia Governor

✉

Rain and Mal,

I can only imagine what advice you're expecting from an accountant. After all, I've been accused of loving numbers and math more than sports, and you know how much I love and miss football.

Mal, I'll be honest with you—I hoped this day would come, but I wondered if it ever would. There have been times I wondered if you'd survive your mistakes, your temper, and your past. But you've done more than survive them. You've done what no one could—you've turned them into strengths. I'm in awe of who you've become this year.

Rain, let me get in line with everyone else to tell you how little he deserves you. Thank you for lowering your standards to take my poor brother in off the streets. He loves you like he's never loved anything. We all love you, too, and I'm happy to call you a sister.

Now to you both. You know that Mon and I have had our share of ups and downs. Things have changed with LJ in the family now and we've never been happier. I think we'll make it—no, I know we'll make it because we've learned to be honest in all things. No secrets and no games. Do that and you'll find yourself writing Wedding Letters as a couple to your own children and grandchildren one day.

Now the best for last. Please enjoy my first and only acrostic poem:

> <u>*M*</u>*ake each other first*
> <u>*A*</u>*lways say, "I love you"*
> <u>*R*</u>*espect him*
> <u>*R*</u>*espect her*
> <u>*I*</u>*nsist on honesty*
> <u>*A*</u>*gree to disagree*
> <u>*G*</u>*et away often*
> <u>*E*</u>*njoy every day like it's your last!*

Monica and I are proud of you both and can't wait to watch our kids grow up together.

We love you,
Matthew, Monica, and LJ

✉

Rain had read them many times since her wedding day, but some of them still brought a tear. The last brought more than one.

CHAPTER 23

The four men returned inside and after another session of stories—some told for the exclusive purpose of embarrassing Noah—Stephanie whispered to her daughter that she was tired from the day of travel and ready for bed. Rachel whispered something back and took control of the room.

"Can I have just a minute?" The chatter stopped all at once and Rachel stepped onto the hearth. "Noah, come up here with me."

Rachel looked down at the crowd and smiled. "The hearth is powerful. I like this!"

"Uh-oh," said Malcolm. "My boy's in trouble for something."

"Not at all. I just want him to hear this at the same time as everyone else."

Noah's lips said nothing, but his eyes said plenty.

Rachel began, "I'd like to make an important announcement—"

"And here we go," Matthew interrupted.

Rain jumped to her feet, and Stephanie was confused by the commotion.

"Hear me out," Rachel said. "I've been thinking about this for a while and waiting for the right time."

A&P held Putin on her lap and quickly covered his ears.

"Oh my, oh my, don't tell us you're *pregnant*!" Rain said with her arms flapping.

"You're *pregnant*?" Stephanie said, and her face flushed red so quickly she looked like she'd been doused with paint.

"You're *pregnant*?" Noah said. "How's that possible?"

"Well, Noah," Samantha chimed in. "You have a girl and a—"

"*Sam!*" Rain shouted.

Rachel threw her hands on top of her head. "Are you kidding me? What is wrong with this family?" She almost giggled the words. "Relax. I am most certainly *not* pregnant. I repeat, *not* pregnant."

Rain fell back into her chair, and Stephanie fussed with her hair, as if the excitement had tousled it out of place.

"You guys are *unbelievable*," Rachel said.

"Welcome to *my* world," Shawn replied, and Samantha stuck an index finger gun in his ribs.

"It's nothing that exciting," Rachel resumed. "I mean it is, but not anything like that. It's about my father."

The room went silent.

"You mean *Daniel*," Stephanie said and the color in her face went from red to white.

"No, Mother, I mean my *father*. My *real* father." She looked at Noah and they interlocked all four hands into a nervous lump. "I've decided to invite him to the wedding."

Stephanie rose from the couch. "How?"

"I'm going to find him. I have contacts now at work."

"That's impossible," Stephanie said.

"It's not, Mother. One of my best friends—Tyler from work; I know I've mentioned him before—he's *amazing* with technology. He has experience with this kind of thing and he told me that if my father is alive, he can find him, no matter how hard he's tried to stay off the radar." Rachel looked into Noah's eyes. "If my father has become who we hope he has, he deserves to know. He deserves an opportunity to come. Even if he chooses not to."

Stephanie felt light-headed and eased back down.

"Mom?"

Stephanie slipped down into the couch until her head rested against the back.

"Mother? Are you all right?" Rachel rushed to one side, Rain to the other.

Rain put her hand against Stephanie's forehead. "Someone get some water, please. And a cold washcloth."

Rachel slid in closer to her mother and began tenderly massaging the back of her neck. Noah rushed back in with a cold bottle of spring water; Samantha followed with a soaked washcloth. Rain placed it against Stephanie's forehead and then asked the rest of the family to leave the room. "Give us a minute, everyone."

They all drifted outside, including Noah, but only after Rachel nodded approval.

"Mother?"

Stephanie reached up, put her hand on the washcloth to hold it in place and felt Rain's warm hand under hers. Water began to drip and run down her forehead until the lines around Stephanie's eyes redirected the drops into tears.

Stephanie stared at her daughter until the drops weren't just water anymore. "I'm sorry, Rachel," she said.

"For what?"

"I'm so sorry, Rachel, dear."

Rachel took a Kleenex from a box on the coffee table and started to wipe away the rivers of water and tears and eye makeup on her mother's cheeks.

"No, let them." Stephanie quivered. "Let them."

Rain gave Stephanie's arm a light squeeze before standing and leaving the two women alone in the room. Seconds later the back door slammed shut and Rain joined the others behind the Inn.

Mother and daughter looked into each other's eyes until the weight of the past was, at long last, more than Stephanie's heart could endure. She pulled the washcloth from her forehead and held it in her hands. "You won't find him, Rachel."

"Why not?"

"Because he's dead."

CHAPTER 24

The Inn was quiet.

Rachel sat back against the couch and covered her face a moment. "You've been lying to me."

Stephanie considered the answer, though she knew there was only one. "Yes."

Rachel took a deep breath and sat up. She rubbed the disbelief from her eyes. "When?"

"Long ago."

"*How* long? How long have you known?"

Stephanie took her daughter's hands and squeezed them tight. "A long time, Rachel, dear. I've known for years."

Rachel shook free of her mother's hands and rose to her feet. "When?"

Stephanie remained seated and studied the washcloth she clutched in her lap. "You were seven."

Rachel felt her fists and jaw clench. "Seven? I was seven? You've known since I was *seven?*"

Stephanie nodded but could not look up.

"Seven?" Rachel began fiddling with a charm on her necklace. "We *left* when I was seven."

"I know."

Rachel sat again. "What about the cards, Mother? The post-cards? I have a dozen of them."

"Daniel."

Rachel heard her heart pounding out of her chest. "No." She hammered the word again. "No!"

"Daniel. He . . . He wanted you to keep believing."

"Daniel? Why? When did he care enough about me to keep me believing in anything? *When?"*

Stephanie repeated the word aloud that she'd been running through her head on a constant loop for almost twenty years. "Believe." Stephanie hiccupped in a gulp of air and composed herself. "He wanted you to believe, and he wanted you to be happy."

"Believe? Believe in what? Believe a lie? Why? Why not just tell me, Mother? You didn't think this day would come? You didn't think I'd want to see him when I was older?"

Stephanie averted her eyes again. "No. No, I didn't."

"So why?"

Stephanie hadn't wiped her eyes and she tasted a bitter

mixture of mascara and foundation on her lips. "Daniel and I wanted you to believe better about him."

"Believe better?"

"About him."

"Why? I knew who he was. I saw the fights, Mother. I saw the anger."

Her voice turned more resolute. "You didn't see it all."

Rachel was back on her feet, but again Stephanie remained still.

"So the cards were from Daniel. My stepfather sent them to . . . what, to repair something? To make me believe my real father was turning his life around, becoming something better? You and that stupid saying. We recited it over and over and over again. *We're different; he's different.*" Disdain seeped into her voice. "*We're better; he's better* . . . Just words, Mother?"

Rachel didn't wait for a response. She left the room and entered the bathroom in the main hallway.

Stephanie began to weep again.

When Rachel returned to the living room, her hair was pulled back and her face glistening from a thorough washing. She sat down next to her mother, imagined the word carefully, and said, "How?"

Stephanie looked into her eyes and her expression answered, *How what?*

"How did he die?"

Stephanie fought the urge to break away, to ask for more water, to escape the Inn and to run into the night. Her leg muscles twitched and her fists clenched around the cloth.

"Your father was not a good man, Rachel."

"How, Mother?"

"He hit me. He lied. He hit *you*."

"Mother."

"He could have done more, hurt us more, hurt *you* more, Rachel. He could have hurt you much more."

"Mother."

"There were good days and you remember those right now—I want you to remember those—but there were also bad days, Rachel. So many bad days when you were at school and I was alone and I had nothing between him and me and his anger and his tool belt and all I wanted was to be safe, to keep my promise that I would keep you safe and end the fighting and the cursing and keep you safe. I want you to remember that."

Stephanie squeezed the washcloth until a puddle of water sat at her feet.

"Mother, *please*."

"I killed him."

CHAPTER 25

The Coopers were milling around the swing outside when they heard an engine start on the other side of the Inn.

"Who's leaving?" Malcolm asked no one in particular.

Noah fast-walked around the side of the Inn just in time to see the tailgate of his truck disappear down the driveway. The others arrived just behind him.

"Not good," said Samantha.

"Was it Rachel or her mother?" Rain's voice was wispy and worried.

Matthew joined them. "I don't think her mother drives."

"Son?" Malcolm said, but Noah had already raced into the Inn through the front door.

"Should we help?" offered Rain but Malcolm strongly suggested they wait and give them space. Shawn and Matthew agreed and offered to walk A&P home, but before they'd crossed the property line, Noah reappeared through the front door and approached his parents.

"Rachel's gone."

"Gone?" Rain said.

"That was her in my truck."

"What happened?" Rain asked. "Where is she going?"

Noah's head swiveled back to the Inn. "I don't know, but her mother is locked in her room upstairs crying pretty hard. I mean I could hear her from the entrance."

"Not good," Samantha said again with more authority. "I'll talk to her."

"I wouldn't," Malcolm advised. "Give her time to get herself together."

"Should I?" Rain said.

Malcolm raised his hands to encourage calm. "No. Just . . . Easy, everyone. Just let it breathe. Whatever's happening probably has nothing to do with us."

Samantha pulled Malcolm aside with a tug on his sleeve. "Should I put a deputy on the truck?"

"Let's not, sis. People argue. Rachel's gone to vent or be alone or whatever. She'll be back."

Matthew stepped into the conversation with his siblings and Noah returned to the Inn. Before they'd even noticed he'd disappeared, Noah bounded back down the stairs, climbed in his father's F-150 pickup with the *Domus Jefferson*'s logo splashed across the side and raced down the driveway.

"What is it with people swiping other people's cars around here?" Malcolm asked.

"Could have been worse," Samantha said. "Could have been my police cruiser. Remember that?"

Neither Malcolm nor Matthew smiled back.

Samantha kept smiling anyway. "Too soon?"

Noah drove up Route 11 to the only place that he would've gone in the same circumstances, the only spot on earth where he'd want to diffuse anger or heartbreak. A short drive later he found Rachel standing atop the Woodstock Tower.

He didn't know what to expect when he ascended the final flight of stairs and stepped onto the tower's silver platform. Stephanie had appeared inconsolable. Rachel, however, looked calm and cool, reserved, measured. He circled around her and stood face to face.

"You all right?" he asked.

Rachel was chewing on the corner of her lower lip. Under other circumstances he would have mentioned how adorable he thought it was. "Rach? You want to talk about it?"

She took a deep breath, and for an instant Noah was sure she had something to say. But the words never came. She resumed chewing on her lip and stepped away from him toward the rail. Her eyes studied something in the distance.

Noah remained where he stood and watched her from behind. It was growing dark and he wondered just how far into the valley she could really see in the blue-gray dusk. He let another minute pass and then stepped up at her side. "You two had a fight, I can guess. I hope it wasn't about the wedding."

No reply.

"Whatever is wrong, whatever this is all about, it might be easier if you let me help you."

Nothing.

"You know that I love you. You also know that the greatest moment of my life will be marrying the woman I love, at the place I love, in the valley I love. We're family, Rachel. Or we're *almost* family, anyway. And this is what families do. No matter how hard it is, this is why we're here for one another."

Rachel began to shake her head left and right, but it wasn't obvious to Noah whether she was responding to him in some way or to her own thoughts. He stayed quiet and waited for another cue. When it didn't come, he leaned in and kissed her on the side of her head. Then he took a few steps backward, sat on the platform with his back against the opposite side. Then he waited.

Noah felt like an hour had passed before Rachel began shaking her head again at the night sky. "Family?" she said, looking up. "This is what a family does? I don't even know what that means. *Family.* My mother is a liar." Her eyes went to the ground below and after several breaths, she continued. "Daniel is a liar, too. And my real father—the one who brought me into the world? Who knows? At least he never lied. I mean maybe, even with all his problems, maybe he was really the most normal of any of the adults in my life. And now he's dead?"

Noah rose but held himself in the distance. He inched back against the rail and held the top bar, fighting every instinct to pull her in and lift whatever heavy weight would make it all go away. "What do you mean?"

"Dead, Noah. Dead. He's gone."

"I thought he had—" Noah breathed and rewound. "I thought he left."

"So did I."

"How? What happened?"

"Killed. Killed by my mother's hands."

Noah could tell Rachel's shoulders were beginning to quiver and he stepped forward to put his hands on them.

"I should go back, shouldn't I? Should I go back?" The words tumbled out awkwardly in stifled breaths. "I should go back. I should ask." The words were nearly unintelligible.

Noah struggled to catch his breath. "Rachel . . . I'm . . ."

CHAPTER 26

Noah left his father's vehicle on the mountain and drove them back to *Domus Jefferson* in his own truck. Rachel said little on the drive except for the words, "No matter what she says, I will not stay there tonight."

Noah took her hand. "When it's over, I'll get your bag and you can stay at A&P's. All right?"

"Mm-hmm." They rode on, the only sound coming when Rachel rolled down her window and stuck her hand into the rushing wind.

They arrived at the Inn, and Noah turned off the truck. After a few more moments of quiet, Rachel put her hand on the door handle and said, "I'm ready."

Noah led her to the Inn and had her wait in a rocker on the porch. "Right back," he said.

"Mm-hmm."

Noah found the family gathered in the dining room. "Could I talk to dad and Aunt Sam alone?"

When the others cleared, Noah asked Samantha and his father to sit. "Where's Stephanie?"

"Upstairs," Samantha said. "Last time Rain checked on her, she was still a wreck, circled up in a ball, refusing to talk."

"How's Rachel?" Malcolm asked. "Where is she?"

Noah set his phone on the table in front of him and spun it in a circle with his index finger. "We've got a problem."

The look from Samantha to her brother said, *I told you.*

"Rachel's mom unloaded some stuff tonight. I guess the wedding and Rachel wanting her dad to be there, all of it pretty much triggered the avalanche, you know?"

"No, son, we don't. What avalanche?"

Noah spun the phone again. "Do you think you can get Stephanie down here? Rachel needs to hear some things."

"You're talking in circles, son."

Noah looked at him. "Rachel has always lived with the idea that her real dad was alive somewhere. Rachel thought he just couldn't handle it all so he left them and started over. I guess he was pretty rough on them sometimes. They fought a lot and whatever. But she's gotten postcards from him, one or two a year since she was a kid." At once Noah realized Stephanie could still be awake, and he knew from growing up in the home how easily voices and secrets traveled from one room to another.

Noah leaned over and said quietly, "Her mother came clean tonight that he's dead." He looked at the door and turned down the volume even more. "I think she killed him."

"What?" Samantha and Malcolm said in unison.

Noah looked again at the door separating the dining room from the living room, as if expecting Stephanie to burst through it before he was ready. "Can you get her down here?"

Malcolm eased away from the table and stood, but Samantha stopped him. "Let me."

During the five minutes before the storm, Malcolm took two Excedrin at the kitchen sink, said a prayer, and let the others know the Inn was off-limits for the time being.

Noah invited Rachel in from the porch and poured her a glass of milk at the table. "Need anything else, Rach?"

Samantha appeared through the door before she could answer.

"Well," Noah said, "how did—"

Stephanie followed a step behind. Her eyes were red and puffy, her cheeks raw, her hair a tangled mess of bottle blonde. She forced a painful smile at Rachel but didn't seem to notice anyone else in the room. Samantha pulled out a chair and Stephanie sat.

"Rachel," Samantha began. "Mrs. Kaplan wants to talk and I think I should sit here with you, would that be OK?"

Rachel nodded.

"And how about my brother and Noah? Would it be all right if they stayed with us, too?"

She nodded again.

"Mrs. Kaplan, you know I'm the Shenandoah County sheriff. I have no jurisdiction and there is no warrant for you here or anywhere else, as far as I know. So you don't need to be afraid to tell us whatever you'd like to. If I feel I should make a call, based on my duty in law enforcement, then I will. But this is just us having a conversation, OK?"

"Uh-huh."

"Why don't you tell us why your daughter is so upset."

Stephanie looked at Rachel and began, her voice thin and constricted. "This isn't how it was supposed to happen, Rachel. When you said you wanted your father to be at the wedding, *your* wedding, I lost myself. I just . . ."

Stephanie turned to Samantha. "I've always wanted to tell her. I have. I've meant to, and I would have before the wedding, I swear I would have. But it just . . . It just happened tonight. Maybe it was right . . ." Stephanie wiped her eyes but found them dry.

"Go on," Samantha said.

"You have a right to be upset, Rachel," Stephanie continued. "You do. All these years of wondering. The lies, so many of them." She looked at Noah. "I didn't mean to hurt her. You *know* I didn't mean to hurt her."

Noah had never experienced the odd nervous energy bursting from his veins. He held Rachel's hands in his and had to remind himself not to squeeze too hard.

Stephanie looked back at her daughter across the table and let the others slide into the background of the Inn. "Your father was complex, Rachel. He loved with passion, and he lived with passion. He had days—weeks, really—when he was kind and so controlled. I loved him." She crossed her arms over her chest and put her mouth against a forearm. "I loved him. Of course I loved him, I married him because I loved him. He was good. And I don't know why he changed sometimes, I don't know what happened inside him, but he *would* change. We would return from an errand or a walk and he'd explode inside the house. Cursing and breaking things. He made lists of the things I did wrong. Long lists. If I burned a meal or forgot to wash a shirt or forgot to reorganize his tool belt, he would sit at the kitchen table and make his list. If I asked him why he was late, he would make a list. If I wouldn't give myself to him, he would make a list. Lists, lists, lists. Always counting and reading and keeping score." She paused and studied the backs of her hands. "I don't know why he did it. He just did. *He just did.*"

Stephanie began to cough and Malcolm brought her a bottle

of water from the kitchen. She thanked him with a broken smile, torn at the edges and tired.

"I tried to make it work. Obviously I tried. But you had seen so much, hadn't you, dear? So much you probably don't even remember, or *want* to remember. You were so young, too young for those things, weren't you, dear? Sometimes you hid in a closet by the front door. Sometimes I sent you to the neighbors. Do you remember Alan Richardson? He lived across the hall. He was a nice old man and worked odd hours. Do you remember him?"

Rachel glanced up at Noah and shook her head.

"I don't know if the other neighbors heard; no one ever said. But *he* did. Mr. Richardson *always* heard." Stephanie took a drink of water and fumbled putting the lid back on.

"It was a Monday. You got on the bus in front of the apartment complex. You were in the first grade with . . . What was her name? Ms. Tinka? Such a nice lady." Stephanie began to peel off the bottle label.

"You got on the bus and I watched you sit by the window on my side so I could wave good-bye. You always did that. You always sat on the same side so we could wave. Then the bus drove off to the other stop on the other side of the complex. That was that. I went back inside and your father had his tool belt on the table. He was mumbling to himself about being late for the job site. He didn't want to be late, he said. He *couldn't* be late. I stood at the sink and tried to ignore him. I figured it would pass, it always passed, somehow, and I knew he didn't have time for a knockdown, so I just stood at the sink and rinsed clean dishes from the dish rack."

Stephanie stopped picking at the label and left it half-dangling from the bottle. Awkward seconds ticked by like ants marching out of order until Samantha reached over and patted Stephanie's arm. "You're doing great."

"I rinsed your cereal bowl over and over, listening to him behind me at the table sorting through his tools and cursing me. Then he slammed something—a hammer, I think; I don't know—he slammed it hard on the table and shouted at me to get him a piece of paper for his list. I turned around and said, 'But you'll be late, dear. I'll do it later. I promise I'll do it for you later.'"

"He stood up and threw his chair behind him. 'You didn't organize my tools, Stephanie. Why didn't you organize my tools, Stephanie?' I kept telling him that I had. I'd done just as he asked. I'd straightened them like I did every night. I know I had. They were exactly where they belonged. Then he slammed the table with both his fists so hard the tool belt popped into the air. 'Then who? Then who? Then who?' he screamed at me. 'Was it Rachel? Was Rachel in my tools?'"

Stephanie had Kleenex in each hand, clenching and gesturing with them, eyes fixed on her daughter. "I told him I didn't know. I said I hadn't seen her in his tools. I said she was a good girl. She wouldn't do something like that. But he was convinced. He was *sure* she'd played with them and he threatened to teach her a lesson. 'That little thing will pay,' he said. 'She'll pay to me and the devil. Where is she? Is she at school? When is she home? When does she get home, Stephanie? What time? Will she be late, too, Stephanie?' I just covered my head and cried. I couldn't stop crying. He threw his tool belt against the wall. 'Where's my paper? Where's my list?'"

Rachel put her head on the dining room table and Noah, not knowing what else to do, cradled it with his hands.

Without warning Stephanie pushed herself away from the table and stood. She circled the table and knelt at Rachel's side. "He picked up a wrench off the floor and threw it at me. Then he got on his knees and lunged for a screwdriver. 'Stop it!' I yelled at him. 'It was me. Me. Rachel didn't move your things, it was me!' But he got up and came at me and chased me around the table screaming and calling you a liar and telling me how we'd both pay. I tripped on a table leg and fell into the refrigerator. He jumped on top of me and I reached for the only thing I could feel on the floor."

Rachel's breathing was quick, and under the table she pushed two nervous clenched fists together.

Stephanie stood and began rapidly tapping on the table with her knuckles. She looked at Samantha and let the words tumble between them. "It was a flashlight. I hit him in the head with it.

He was stunned, so I hit him once more. Then I jumped up and hit him again. It was so heavy and the sound bounced around that tiny kitchen. I struck him five times or ten or more until blood came out of his ear . . . until . . . He stopped." Stephanie ran out of breath and sputtered, "He just stopped." Then she lost her balance and fell back into the glass doors of the china cabinet.

Samantha and Malcolm leapt to catch her and guide her to the floor. She leaned against the cabinet and put her head in her hands.

"I'm so sorry, Rachel." She gripped onto two dry tissues. "But he's not looking at me anymore. He's not talking. He's not breathing."

"It's OK, Stephanie," Samantha said.

"He's not anything."

CHAPTER 27

Rachel wanted to ask questions, but none would come. She could only sit and relive the day her mother described. She still tasted the confusion at being picked up from school, the race out of town in her mother's rusty car, the snack machine at the motel where they slept that night.

When she felt steady enough to stand, she lifted her head from the table and left the room. She walked with her arms folded to hide the quivering.

Noah retrieved her bag and caught up with her halfway to A&P's. She was, of course, honored to host Rachel for the evening and had tea brewing for all three of them before the couple could even say thank you.

"One night, two nights—whatever you need, Rachel. You're always welcome here," A&P said.

They sat in A&P's large, lodge-style living room with exposed, thick wooden beams and lodgepole pine furniture. Rachel sipped her tea and eventually relaxed enough to kick off her shoes and slide back into the soft cushions. A&P described the history of her home, how she found it, and why she ended up in the valley to begin with. She stopped when it became clear Rachel wasn't listening anymore.

"Would you like to talk, dear? I'm an excellent listener."

Rachel took another sip and set the mug down on a cork coaster on the coffee table. She looked at Noah, but her eyes drifted to photos on the wall over his shoulder. "I feel like I've been stabbed."

She looked at A&P, crossed her legs, pulled at her shorts, looked at Noah and tried to smile but could only shake her head. She looked back at A&P and pulled her feet onto the couch and hugged her legs.

A&P also put her mug down and sat up. "You want to talk?"

Rachel didn't answer.

"Noah, sweetheart, maybe the two of us could be alone for just a little while. Just the girls."

He shook his head. "No, I should stay. I should be here, Rachel."

Rachel looked at him and touched his arm. "It's all right," she whispered. "Go talk to your parents."

"You're sure? I think I should be here." He looked at A&P. "I need to be here."

"Just a spell," A&P assured him.

Noah looked back to Rachel.

"It's fine," she said.

"Yes, we'll be fine," A&P said. "I'll take good care."

"Call or text, OK?" he said to Rachel. Then he kissed her on the cheek and mouthed a thank-you to A&P.

A&P locked the door behind Noah. She took his spot on the couch but kept a safe distance. Then she waited. She didn't mind the silence.

Rachel rocked back and forth, still hugging her legs, still battling the distinct pain in her gut that only the razor edge of truth can deliver.

"I don't understand," she said, resting her head on her knees. "I just don't understand why she did this. Why she did this, and why she lied for so long." She began chewing on the corner of her lip. "What do I do now?" she said, and A&P remained, as promised, completely quiet. "What do I do? How do I talk to her? How do I trust that any of this is real?"

Rachel turned her head the opposite direction and felt tears beginning to whisper to her eyes. *No tears for her,* she thought. *No tears.*

A&P left the room and returned with a box of Kleenex. She took one for herself and set the box on the coffee table.

"I know he wasn't a perfect man," Rachel said to the empty side of the couch. "He wasn't. And I was just a child, obviously just a child, but I saw things. I heard the words he used and the cold fights he had with her. But they didn't last that long, did they? Didn't he always warm to her after? Didn't he always kiss her and clean up the mess?" She turned back to A&P, eyes dry, but her voice was beginning to waver.

"We had a tiny coat closet in the apartment. Very small, just big enough for a broom and a mop. We didn't even put coats in it. I hid in there sometimes during the fights if I could get in there fast enough. Then I stayed until my father opened the door. I remember he would pat my head and send me away. Then he'd take out the broom and clean up whatever damage he'd done. In the morning I'd step into the kitchen and it was new again. Always new again."

Rachel looked over A&P's shoulder and again found the arrangement of family photos on the wall. She saw A&P with a man Rachel presumed was her husband; Rain and Malcolm on what must have been their wedding day; Malcolm and a baby; Malcolm, Rain, and a baby; A&P and Noah on what she guessed might have been his prom night; Samantha as a teenager in a nun's costume standing with her father on a dark stage somewhere; and A&P with a cat on the Cooper's backyard swing.

"People make mistakes," she said, and A&P replied with a subtle nod. "Don't they?"

"Mm-hmm."

"He made mistakes. He hit her—I saw it—but he always

loved her after. Then he would hold me in his arms for a long time and apologize. But I don't remember him ever hitting me, Anna Belle, I don't." Again she turned the other way and this time closed her eyes tight and hugged her legs ever tighter.

"People make mistakes, but they change. They change. He could have changed. He hit Mother—I know, I saw. He broke that broom on her head once and he stabbed her foot with the end, I remember. I saw it. He cursed her and stabbed at her feet while she screamed and ran around the kitchen. I saw it."

Rachel gave way to tears that gathered into heavy sobs.

A&P slid close and put both arms around the broken young woman. She cradled her and whispered. "People make mistakes."

CHAPTER 28

While Stephanie slept in medicated peace for twelve hours at *Domus Jefferson,* Samantha hunkered down all night in her Shenandoah County sheriff's office doing research into Stephanie's background. She scoured the Internet and the law enforcement databases for any unusual police reports from Kansas City, Missouri, around the time of the altercation, looking for any related wire stories.

There were no missing-person reports that came close to matching Stephanie's account and no open case files that might sound alarms. She researched the neighborhood that Stephanie and her family had lived in and accessed a federal database of unsolved homicides in the area. There were many to peruse, but none matched the details she needed to connect any dots. She sat back and once again felt grateful she lived in a town and county where the serious crime statistics barely filled an index card.

When she couldn't keep her eyes open anymore, she locked the door and dozed off on a couch in her office.

None of the other Coopers slept much either. Malcolm shared the story with Rain in full detail, careful not to embellish or exaggerate, but intent on fairly representing the horror the Kaplan family had lived through. When Malcolm finished, Rain called A&P and was assured Rachel was safe and comfortable.

Matthew spent much of the morning in his brother's office at the Inn with the door closed. He exchanged e-mails and phone calls with three disgruntled clients in Boston who had questions about their portfolios. He booked an airline ticket for that evening and committed to spending the next week in the office, catching up. Before logging off Malcolm's computer, he sent Monica an e-mail telling her the family said hello and hoped she was well. Then he wished her well, too.

Noah slept less than anyone. He'd received a text message from Rachel saying she was exhausted, he needn't return for the night, and they would speak in the morning. He tossed from one side to another, flipping his pillow even more often than he usually did, and wishing Rachel would change her mind. At first light he went downstairs to fix his own breakfast. While he sat at the smaller table in the kitchen, he sent Rachel three texts but got no reply. He took his time eating, washed his own dishes as well as the dishes from the night before, and wiped down the counters before deciding he couldn't wait any longer to check on her in person.

He breathed a sigh of relief when he walked out the back door of the Inn and saw Rachel walking across A&P's property toward him.

Noah stopped at the swing and waited. He hadn't often seen her dressed so casually, and he smiled at how beautiful she was, even in gray sweatpants and a tight-fitting T-shirt. Her arms were folded across her chest and she looked down with each step she took as if navigating a minefield.

"Morning," Noah said and he hugged her. It was obvious she hadn't slept much either, if at all. "Long night?"

"You could say that."

"Me, too."

With his arms still around her, Noah's eyes caught a black sedan arriving and stopping in front of A&P's front door.

Rachel let go of him and buried her hands in the pockets of her sweatpants. She forced herself to look up. "I love you, Noah."

"I know you do, I—"

"Wait. Just let me have a minute. I really do love you. You know that's true. And you know what happened last night doesn't change that."

"What is this, Rach?"

"I had this all figured out," she stammered to herself. She closed her eyes and tried to clear her mind with a deep breath of morning air. Then she took his hands. "It's just too much, Noah. It's too much right now. It's too fast. Last night, the wedding, my mother, the new job—all of it. It's just . . . It's just that I need some time. I just need to figure everything out, you know? I need time, Noah, time to myself."

Noah let go of her hands and sat on the swing. He rubbed his eyes and tried to shake the scene. When he opened them again, she was standing in front of him taking his hand in hers and pressing the engagement ring into his palm. She closed his fingers around it. "I can't," she said.

Noah looked in her empty, tired eyes and would have cried, or begged her to stay, or torn the swing apart if only he hadn't felt so numb.

Rachel put her hands on his face and leaned into him. "Good-bye," she said with a kiss on his cheek.

Noah felt like a shot soldier. In shock he watched her walk back across the wet, grassy field. When she reached A&P's, she said something to the driver of the sedan and reentered the house. A minute later she returned with her overnight bag. When the driver saw her coming he started to get out but Rachel put her hand on his door and pushed it shut. Then she opened her own door, got in, and left.

Noah sat motionless on the swing and watched the car reverse, turn around, and roll down the driveway. He kept staring into the space Rachel should have been in until the dust cloud from the gravel and dirt settled back to the ground. He opened his hand and realized he'd been holding the ring so tightly that it had left deep, red lines in his skin. He balanced the ring on his leg and let the breeze ease the swing forward and back.

His mind saw spring again and the beginning of the greatest summer of his life. His hands held a degree from the university he loved. His eyes fell in love with the most fascinating, captivating smile he'd ever known. The sketchpads in his apartment were filled with images of that smile and the face it belonged to.

He'd been spending his most important summer drawing the perfect life for himself and a future that couldn't fade or be erased with time or pain. But as the swing came to a subtle, silent stop, pain was all he felt.

He looked again at the ring balancing on his leg.

His mother found him there an hour later.

CHAPTER 29

Noah swam through the next few days more than he lived or survived them. After a night of unloading years of baggage and heartache with A&P, Rachel convinced herself she needed time alone to sort through the pain and lies.

A&P neither encouraged nor discouraged her to cancel the wedding and return to the city alone. She did exactly what she'd promised: she listened. When the sun rose and it was clear Rachel's decision was set, A&P offered to drive her home or let her borrow her car. Rachel again refused the help and said she'd prefer to take a cab or a bus and quietly escape the valley.

A&P ignored her, called a car service she'd used before and left Rachel no option.

Noah chose to remain at the Inn. He wasn't sure he could face his apartment in the city and the task of re-sketching his future. While still at home he sat around the table with his mother and A&P to begin the process of un-planning a wedding.

The to-do list seemed longer than ever. Several hundred people had been invited. They lived down the street; they lived across the valley. They lived in all orders of the Commonwealth of Virginia and as far away as Sacramento. Some would have to be called, some could be e-mailed, others would simply receive an un-invitation in the mail. Rain and A&P offered to do most of the work and apologized repeatedly that Noah was experiencing what no one should have to live through.

"It's not your fault," he said. "Please stop apologizing."

As they sat and planned out their strategy, Malcolm walked in and out of the room offering assistance and suggestions. Mostly he just wanted to keep Noah's mind and mood occupied. It was difficult; all Noah wanted to do was lock himself in the cottage he'd grown up in and come out some time around the holidays.

Noah sent text messages to Rachel and received short, simple replies. She'd returned safely to the city and was taking some time at home to sort through her new reality. Noah was anxious to see her again and offered that then, more than ever, she needed someone to help her get through this tough time.

Malcolm and Rain drove Stephanie to the airport and wished her well. They also made her promise to stay in touch as the days unfolded.

Three days after Rachel returned the ring, A&P walked in to the bed-and-breakfast carrying a leather-bound binder with *Noah and Rachel* engraved on the front.

"Where's Noah?" she asked Rain.

"He's gone into town with his dad. I think Malcolm is trying to get some of the catering deposit back."

"About that." A&P began flipping through the laminated pages. "I know it's supposed to be bad luck for Noah to read his Wedding Letters before the actual wedding, but given that there isn't going to be one, at least not right now, I'm going to let him. Reindeer, there are some special notes here. I mean you never really know what people think or have experienced until you see it in writing. So why not? Right?"

"I'll leave that completely up to you, Anna Belle. This is your project."

"There's more."

"Should I be worried?" Rain tried to force out a laugh for the first time in days, but it was so awkward and unnatural that both women wished she hadn't tried.

"No, not worried, but you might want to call your husband and have him stand down."

"All right. I'm listening."

"Rachel is suffering right now, and heaven and the desert know her mother is suffering, too. I can't imagine their grief, and I've survived plenty of my own. That girl wept her way through the night until I thought there wasn't another teardrop left in the clouds. Then she found another. . . . Sweetheart, I love Noah, he's my family like the rest of you are, and it pains me to know he's hurting. But he's a strong young man—you've raised him so well, but that's not news to you, of course—and he's going to get through this like everyone else who's had a heart broken. And Rachel may well come back when she figures all this out."

Rain knew A&P was right. Noah was well-grounded and the Coopers had enough experience with family drama to know that even the most painful family wounds can be healed with time and patience. "I hope you're right," Rain said.

"And even if I'm not, even if they drift apart, he's *still* going to survive and thrive and find someone else. But the Inn . . . now that's a different story. It's ending is written, right?"

"Why do I know where this is going?"

A&P grinned and raised her eyebrows up and down. "Because you know it's a great idea."

"Quit stalling," Rain teased. "Let's hear it."

"Malcolm's building a gorgeous gazebo that belongs in a magazine. You have a caterer and a photographer. The tents are rented. You've invited a million people who have cleared their schedules. Some of them have bought airfare, booked rooms in town, taken vacation days, all that. And it's not like the wedding is—*was*—a year away. It's in thirty-five days."

"You counted?"

"Didn't you?"

"Maybe," she sighed.

"Rain, let's take that invite list and double it. Let's invite everyone who's ever stayed at the Inn. Let's invite the new owners, whatever their names are—"

"The Van Dams."

"The Van Dams, yes, and anyone else who wants to come. We'll celebrate the Inn, the history, Jack and Laurel, the friendships, and we will bid farewell to this place in the way it deserves." A&P finished with a flourish.

"A celebration," Rain mused.

"A celebration."

"A party in place of a cancelled wedding," Rain added.

"A *celebration*," A&P repeated. "And I'll cover whatever added expense there might be, since it's my idea. I'll re-invite, I'll re-mail, I'll re-do it all."

Before Rain could answer, A&P slid the open book across the table. "Read this."

✉

Noah and Rachel,

I am honored to be requested to write letter for your grand wedding. We have good memories of our visit to the bed-and-breakfast of your family. When we visit in 1997 Noah drew picture of my wife on the porch in a rocker chair. Do you remember this?

We stay three days with you on the trip to America. We visit

five states and stay almost one month. We stay in diamond hotels
and resorts. We make many memories.

On the wall in Tokyo in our home we have one memory from
the trip that is the most happy of all. It is the drawing of my wife on
your porch. It remind my family what we love about America and
what we love most about our trip.

We want to return, but my business is bad now. Someday we
try, but until that day we have very best memories. We have you.

My family will pray for God to bless you and your wedding.

Yee-Quon Lee

✉

"I remember them," Rain said, still holding and studying the
letter.

"And they remember you. Isn't that wonderful?"

"That it is."

"And there are others like it. The Inn has been so important
to so many people. And I know it's presumptuous, Reindeer, but
we owe it a good-bye."

Rain read another letter, then another. She removed one
from its sheet protector to admire up close. She held it up against
the light and wondered how much A&P had spent on the cus-
tomized, embossed stationery. "You're too much," she said, slid-
ing the letter back into its home.

A letter from Layne Birch reminded Rain that a life had

ended in the Inn. She retold A&P how young Cameron, a Civil War buff and cancer patient, had stepped from this world to the next in an upstairs bedroom when Jack and Laurel still ran *Domus Jefferson.*

"Trust me, if you go ahead with the plans and we honor the Inn and the people who've stayed here through all these years, I promise you'll see more guests and friends than you can imagine. But there will also be others here you *won't* see."

Rain closed the binder. "I love you, Anna Belle. And you had me at *celebration.*"

CHAPTER 30

A&P and Rain made the same pitch to Noah and Malcolm later that afternoon in the living room. Malcolm was an easier sell; Noah needed convincing.

"Why do I want to be reminded that the wedding is off?"

"Don't think of it that way," his mother said. "If you'd decided to get married next spring, or next year, or never at all, we might have decided to do this anyway."

"And Rachel's still welcome to come; we'd love that," A&P added.

"Son, this is your call. Maybe it shouldn't be, I don't know, but I'm making it so. This was your wedding, your day. If you'd rather not go ahead with this, or if you'd rather do something on a smaller scale, we'll support that. And hey, you'll be saving your mom and me some money, right?"

"Good point, Corn Pops."

Rain removed and threw a hairclip at him.

"What?"

"Noah, can I show you something?" A&P produced the couple's Wedding Letter binder from her bag and set it on his lap.

"I don't know, A&P—"

"Don't say *no* yet. . . . This is just some of them, Noah. I have others at the house and more I haven't even opened yet. I bet I have thirty letters yet to read, and we're not even in September yet. Who knows how many we'll end up with."

"But what's the point?"

A&P shooed Malcolm down the couch and plopped between father and son. "I know it seems useless to keep these right now, what with the wedding off and everything else—trust me, I know—but the advice and the stories are still meaningful. You've got to keep this anyway."

"Are you out of your mind? I'm not keeping a book of letters about a wedding that isn't happening."

"So let your mother keep them. Or I'll keep them in my home and you can read them whenever you want. The point is these people love you and your family regardless. And some of the letters are from Rachel's side, too. You can't just throw all that away."

Noah opened the binder and scanned the letters. Though he tried to imagine them being about some other couple and some other wedding, each letter felt like he was holding a torn sketch of his lost summer.

✉

Dear Noah and Rachel,

Every parent dreams of their child's wedding day, right? Every parent hopes and prays that their child will find someone special who will treat them as the most important gift in life. I do hope that you will be that person for each other.

It wasn't that long ago that I was in your parents' shoes watching Angela walk down the aisle. With her permission I'd like to share with you some of what I wrote in my wedding letter to her.

When I married Angela's father there was never any question in my mind that it would be for forever, or until death do us part. I always thought my life would play out like a fairy tale from "Once upon a time" all the way to "Happily ever after."

Life doesn't always go as planned. Some of the most difficult times of my life were during my first marriage. It was filled with yelling, heated discussions, name calling, long periods of silence and tears. It wasn't always like that. For years we laughed; we enjoyed each other's company. We were inseparable, and we were never afraid to express the love we had for one another.

Things changed. The stresses of daily life began to take their toll. There was a child to raise, bills to pay, and careers to build. The problem became that we took care of all these other things instead of tending to our own relationship. The marriage failed.

Don't make the same mistakes I made. Learn from them. Put your relationship with each other first. Even after you have children, accept nothing less than being a priority to each other.

You already know life is hard. Marriage is hard, too, and no marriage is perfect, no matter what you think. Every marriage has its ups and downs. The "Once upon a time" can end in "Happily ever after," but it takes work, it takes compromise. It's about give-and-take. It's knowing that it won't always be 50/50. It takes love, communication, a strong commitment, and knowing that at times there will be hurt feelings because we're flawed and our words are sometimes flawed too. If you enter into your marriage knowing and accepting that each of you will make mistakes, then you will be armed with one of the most important gifts you can give each other: the power of forgiveness.

If, through the years, you can forgive each other for being imperfect, then you will guarantee yourselves the opportunity to grow old together.

I am so fortunate that I got a second chance at marriage with Shawn. I've learned to make every day count.

Trust in each other and fight through the difficult times. There will be many. But at the end of the day, when you lay your heads down on your pillows, reach out across the bed and take each other's hand and know that, despite the difficulties of the day, you are still one, still together—and together for the long haul. And finally, don't ever be afraid to wear out the words, "I love you."

Congratulations!
Samantha

✉

Dear Noah and Rachel,

   This is the first Wedding Letter I've ever written, and I'm not really sure what to say. Isn't that weird? I mean, I have my own book of them from my wedding day, and I'm still sitting here at my kitchen table trying to figure out what to say.

   I guess I envy you guys. That's weird too. I am happy and I love my dear husband more than anything, but I still wish we could go back to the day you're having now. It's one of the few days in your life you will always remember. What you ate, who was there, who made the toast at dinner, who you danced with, what the food smelled like. I remember all of it.

   But then you get to the busy business of being married instead of getting married and things change. You work all day and then you come home and work some more to make a home and a family. You worry about money (which we have to constantly), and you fight about money (which we do sometimes). You try to build the best life for your children (which we try to do morning and night).

   But the beautiful thing about your wedding day is the why.

Today is all about the why. Why you love each other, why you want to be together forever, why you're getting married at the Inn, why Noah asked and why Rachel said yes. Enjoy the whys.

A lot of my own Wedding Letters are gooey and filled with sweet thoughts about love and how perfect it all is. I wish I had a few that said how hard some days would be. That sometimes I would want to pack up my stuff and bundle up Taylor and come home to Mom and Shawn so they can take care of me. It's OK to have those days; everyone has those days. Just make sure you have more of the other kind of days.

The kind when, after a long day without seeing your husband or wife, you stand in the living room or kitchen or by the front door and just hang on to each other. You don't have to talk about the day, or what's bothering you, nothing. You just hang on to each other and remember what a blessing it is that God gave you someone to hang on to.

Darn it, I got gooey when I didn't mean to! I guess I'm Grandpa Jack's granddaughter, huh?

Congratulations, guys. I can't wait to share this day with you.

Love,
Angie

✉

Rachel and Noah,

Anna Belle Prestwich—whom I presume you both know, otherwise this is an elaborate prank—has invited me to give you some advice.

I'm divorced, as you may not have known or remembered, and I spend most of my waking hours preparing for our work together at the Department of Justice. It's an adventure I cannot wait for our team to begin.

It's odd writing this letter to you and to a man I've not yet met. I do hope by the time you read this I will have made his acquaintance.

My counsel for you comes from a song that was popular when you were in diapers. Andy Gibb recorded a song in 1977 about his new wife called "I Just Want to Be Your Everything." The song has a line that I've always appreciated:

"If you give a little more than you're asking for, your love will turn the key."

In marriage you need to give a great deal. Be sure that you are doing enough, always giving more than you're expecting. People speak and write about the best marriages being built on give-and-take. The key that opens that kind of relationship is pure love, and pure love comes from giving. If I'd done more of that, I might be married to a woman instead of to a dark office and a laptop.

That is the advantage of friendships and mistakes. Because we are friends, I hope you may learn from mine. And you will likewise teach others down the road.

As my mother used to say, "Always remember who you are and what you stand for."

John Fletcher

✉

Dear Rachel and Noah,

I write this letter from a restaurant in Phoenix. I have had this lovely stationery from your friend in my purse for a week or more but have not known what to write.

I've come to dinner with a woman from my complex who was lonely tonight and asked if I would join her. But she saw two friends from her church and is now across the restaurant visiting with them. I do not mind. Being alone is something I've grown accustomed to.

You're getting married. The thought rarely leaves my mind these days. When Rachel's father and I were married, we felt as if the world was telling us we had no choice. But we did have a choice, and we married because we were in love, very much so.

I was expecting Rachel but if her father felt obligated to marry me, he didn't show it. I believe he loved me then and I still believe it now. He did not always show it but when he did, he was kind and he was compassionate, particularly during our early years together.

I loved him, too. He was handsome and a hard worker. He did not always enjoy the labor, and it was hard on him physically. But for most of our lives together, he put food on our table.

He had other qualities to be certain and I tried to recognize and point them out. I hope you will do that with Rachel each and every day you are married. I don't know when I stopped doing that with your father, but I did. That could that have been part of our ending.

211

Being kind was not always easy. Rachel, you saw this. You saw that his anger was his undoing. I am not someone who prays. I have not been a woman who believed there was anyone listening. But, Rachel, I pray every day that Noah will not have a temper like your father did. If there is a God and if He loves you, He will see to it that you are not subjected to another angry man. I forgive your father for his anger fits. I forgive him for his lists. I do not and cannot forgive him for the way he treated you.

I feel peaceful when I think of what your future will bring. I believe Noah and his family to be good people. I know they have their own past, and so do we. But the future has no secrets.

I wish for your health. I wish for your happiness. I wish that your father could see what you have become and the kind of man you have chosen to marry. I wish that Daniel would come home to me. To all of us. If we are lucky, he will join us on September 27 and celebrate the day with us.

I have more to say but no more energy to say it. I love you, Rachel. I thank you for standing by me when I am difficult to stand by. I know I am often difficult to stand by.

Congratulations,
Stephanie Kaplan

✉

Noah closed the book and looked at his mother. "Let's do it."

CHAPTER 31

34 Days to the Celebration

Rachel left four messages for Daniel before he returned her call. He was apologetic, and though Rachel wanted to disbelieve and distrust, she couldn't ignore the sincerity in his voice.

"How have you been?" he asked.

Rachel paced around her apartment in the same sweats she'd been wearing on the day she had left Noah in shambles. The television was muted, but she turned it off anyway. "Where are you calling from?"

"I'm in town actually. I'm at the Mayflower."

With all the time to prepare for the call, she hadn't been prepared to hear he was in the states, and certainly not just across the bridge in DC. "How long are you here?"

"A few days. I'm arm wrestling with a Congressman. . . . Did you get my wire transfer for the last of your student loans?"

Rachel resumed pacing and picked up the stuffed squirrel Noah had given her after their accidental meeting. "Yes, thank you." She set the squirrel down. "I'm paid off. In the clear." She picked up the squirrel again and moved it from one shelf to another. "I didn't expect you to be so close."

"Honestly, Rachel, that played a role in me not calling sooner. I knew I'd be stateside and close enough for lunch or dinner, if you're interested."

Am I interested? she thought.

"That would be nice," she said before she could talk herself out of it. "I have something I'd like to talk to you about."

Daniel was silent, and Rachel heard a woman's voice in the background. "Sounds important," he said and the background noise became an echo. "I can meet whenever you like, Rachel. Just tell me when and where."

They met in the lobby of the historic Mayflower hotel for breakfast the next morning. Daniel stepped out of an elevator wearing an Armani powerbroker suit, crisp blue shirt, and no tie. The ensemble made him feel strong and in control; he wore it often. His black hair was slicked back and graying at the temples, but as thick and full as ever. Rachel wore her favorite spring dress, one that made her feel more beautiful than anything she owned. She reminded herself in the mirror before leaving her apartment that she could stand to wear it every day.

After a clumsy hug, Daniel kissed her awkwardly on the cheek. "You look amazing, Rachel, as always."

"Thank you."

He walked past the hostess and led them to a table in the furthest corner of the restaurant. "This all right?" he asked, and he pulled her chair out for her.

She nodded, sat, and put her Blackberry on the table next to her silverware. She wasn't sure if she wanted it to ring at some point or not, but seeing it there made her feel connected to something when the rest of the atmosphere seemed surreal.

Daniel began the visit by making conversation so rote and uninteresting Rachel wasn't sure it even qualified as small talk.

After they'd ordered, Rachel used the break to change course. "You're not here alone, I assume."

Daniel rearranged his napkin on his lap. "No, I'm not. My friend is here in town."

"You don't have to call her a friend, Daniel. It's been a long time, and I'm not a child."

"We're not married, Rachel, and we're more friends than anything. We take good care of each other."

"So how is she?" Rachel asked because she thought she was supposed to.

"She's good. She's good."

"You know I've never met her."

Daniel studied her eyes. "Would you like to?"

"I'd like that," Rachel said with a firmness that surprised her so much that she said it again. "Yes, I'd like to meet her."

"Fair enough. I'll call her when we're done. She's up in the room."

They both took drinks and settled their nerves. Then Rachel noticed Daniel angling for a better view of her ring finger. "You knew?" she asked.

"About the wedding? Yes, I wrote a letter for the friend of yours, A&Something? I thought I might see a ring."

Rachel looked at her own finger and frowned involuntarily, exactly as she had more times than she could count since last weekend. "I meant to call and tell you myself." She said the words without breaking her gaze away from her hand.

"Don't be embarrassed about it. I'm the last one who could file a complaint for not being kept in the loop."

Well that's true, she thought.

"Everything still set?"

"Not exactly," she said.

"Do you need funds? Can I help?"

"*No.* No money. It's not that." Rachel's phone rang and she hit the ignore button without seeing who it was.

Daniel slid the fresh flower arrangement between them to the side. "Is there something you want to talk about?"

"There is," said Rachel. "I'm not getting married. It's . . . I called it off. . . . At least for now."

"Oh. Well, I'm sorry to hear that, but it happens. It happens all the time, so I've seen myself. Is it something that can be fixed?"

Rachel sat a little straighter and tucked a rambunctious lock of hair behind her ear. "May I ask you something? Something blunt?"

"Of course."

"When did you know about my mother?"

"When did I know *what* about your mother?"

"When did you know what she'd done?"

"What she'd done?"

"Yes, Daniel. When did you know about my real father?"

Daniel took another drink of cranberry juice. While he wiped his mouth, Rachel retrieved a small stack of postcards bound in a rubber band from her purse. She placed them on the table.

"She told you," Daniel said.

"She told me everything."

Daniel picked up the postcards and removed the rubber band. He flipped through them and remembered the places he'd been with an odd mix of pleasure and regret. "When did I know?" he said. "I knew after a few dates with your mother."

"She told you *that* soon?"

"Of course. Those are things that come up in a conversation with someone who's been married before. I hadn't; she had."

"And you weren't alarmed?" Rachel lowered her volume. "How? Why?"

"Alarmed? She was a widow, Rachel. A lovely widow who'd been through a tough marriage and who had this precious daughter who missed her father. Sure, I was alarmed—I was alarmed at how alone you were."

The server arrived with Daniel's omelet, croissant, and salsa and Rachel's oatmeal with fresh fruit. They each offered a polite thank you and waited for the privacy to return.

"You knew he'd died," she said, fearing the truth was only half-told.

"Yes, Rachel. . . . Are you all right?"

She pushed her oatmeal away. "Did she tell you how he died?"

"Of course," he said. "It was an accident."

"What kind?"

"He fell at work?" Daniel hadn't meant for it to come out as a question.

"Sure, he fell. But not at work, Daniel, at home. My parents fought and they *both* fell. But the fall didn't kill him."

Daniel felt the hair on his neck come alive.

"She killed him, Daniel. She killed my father."

Daniel's hands wanted to fumble with something and his eyes felt tempted to dart around the room. His stomach spun and churned, but he remained frozen, his upper body rigid, his muscles tense.

"She killed him," she said again.

Hearing it twice doesn't make it more true, he thought.

"They had a fight, like they had plenty of times before, but this one was different. They struggled and she killed him. That's all I know."

Daniel's mind raced like a flipbook.

"Daniel?"

He fought through the paralyzed static and removed his glasses. He tucked them in his coat pocket and pulled at the corners of his forehead, tightening the wrinkles but loosening the tension. "I didn't know, Rachel. I didn't have any idea. I really didn't."

"I don't know whether to be sorry for you or angry. How could she keep this from us? How does she sleep?"

"I think you know well enough that your mother has had more sleepless nights than both of us put together." Daniel flashed through the memories of restless midnights, Stephanie's winding and rambling bedtime conversations, her crying fits, and her chronic depression. He closed his eyes but could still see the vacancy in hers. "How did she . . . um . . . How did . . . Did no one know? Does no one know?"

"Evidently not."

Daniel leaned in. "I didn't know, Rachel. I couldn't have kept that inside."

Rachel tapped the cards. "But you did know something, Daniel. You knew he'd passed away. You lied to me."

He made eye contact and allowed the words to spill out in a way that scared him. "I wish I could defend myself, Rachel. I wish more than anything in the world this moment wasn't happening. I was uncomfortable, I was literally *sick* when I wrote the first card. I could barely breathe when I put it in the mailbox. I was out of the country, completely alone on some business trip. No one to talk to and no one to talk me out of it." He picked up the cards and spun them over. "I carried it in my pocket for weeks. When I finally mailed it, I wasn't even sure it would survive, it was so haggard and worn out already." He flipped through the postcards until he spotted it: A well-traveled card boasting a picture of the Leaning Tower of Pisa on the front and a scribbled paragraph on the back.

"I remember the day it came," Rachel said.

"So do I. I hadn't paid attention to the time change and I called home early in the morning from my hotel. You answered the phone and I knew immediately you'd gotten it. Your spirit was there. It was . . . I don't know. It was special."

Rachel took the card from him and reread the words she'd long ago memorized:

Dear Rachel, I hope this card arrives to you and that it makes you happy. I'm sorry I had to leave you but I am not the daddy you deserve. I need time, my dear daughter, to find out who I really am.

I love you and miss you. I'm sorry. Be good to your mother, she loves you too. Love, Dad.

Rachel returned the card to the stack and rewrapped them with the rubber band. "I deserved to know."

"I know."

"All those years."

"I know."

"I deserved to know, Daniel. I deserved to know he wasn't becoming a better man somewhere."

"Rachel—"

"I should have known who he really was from the beginning *and* at the end. I should have known he wasn't going to change and show up someday at my school play or graduation or wedding. Do you know what it's like to believe someone can change? To believe someone is finding redemption, even if you can't see it? And then to find out he never did? He never did."

Their server returned and, seeing the food untouched, asked if everything was all right. Daniel assured him it was and with a subtle tilt of the head sent him away.

They sat in silence and Daniel continued apologizing with his eyes. Rachel picked grapes from the fruit bowl. The server slipped the check on the table without either noticing.

Daniel's phone rang and he asked, "It's her, do you mind?"

Rachel shook her head.

"Hi," he said with the phone to one ear and a finger in the

other. "Sure. . . . Do you want me to get you? You sure? All right then. We'll look for you in the lobby."

He put the phone in his coat pocket and dropped two twenties in the check folder. "Rachel, I understand if this changes things, changes our . . . relationship. I can't say enough how sorry I am to have hurt you. And I don't know what to say about your mother. I can't begin to process what you've been through, what she's been through. But know this. I will continue to support you however I can. I'm not the best stepfather—you don't need me to tell you that; I know—but I try. I do try."

Rachel put the postcards back in her purse and held it with both arms across her chest. "I don't know what this changes either. I don't."

"Can you promise to take time? Time to figure things out?"

"I can."

"And would you still like to meet my friend? She's coming to the lobby." He stood and pulled Rachel's chair away from the table.

"Why not?" Rachel said, and she followed Daniel out of the restaurant and toward the historic Mayflower's grand lobby.

A moment later one of the elevators opened and a short, middle-aged-but-fighting-it woman appeared. She stood no more than five feet tall with short, red hair, fair skin, and Jackie Onassis sunglasses. The blind woman swiped at the ground with a cane as she stepped into the lobby.

"Over here, Isabella," Daniel said. Then he met her with a kiss.

CHAPTER 32

It wasn't a hard sell. Once again Stephanie found herself driving Arianna, her slot-thirsty neighbor, to an Indian reservation in the Arizona desert. The friendly, chatterbox friend provided noise in Stephanie's quiet head.

By midnight Arianna had won almost five hundred dollars in quarter slots and, because the hotel was quiet and the hour late, a manager offered to comp her a deluxe room with two king-sized beds. Arianna called and interrupted her husband's evening of watching *Leno* and eating pretzels to ask permission to stay. He agreed it was wiser than driving home in the middle of the night. Arianna withheld the surprise that she would come home in the black.

They lay in the dark, Arianna comfortably tucked into her bed and Stephanie on top of hers, staring at the stucco ceiling.

"Are you awake?" Arianna asked two minutes after Stephanie had turned off the light.

"Yes."

"I won five hundred dollars tonight."

"I know."

"Five hundred dollars. I've *never* won that much."

"That's a lot of money," Stephanie said.

"I can't wait to tell Lew. He'll be so excited. Won't he be excited?"

"He will."

"Maybe he'll let me get a new chair. I would just love a new chair. One that vibrates would be nice. Have you seen the ones that vibrate?"

"Uh-huh."

"They have a controller attached and it has different speeds. Have you seen them?"

"I have."

"They have them at the mall. I don't know the store, but they're right there by the food court. They're right up front. Anyone can try them. Lew thinks they're too much money. But maybe now he'll say it's OK. Do you think so?"

"He might."

"He might. I hope he does. You know, I've won up to a hundred dollars before. But I always lose it again. I've never, ever been up five hundred dollars. Lew doesn't usually let me play the quarter slots when we come. Only nickels and pennies. It's hard to get up that much on the nickels, you know?"

"Uh-huh."

"Five hundred dollars. Lew will be so excited."

"Uh-huh."

Arianna continued chatting until the blackness swallowed her rhythm and the words were replaced with snores. Stephanie looked in her direction and tried to remember the last time she'd heard the sound of sleep.

When she turned back to the ceiling, she saw her husband's face lording over her. His breath smelled like corn chips and anger. His eyes were wide and dark and the blue-gray bags below them were so thick they overpowered his face. His face. His long, narrow horse-face. He hadn't shaved in a week and when he forced his mouth on her neck, it left her skin red and itchy.

Stephanie closed her eyes and pushed the anxious air from her lungs. But the new air wasn't any calmer and she felt familiar panic. She breathed out again and squinted. Her husband's eyes were glassy, like marbles the color of dirty ocean water. They rushed at her and she flinched.

Sleep, her thoughts begged.

The eyes rushed again and she rolled over on her side away from Arianna. "Sleep." She said the word aloud. But the eyes were on her now, so close she couldn't tell which set was hers and which were his. She felt the cold crack of a wrench against her collarbone and the snoring from across the room became curses and taunts.

Stephanie was on her back again. She put her hands behind her pillow and wrapped the sides up over her ears. She clenched her jaw until her teeth hurt. A chair fell. He fell. The threats began. *Rachel, Rachel, Rachel.* She saw his tool belt scatter. *Was she in my tool belt?* A level, tape measure, sockets. *Was she in my tool belt?* A pencil, plastic goggles, a list on a folded up fast-food napkin. *Was Rachel in my tool belt, Stephanie?* The screwdriver came at her and she yanked her hands from underneath the pillow. One of them held a flashlight. *Crack, crack.* She flinched and swung it again. *Crack.* Blood came from his ear. Tears came from her eyes.

She ran away and knocked on her neighbor's door across the hall. Mr. Richardson's eyes were warm. He put a hand on her shoulder and followed her back to her kitchen. *Ten minutes,* he said. *Don't cry. Get what you can in ten minutes and go.*

She ran. She packed two bags, left the building, ran to pick up Rachel from school, ran away from Kansas City. She stayed off the interstate and checked into a motel not far away in Independence, Missouri. She paid cash.

She called Mr. Richardson that night from a pay phone in the parking lot after Rachel had fallen asleep.

Just go, he said. *Go start over. Take care of your little one.*

Back in the motel room, Stephanie cuddled up next to her daughter. *Dad's left us,* she whispered. *But we're all right. We're all right.*

Arianna woke Stephanie up at 9:00 A.M. and they ate at the elaborate breakfast buffet together before checking out.

"Did you enjoy your stay?" the clerk asked.

"Very much," Arianna gushed.

"You have some luck?" the young man gave a condescending wink.

"Did we ever! I'm going home five hundred dollars richer."

"Lucky young lady," he flashed a bleached-white smile.

They walked away from the registration desk and noted how the lights and sounds of the casino were already tempting gamblers to the tables and slots. "I'm going to use the ladies' room before we go." Stephanie excused herself to a lobby restroom.

"I'll wait."

When Stephanie returned, Arianna was loading twenty dollars into a nearby slot machine. "We might not be back, right?"

"Whenever you're ready," Stephanie said.

"You're sure? You drove, I don't want to keep you." Arianna was already watching the wheels spin.

"I've nowhere to be."

"What if I could win enough for two chairs? Imagine!"

"Why not?"

When the first bill was spent, Arianna turned and asked, "How about we try the dollar progressives this time?"

"Sure."

"Look at how much it's up to!" She pointed to another bank of blinking machines.

"That's a lot of money."

"Maybe we could win that car."

"Uh-huh."

Stephanie sat in a chair next to Arianna while she hit MAX BET and lost her money three dollars at a time.

"I'll get it back," she said. For an hour she won ten dollars for every twenty she lost. When she'd finished, she'd spun away every dollar she'd won the night before.

They walked quietly out to the parking lot and buckled themselves into Stephanie's car. No one spoke until they were clear of the reservation and well on their way out of the desert.

"Please don't tell Lew."

"Of course not, Arianna."

"Please?"

"Of course."

CHAPTER 33

25 Days to the Celebration

It wasn't an accident. Malcolm told Mr. and Mrs. Van Dam, the soon-to-be-owners of *Domus Jefferson,* that the first weekend of September was a good time for them to stay the weekend as guests. He knew the Inn was booked and was anxious to have them experience the buzz of a busy night and morning.

Mrs. Van Dam spent the early evening under Rain's feet as she made preparations for the next morning's breakfast. She admitted to not being a very good cook and let slip that they were considering going with a more *packaged* breakfast. Rain didn't know what that meant, but it scared her all the same.

Mr. Van Dam shadowed Malcolm as he checked in guests and shared the history lesson behind the Inn, the furniture, and the art to those who wanted it. The new owner took notes and captured as much as he could before deciding much of it might not be useful for them.

After the guests were checked in, Malcolm suggested the

two couples head out for a late dinner at Joe's Steakhouse in Woodstock. Malcolm texted his friend Joe from the car to alert him they were coming. He also asked for a quiet table upstairs and mentioned that he hoped Joe might have some time to swing by and introduce himself to the new owners of the Inn.

Joe's manager, a woman Malcolm had long-referred to as Bubbly Ashley, met them at the door and led them upstairs to a table on the balcony overlooking Main Street. "Joe says he won't seat anyone else out here. It's all yours." Malcolm and Rain's drinks were already on the table.

"You're regulars?" Mr. Van Dam said.

"You could say that," Malcolm answered. "But we try to support all the locals. Frankly there aren't many options for dinner in town. The Café stays open late on Thursdays for a very nice dinner, which you should certainly try, and there's the deli and some pizza places in town. Seafood by the freeway, some Chinese, but not much else besides fast-food row. Oh, Edinburg has a tasty Italian place—Sal's. And there's a Mexican place in Mount Jackson you'll want to try."

Rain broke in. "We've always felt as though we should support the local establishments and make sure we feel good about recommending them to our guests. Every weekend couples will ask about nearby restaurants and we do our best to spread the recommendations around."

"Spread the love," Malcolm said. "Spread the love."

"Um, I see." Mr. Van Dam resumed taking notes on his legal pad.

They discussed the evolving menu, and every now and then another of Joe's friendly servers came by to introduce themselves to the future of *Domus Jefferson*.

"Everyone seems to know you," Mrs. Van Dam said. "Is that normal?"

"Is *that* normal or am *I* normal?" Malcolm asked.

"Oh, stop." Rain saved the confused woman across the table. "Yes, it's small town America. It's an exaggeration to say everyone knows everyone, but you hear that saying a lot in a town like this. And to a certain extent, I suppose it's true. Particularly with the Inn. Many of these people, even though they're lifelong residents, have stayed with us. They have ladies' weekends, church retreats, that sort of thing. And remember, *Domus Jefferson* has been a part of the community for a long time. Even before Malcolm's parents bought it in '68."

"How often does that happen?" Mrs. Van Dam said.

"What?"

"How often do the local people stay?"

"Malcolm?" Rain tossed it to him.

"In actual numbers? I couldn't say. We book group events like that—multiple room stays—once a month. Maybe every two months, depending on the season."

Mr. Van Dam scribbled more notes.

His wife spoke up again. "Do you ever feel like you've lost, I don't know, your privacy?"

Rain smiled. "There isn't much privacy in our world, I'm afraid. It's part of the lifestyle. We live at the Inn, as you know; we've raised our son there. It's home and every few days or every weekend people come to that home. We like that aspect, don't we, honey?"

"We've *learned* to like it," Malcolm corrected. "It takes time, no doubt about it."

More notes for Mr. Van Dam. Then a question, "We've talked a lot about your marketing, but what have you done to attract more of these *group* events? Receptions? Corporate retreats? High-dollar guests?"

"Well, not much. They come when they come. A lot of our success has been word of mouth, and that's easy with forty years of history here. We've had couples conceive their children in our Inn and then welcomed those children back with their own spouses."

Rain covered her eyes and Mrs. Van Dam blushed. Her husband did not write down that note.

Bubbly Ashley brought their dinners and paused to refill their drinks for the third time. Malcolm had a New York strip, Rain had barbeque ribs, and the Van Dams had chicken Caesar salads. As they ate, the Coopers continued downloading years of expertise and experiences. They highlighted the highs and were honest about the lows. Mr. Van Dam filled two pages with notes, and his wife tried to count how many people Malcolm waved at and called to on Main Street.

Joe stopped by and introduced himself with several quick jokes. "So, are you two actors?" he said to the Van Dams.

"I'm sorry?"

"Do you act? We have this mystery dinner evening we do a couple times every year. Last few shows have been decent, but some of the cast members are just lousy, right guys?" He punched Malcolm playfully in the arm. "I've been trying to get the Coopers here to try a show for years. Malcolm's sister, Samantha, our honorable sheriff, is a regular star in our shows, and a big-time scene stealer, too, but Malcolm and Rain haven't signed on yet."

"And we're not going to anytime soon, Joe. Don't you want people to keep their food down?"

Joe made another joke, and Mrs. Van Dam began fiddling with an earring. "Actually," she said, "truth be told, I did try some theater in college, but that was a long time ago."

Mr. Van Dam turned abruptly to Joe. "We won't be acting in a murder mystery show, I'm afraid, but we'll gladly tell our guests about them, if you'll drop off some literature."

"Consider it done," Joe said and insisted the meal was on the house.

"You don't have to do that," Mr. Van Dam said.

"I know I don't," Joe said, slapping his back. "I wouldn't offer if I thought I *had* to."

They thanked him and began to leave the restaurant, a process slowed by half a dozen introductions to other diners the Coopers knew. Mr. Van Dam tried to capture as many names as he could, but Malcolm spoke so quickly and moved from handshakes to the latest gossip in such rapid fire it was difficult to keep up.

Rain suggested dessert at Katie's Custard on the way home, and the couples sat at a plastic picnic table at the edge of Route 11 enjoying a custard that melted faster than they could eat it. There were more questions and more answers longer than they needed to be. Then came more concerns about profit and loss and even more assurances the Inn was on solid ground.

"You should be mayor," Mrs. Van Dam said to Malcolm when a passing car honked at them for the second time and a hand appeared out the window.

"Nah, not for me. I prefer to stay under the radar."

"Yeah, right." Rain tapped the end of his nose with her drippy chocolate and vanilla twist. Another car passed and honked.

Mr. Van Dam wiped custard from his chin and looked at his wife. "Do you think something like this would ever work in the city?"

"Ice cream?" she said.

"No, a stand like this—an old-fashioned, walk-up style. Not

a strip mall shop." The discussion evolved into Mr. Van Dam's vision for Woodstock. "It's fine here, very welcoming. But how do you take a community like this and infuse it with city conveniences, better restaurants, more variety, without losing the small town . . . what is it . . ."

"Charm," Rain offered.

"Sure. How do you do that? How do you make it more of a bedroom community for northern Virginia? How do we attract more money from the city—maybe even more commercial development—but without upsetting the locals?"

Rain squeezed Malcolm's leg under the table. "Honey?"

Malcolm shoved the rest of his cone in his mouth and wiped his hands on what was left of the napkin. "Good luck with that."

"What do you mean?" Mr. Van Dam said.

"He means it's a balancing act," Rain said.

"I do?" Malcolm said.

"Yes," Rain answered. "We walk a fine line between maintaining what makes the valley unique and emphasizing what tourists want. But I think you'll find the most important thing is the people. It's the *people* who make the valley special, not the restaurants or the businesses or even the changing of the leaves."

Malcolm furrowed his brow like a cartoon character. "Is that straight from our website?"

"Yes, but I wrote it, so I can use it whenever I want."

The night ended in the living room with Rain making plans

with Mrs. Van Dam for the good-bye celebration. Their husbands sat in Malcolm's office discussing building permits, county politics, and revisiting the list of furniture the Coopers had chosen to take with them to their new home.

After a breakfast the next morning that Mrs. Van Dam called both chaotic and delicious, her husband checked his watch and excused himself to the yard where he met a Fairfax-based general contractor.

Malcolm watched from the porch as the other men walked the property and Mr. Van Dam added another page of notes to his legal pad. Malcolm overheard talk of a paved driveway, a new building with meeting rooms, Wi-Fi, and a pool. When they walked around to the back of the house, Malcolm didn't follow. Instead he returned inside and reread a letter from his parents' collection. Then he debated whether to let the Van Dams read it, too.

✉

July 10, 1968
Laurel,

I'm not even going to try describing how this place looks. You'll have to admire it with your own eyes. It's heaven.

I am spending the night in one of the guest rooms at the Inn at the absolute insistence of Mr. and Mrs. Condie. They thought I should experience the Inn at night. I'm afraid it might have closed the deal for me. It is so calm here, Laurel, a reverent feeling I don't want to lose. I expect when I open the shade in the morning I'll see fog rising in the field below the house and ghost-soldiers marching silently through it. I feel like I'm sleeping in a history book tonight.

I spent the afternoon and evening downtown at a diner on what I suppose is called Main Street. There is really only one street in the town and it runs through the center of everything. It's also called Route 11 or Old Valley Pike, and it goes for miles and miles north and south connecting a whole string of other small towns to Woodstock. I believe Woodstock is the county seat.

This place has some fascinating history. I learned from a woman at the diner named Tiffanee (sp?) about a man named John Peter Muhlenberg (sp?) but who everyone called "The Fighting Parson." Now that's a nickname.

He came to Woodstock in the late 1700s to be the pastor. In 1776, which is just about my favorite year as you know, he delivered a sermon calling for volunteers to join the militia to the Continental Army. At the end of his sermon, he ripped off his church robe and revealed an officer's uniform underneath. He shouted, "There's a time to pray and a time to fight!" What a man he must have been!

The town hosted generals and soldiers from both sides of the war. And one guess who designed the town's courthouse? Jefferson. It's the most beautiful limestone I've seen.

Hon, this place already feels like home to me. The Inn needs some work in a few spots, but nothing your man cannot do alone or with help from Matthew and Malcolm. I see new art for the walls, some new furniture in the rooms, and new mattresses for the cottage. They look like one too many kids have jumped and peed on them, probably in that order.

And it's silly, I know, but I can't wait for you to see the mailbox. It was the first thing I noticed. It's sort of rusty-red with a white dove carrying an envelope in its mouth. It's the kind of mailbox that knows secrets. It's the kind of mailbox that will hold our Wednesday Letters proudly and then beg you to read them aloud. See? I told you it was silly.

We probably don't need to decide for another week, but we can't wait long. The Condies would like to close the sale and be in Boulder within a month, tops.

I could die in this house. It's got to be close to God.

> See you in a few days,
> Jack

CHAPTER 34

22 Days to the Celebration

Rachel's first day of work at the Department of Justice was a whirlwind of paperwork, meetings, department orientations, and more paperwork. She met the remaining members of her team at a special lunch in a posh restaurant in Union Station next door to their building. There were eleven of them in total, all covered under the same grant Rachel had helped secure, and they came from myriad backgrounds in government, business, and academia.

Rachel relied heavily on Tyler to understand and adapt to the DOJ culture. Even though they were equals, Rachel often bypassed her boss to approach Tyler with questions about her new responsibilities. She appreciated his patience and willingness to hold her hand through the transition from full-time student to full-time employee of the federal government.

When they weren't talking about work or sharing private opinions on their colleagues, Tyler casually reminded her of the good, stress-free times they'd shared in college. Rachel was amazed—and impressed—at how many memories he'd captured and was eager to recount.

Tyler didn't know every detail of her private life, but he knew enough to know a door had been opened. One afternoon over a snack and soda in a conference room, he'd asked if the wedding was cancelled or simply postponed, and Rachel admitted she wasn't sure which anymore. All she knew is how much she appreciated his willingness to listen. She'd always known he was intelligent and well-traveled, that he spoke French—badly—and had no baggage. But she'd never known what a good listener he was, and he offered to listen often.

They only touched on the topic of Rachel's father. She couldn't bring herself to tell Tyler everything, but she at least told him he could stop looking. Rachel was glad Tyler just said OK and didn't press her for details. She wanted to imagine that her father might still be alive somewhere, still scribbling and sending the occasional postcard, but she knew that was impossible.

Rachel called Noah on the way home from work at the end of her first week. His eager, boyish voice made her smile. "Hey you."

"Hey back. How are you? Where are you?"

"Heading home from work."

"Everything all right? You survived?"

"I survived. It's pretty nuts already, but I'm making it."

"Good. Nuts is busy. And busy is good, yeah?"

"Busy is good. That's true."

"So what's it like?" Noah asked.

"It's a little frightening, honestly. It's reports and meetings and calls." She paused before adding an "Oh my!"

"Ha," Noah grumbled.

"Just one?"

"Not even—I just don't know how to give half a *ha*."

Rachel enjoyed a laugh and sat on a bench by her downtown metro stop.

"What are the people like?" Noah asked.

"They're fantastic."

"How's Tyler Clingman?"

"Clingerman."

"Whatever."

"He's fine, Noah. He's actually been a big help to me."

"Oh, I bet he has."

"He's been a good friend to me, you know. He's handled a lot for me this first week to help me get settled."

"What a gentleman," Noah said, though he was actually thinking, *What else has he handled?*

"Anyway. Next topic. How about you? What are you up to, funnyman? Watching *Dr. Oz*? *Ellen*?"

"How dare you, Rachel Kaplan. You know I'm a *Rachael Ray* guy."

"Tsk-tsk, Noah," she said and admitted, if only to herself, she missed the banter.

He switched the phone from one ear to the other. "I've missed you, Rach."

"Thank you."

"Thank you?"

"I've missed you, too, Noah."

"You get my e-mails about the party?"

"I did."

"And?"

"I don't know yet."

"Rach, it's coming up quick. And it's important to me. It's going to be a big day for everyone. People are coming from all over to say good-bye to the Inn."

"I know, but it's a weekday, Noah. And I just started work. I don't know if I can really disappear for a whole day."

Noah counted yet another reason he wished they weren't having this discussion by phone. "You do realize you were prepared to take off an entire week for a wedding and honeymoon, right?"

Rachel replied with an embarrassed silence.

Noah sighed. "I'm sorry. I just want you there."

"But does anyone else?"

"*Of course* they do. They want to see you. They want to share the day with you."

Rachel unbuttoned the jacket on her power suit and took a big breath. "I seriously don't get that."

"Get what?"

"I don't get why they'd care to share the big shindig with me. Or why they'd want to share *anything* with me. Not after all this. Not after the way I left." She measured and remeasured her words. "The Inn scares me now."

"Why?"

"Truthfully? It reminds me I haven't seen my mother since . . ." She cleared her throat. "I'm embarrassed about it. I'm embarrassed about *all* of it."

Noah stepped outside of his apartment and looked up at the overcast sky. "Are you outside?"

"I'm getting ready to hop on the metro and ride home."

"Look up."

She did and noticed for the first time all day how dark and overcast it was.

"What do you see?"

"Probably what you see. We're only what, five miles apart?"

"Is it cloudy?"

"Yes, Al Roker, it's cloudy. But no rain. At least not downtown."

"Here either. But it's super dark."

"Same here."

"Remember what I said about overcast skies?"

Rachel flipped her metro card between her thumb and index finger. "Yes."

"We're still here, Rach, whether you see us or not."

"I know."

"Come to the party. It's important to me."

"I can appreciate that."

"A&P wants you here, too."

Rachel laughed again. "I know. She's been leaving me long and bizarre voice mails every day."

"But they're hilarious, right?"

"That they are."

"I get them, too. It's an A&P thing." Noah took a beat and then a chance. "She's still putting together our Wedding Letters, you know."

Rachel breathed that in.

"She's got more than ever, she says. More than my mom and dad. Way more than Samantha and Shawn. Might have to go to another book it's getting so fat."

Rachel's voice was soft and with the ambient noise near the metro, Noah had to ask her to repeat herself. "I said, why is she still worrying about it?"

"Because she's A&P. Because she has hope like the rest of us."

"Noah—"

"And because she didn't want to tell all those people not to bother. The letters are keepsakes no matter what. You'll like them, I promise you will. I'm illustrating a cover even."

"Noah—"

"And Angie's said she's still coming regardless. Wedding or no. They'd already bought the plane tickets. And of course they're bringing the baby. I remember how well you and Baby Taylor hit it off."

"Ha," Rachel said. Then she stood up, wedged the phone between her chin and shoulder and rebuttoned her coat. "I don't know. I'm just starting to put things together, to feel normal again. I'm finding some . . . I don't know if it's peace or what you want to call it, but it's . . . it's an understanding. Like finding out who I am again."

"You know who you are, Rachel Kaplan. That never changed."

But it did, she thought.

"All right," Noah said after a moment of silence. "Think about it?"

"I will."

"Dinner soon?"

"I'd like that."

"I'll call you?"

"Sure."

"I love you, Rachel. You know that, right?"

"I do."

It was not the *I do* he wanted to hear, but he couldn't deny it felt better than nothing at all.

CHAPTER 35

13 Days to the Celebration

Malcolm was sitting at his desk when headlights lit up the front of *Domus Jefferson* and the Shenandoah County sheriff's SUV came to a stop in the spacious gravel parking area. Malcolm watched his sister kill the lights and sit in the car for a minute or two before opening the door and stepping into the night air. He moved to meet her at the front door, but when he pulled it open, she wasn't on the porch, she was walking across the north side lawn heading toward the guest cottage. He watched her open the front door, flip on a light, and shut the door behind her.

"Who's here?" Rain startled him from behind.

Malcolm pointed at the guesthouse. "Sammie."

"She need something?"

"I don't know."

"Is she all right?"

"I don't know that either." Malcolm turned and kissed her forehead. "I'll find out." He descended the porch alone and made his way to the small two-bedroom guesthouse he and his sister had once shared as children.

"Knock-knock," he said, opening the door. Malcolm found Samantha in full uniform lying on her back on a double bed in her old room. "Do you have a reservation?"

"Don't need one." She smiled.

"Oh, really?" Malcolm leaned against the open door.

"Nope, I know the owners."

"Ah, yes, the owners. Good people."

"Eh. The wife's sweet," Samantha said, "but the husband's a hoser."

"Hoser? What are you now, a Mountie?"

"Shut it."

"So why the visit? Shawn finally kick you out?"

"You wish."

"I do?"

"You know you'd love to have your sister back here tormenting you like the good ol' days."

"I thought *I* did most of the tormenting." Malcolm slapped her hip. "Slide over, sheriff." He laid down next to her and pulled the pillow out from underneath her head.

"You're such a doof," she said, yanking it back and doubling it over so there wasn't enough to share.

"Doof," Malcolm chuckled. "Haven't heard that one for a while."

"Yet it never goes out of style," she said. They laid side by side, looking up at the ceiling.

"Everything all right, sis?"

"Yeah, just been meaning to come by all week. Been thinking about this place."

"The Inn?"

"The Inn, the cottage, the hill, Mom and Dad. . . . I haven't been in the old room in a long time."

"I'm surprised you recognized the place. Rain took down your Johnny Depp and Heathcliff posters years ago."

"It was Tom Cruise and Garfield, thank you very much. And that was a *long* time ago. Long before Katie Holmes and long before he became a Scientologist."

"Garfield's a Scientologist?"

Samantha pulled her pillow out and whacked him.

"What?" he protested. "I don't judge."

Laughter filled the cottage and Samantha put the pillow back in place, this time leaving half for Malcolm and inviting him to take it with a pat. They looked back up at the ceiling. "Remember those glow-in-the-dark stars I had?"

"Uh-huh. Mom bought them for you to make you like the room."

"Yep. We went to Ben Franklin. Must have been just a couple nights after we moved here. I actually liked the room just fine, but I kept telling her the more stars I had, the more I'd like it. So she kept buying them. Had my own little galaxy up there."

"I remember. They were still there when you and Will split up and you and Angie moved back here for a while. No glow left, but they were there."

"How appropriate," Samantha mused.

They lay in silence, both following thoughts to stale memories.

"Angie loved it here. She missed Will, but she loved living here. I had to drag her away and into that townhouse."

"I think Mom and Dad spoiling her to death had something to do with that."

"Maybe so."

Another verse of silence came and went between them.

"Funny how much you hated this place at first." Malcolm turned to her. "Now look at you."

"Of course I did. That's what you're supposed to do when you're ten and you get ripped from your home."

"Ripped from your home? OK, John Walsh."

"What? It was tough moving here. My life was in Charlottesville."

"Uh, Sammie, you know I moved too? And I was a teenager with actual friends. Most of yours were imaginary."

"Most of yours were imaginary." She mocked his voice. "I had friends. Theater friends mostly, but good friends."

"Maybe so, but you settled in quickly. We all did."

"This place sure helped," Samantha said.

"It sure did."

They reminisced in familiar rhythm about sleepovers and fights, holidays and snowstorms, pranks and parents.

When Malcolm sensed the beat slowing, he went where he least wanted to. "You know I have to ask you this, right, Sammie?"

"What?"

"Rachel's mom."

"What about Rachel's mom?"

"Nice try. What have you decided?"

"Decided? That's a tricky word. It's more like settling."

"Settling?"

"I've settled on not doing anything right now."

"Really?"

"See, I *told* you it was tricky." Samantha closed her eyes. "I've settled on not deciding until after all this winds down."

"Can you do that?"

Samantha smiled and opened her eyes. "I don't know, I can't decide."

"Nice. . . . Well, I'm just glad it's not me who had to figure it all out."

"Tell me about it. It's been weighing on me. I've researched it, had a few confidential and extremely hypothetical conversations with the commonwealth's attorney, made a few calls to Kansas City. How do you report a crime years later that you know was self-defense when no one seems to know, or care, if the victim is dead? I can't find the neighbor; I can't find a report. I can't find a single reason to make that poor woman have to relive a second of that nightmare. All I've got is confirmation from Rachel's school that her mother called to withdraw her from school and requested her records be transferred. That's it."

"And yet you're obligated," Malcolm said.

"That I am."

"So you settled."

"Just until after the party, until Rachel gets things figured out for herself."

"And then what?"

"I guess I'll decide then."

The conversation went to Rachel and Noah, Noah's broken heart, and Rachel's unwillingness to face the family again.

"Can I ask you another question, Sammie?"

"Shoot."

"You think Mom and Dad are cool with this?"

"Cool with what?"

"With selling. With moving on. Do you think they'd be OK with it?"

"Ahhh . . ." She let the word fade into a sigh.

"I worry about that sometimes," he added.

"Honestly? I wouldn't let it bother you."

"Wouldn't you do the same?"

"Definitely."

"That's helpful, thanks."

"Look, Malcolm, I was ticked off when you told us you'd sold the place—"

"I noticed."

"And did you notice I didn't come around for what—a week?"

"Something like that," he said.

"Then it hit me one day. Dad wouldn't have taken a poll. He would have done what was best for him and Mom. And that's exactly what you did. How can I be angry about that? And you said it that night, right? Am I going to run it? No. Is Noah? No."

Malcolm sat up. "But did I do what's best for me and Rain?"

Samantha also sat up and they faced each other across the bed. "Of course you did."

Malcolm looked out the bedroom window toward the Inn. "I don't know."

"Uh-oh, is my older brother having second thoughts?"

"Not second. More like fifth."

Samantha circled the bed and sat next to him. "It's just cold feet, Mal, that's all."

"Is it? I've started having these weird dreams, sis. These dreams where I wake up every day bored out of my mind with nothing to do. And what if Rain and I don't have anything in common without the Inn? What if we sit at the table every night and just stare at each other? This is all we've known. We've never lived any place but here."

"You're being ridiculous. You know as well as I do that isn't going to happen. If anything you guys will be even *stronger* without this place. This is just a spot on a tourist's map, Mal. You and Rain will be great wherever you end up. You know that."

"I guess. It still feels like a member of the family is dying, and I don't want to say good-bye. Is that weird?"

"Not at all. Come on, Mal, you fell in love with Rain on that swing out there. You raised your son here. We're all going to miss it, and if we didn't feel that way there would be something seriously wrong with us."

"You're probably right. It's just gotten tough lately."

Samantha held up a hand and began to count. "Let's see. Number one, you started the summer with an exciting engagement. Number two, your knuckleheaded brother Matthew announces he's lost a small fortune *and* his wife, which would have completely devastated our parents. Number three, you decide to sell the Inn. Number four, your almost-daughter-in-law found out her mother had been lying to her most of her life. Number five, wedding's off and a gargantuan celebration that—thanks to A&P—has completely grown beyond our control is on. That's a busy summer."

"Was that supposed to cheer me up?" Malcolm playfully slapped her hand out of the air.

"Did it work?"

"Not so much."

"How about ice cream?"

"That would help."

They turned off the lights and slowly strolled back to the Inn.

"I love you, Mal."

"I know, sis. And I kinda love you back."

"But you're still a doof."

CHAPTER 36

11 Days to the Celebration

Rachel watched a tape-delayed town hall meeting on C-SPAN and ate takeout from her favorite Indian restaurant.

Noah watched *America's Got Talent* and munched Taco Bell.

She'd spent another day proofing a twelve-page memo on the history of the drug trade in Washington's Anacostia neighborhood.

He'd seen a movie with a roommate, spoken to his mother on the phone for an hour, and worked on a painting of the Shenandoah River A&P had commissioned for no reason other than to keep him busy. Noah sent Rachel a text from his couch.

Noah: tacobell for dinner . . . you?
Rachel: tandoori chicken
Noah: hot date?
Rachel: c-span
Noah: me too!!!

Rachel finished her dinner and replaced the noise of the television with the music of Ingrid Michaelson. She changed into pajamas and lay on the couch, not ready yet for bed but tired from an early morning and a commute home made longer by a broken-down metro car. She propped her head on a throw pillow and hummed along softly to the music.

Noah ate his second Beefy Bean Burrito in one hand and held his cell phone in the other. He laughed out loud as a comedian in her eighties made jokes about NASCAR and monkey space travel.

Noah: AGT funny tonight!!!
Rachel: Zzzzzz tired
Noah: go on txt date?
Rachel: short one :)
Noah: what time u have to b home?
Rachel: :)

Rachel and Noah had continued to see one another since the *incident,* as Noah half-jokingly called it in order to cope with his daily painful reruns. But the dates had been much less frequent and much more awkward than a couple in love should expect. Rachel missed him—she couldn't deny that—but she didn't miss the roller coaster of planning a wedding with people she hardly knew in a town in the middle of nowhere to someone she hadn't known very long.

With the lights dimmed and Ingrid singing in the background, it was easy for Rachel's mind to wander to less murky memories. Mountain biking alone in West Virginia. Her first day in an exclusive private school outside Denver. Sightseeing in Athens as a twelve-year-old.

As he often did, Daniel had brought Stephanie and Rachel on an extended business trip during the middle of the school year on the promise his stepdaughter would get assignments from school before leaving and work on them as they traveled. She always did what was given her and more. While Daniel spent his days wooing a prospective high-dollar trade client, mother and daughter would enjoy a private tour arranged by the concierge at their four-star hotel. They took pictures at Hadrian's Arch and the Roman Forum. They ate lunch near the Theater of Dionysus and walked the ancient cemetery of Kerameikos. Over a decade later Rachel still remembered the awe she felt at the archeological site.

Noah: what you thinking about right now?
Rachel: Traveling.
Noah: where?
Rachel: Greece.
Noah: when?
Rachel: Long long time ago w/mother and Daniel.
Rachel: What are you thinking about?
Noah: you
Rachel: :)

Rachel rolled to her side and picked up her stuffed squirrel from the coffee table. She remembered the day it had arrived with her repaired bike and brand-new Oakleys to replace the pair broken in the accident. She pinched the squirrel's fat cheeks and smiled. No one had ever gone to such lengths for her and she wondered how different things might have gone during the summer if Noah had simply written a check for a new bike and disappeared. "You know how much drama you created, chubby?" she said to the squirrel.

Noah also wondered how differently his summer would have unfolded. The thought crossed his mind every single day as the *Good-bye to Domus Jefferson* celebration neared. He toggled the menu on his phone and flipped through photos of Rachel on the National Mall, both of them at the Newseum, at Arlington National Cemetery, and sitting on the swing in the backyard that he would soon bid farewell to forever.

He imagined life without the accident, without the initial trip with Rachel to Woodstock when she first fell in love with the valley, and, he suspected, with him. He hoped she regretted none of it—not the engagement, not the friendships. Not even learning the truth about her past.

> Noah: I miss us
> Rachel: You mean usa?
> Noah: no a, just us ;)
> Rachel: Not fair to the a :)
> Noah: I miss you and me, better???
> Rachel: :)
> Noah: talk to your mom?
> Rachel: Not yet
> Noah: :(

Rachel knew she needed to reconnect eventually. She couldn't live her life forever without her mother in it, and she feared what might happen if Stephanie were left alone for too long. Her mother's friend, Arianna, had even left a voice mail begging her to call her mother back. Rachel wiped the face of her Blackberry on her pajama top and committed to herself once again to make the call home and take the first step, no matter how painful it might be.

The phone chimed again as she gave extra attention to a makeup smudge on the screen.

Tyler: Hey
Rachel: Hey back
Tyler: Plans tomorrow after work?
Rachel: Not sure
Tyler: Make some with me?
Rachel: What?
Tyler: Dinner, dancing
Tyler: Hello?
Tyler: You in a tunnel?
Rachel: Maybe
Tyler: Maybe in a tunnel or maybe to plans with me?
Rachel: See you at work :) I'm tired. Long day
Tyler: I'm patient ;)

Rachel deleted the messages immediately and began scrolling through her missed calls. She felt guilty. Guilty that she hadn't shut down Tyler's increasing interest in her, guilty that she wasn't sure if she wanted to, guilty that she'd avoided her mother but had taken several calls from Daniel and twice found flowers on her doorstep after work. She and Daniel had promised to share a meal together again and resume their conversation on his next trip through town. He was in a constant state of apology about deceiving her. Rachel looked around her apartment and was reminded that Daniel had furnished virtually everything she owned. She made another commitment that one day she'd have the money to replace his generosity with items of her own.

> Noah: heard from a&p?
> Rachel: Yes
> Noah: me too. almost every day now
> Rachel: She has a crush? ;)
> Noah: who doesn't?

Rachel rolled to her back again and readjusted the pillow. As she had many times since learning the truth about her mother and father, Rachel pictured the funeral. *Was he in a plain brown wooden box in a Kansas City cemetery? Was he cremated? Did they look for us? Where is he now? Is there a heaven or hell or someplace in between for people like him who don't know which they are? Or who they are? Is there a place for people who deceive their family, even in love? Is there a place for someone like me?*

> Noah: u there?
> Rachel: Still here
> Noah: what r u thinking?
> Rachel: Not much
> Noah: fibber
> Rachel: :)
> Noah: then ask me
> Rachel: What are you thinking about?

Noah: u
Noah: that I hope one day we're normal again
Rachel: What's normal again?
Noah: normal is me and u . . . as long as we're together
Rachel: That's sweet
Noah: it's true
Rachel: Fun date, off to bed now
Noah: kiss at door?
Rachel: No way!
Noah: xoxo
Noah: too late

CHAPTER 37

7 Days to the Celebration

Rachel? This is Anna Belle Prestwich calling—A&P. Your voice mail must really like me by now because it always picks up. . . . I have my calendar here on my ample lap and I see the big day is getting close and I don't have a commitment from you yet. Are you coming? Please tell me you're coming, dear. I just got a call from the caterer and they need to know immediately whether you're coming. I know, it's very pushy on their part, but they're professionals so I can't argue with them. I promised I would call you and ask—

"Putin! Get off the stove! Sorry, dear, the cat was on the stovetop licking something from the burner. Remind me to scrub that later, would you?

"So the caterer asked me to call you. They really, really want to know if you'll be there and, if the answer is yes, will you be eating the chicken, steak, or fish? We're doing all three. And why not? A day like this doesn't come around that often. It's a good-bye to a home away from home for this old lady and plenty of others.

"Come join us, dear. The past is the past. Noah says you're still speaking to him and messaging and working things out. That's the best news I've heard in such a long time.

"So come to the Inn and celebrate with us. It's the end of a chapter, isn't it? The end of one, the beginning of another. Wedding or no wedding, you're a member of this family now. Everyone who spends a night at *Domus Jefferson* becomes a member of the family, doesn't matter your last name.

"I think Putin is having some type of Cat-heimer's disease—I don't know if there's such a thing—but he is back up on the stovetop licking the same spot of something that he's already cleared off. PUTIN!

"All right, dear. I hope you're still listening. This little celebration is important to a lot of people. I am still hoping your mother and stepfather will join us. Your mother has not returned my calls, but Daniel did and he was very kind. I told him we'd like to meet him and even though he's never been out here, he's still welcome because he's a part of your family and you're a part of ours. If you speak to him, please make sure he knows that I wasn't pulling on his chain or rope or whatever the expression is; the offer is sincere. We would love for him to come. Also tell him I need to know whether it's chicken, steak, or fish.

"I saved the best for last, dear. It's a little surprise I've been holding out. This is my final card up my sleeve. I've spoken to Noah's parents and they agree that if you come, you should get one of the guest rooms in the Inn. How about that, Rachel? My Land-a-Goshen, I pray this voice mail thing is still voice mailing all this.

"It's quite an honor, Rachel. The Inn rooms are being saved for family and the closest loved ones. Noah, Angie and her husband, Matthew—and did I tell you Aunt Allyson is coming from Vegas? A few others, too, and you. You! Everyone else is staying at one of the hotels. I've booked most of the Hampton Inn just in case we have last minute RSVPs who need a place.

"As I've already said, you can come Saturday, Sunday, Monday, even Tuesday. I don't care. Of course, dear, we'd love to have you as long as you can be here. But this has turned into quite an affair; we could put the county fair to shame with this extravaganza. Samantha says she might have to have the sheriff's department handle some traffic congestion on Route 11 because there's not enough parking up by the Inn. Imagine that!

"We have some people who are coming for the entire thing. Steve and Gail at Blue Canoe Crew are putting together a river rafting adventure for Monday. The water will be cold, but we already have some people on the list for it. There will be some people fishing, of course, and I suspect a lot of others will drive up and see the leaves.

"But really Tuesday is the big day and we want you here. Food, games for the younger kids—I've even ordered one of the moon bouncing, space blowup things. Noah wanted one, can you believe it? Yes, you can.

"Oh, and the gazebo is just about done! You must see what Malcolm has done with it. It's about twice as big as he originally thought. You could marry a whole crowd of people in there at once if you wanted to. It's really so lovely sitting on the hill. He's even gone and repainted the swing a fresh clean white so it matches. Those people taking over here have no idea what love and sweat that man is leaving behind.

"Oh, and you will not not *not* believe the letters I have here for you and Noah. You should have the book, Rachel. Maybe one day things might change, or not, but the letters are very touching. There is good advice here. Sound advice from people who love you two kids. Even if you decide it's not right to keep them with the wedding off and all, you should read them once anyway.

"Will we see you? Please call me. Or message text me. I don't much know how to reply to those, but I see them on my phone. Nothing would make this widow happier than seeing you. I know a young man who feels the same way. He misses you. He wants you close whether you're on the trail to the altar or not. . . . I'm sorry, I promised myself . . . Forget it . . .

"Let me leave you with a joke. Knock-knock? You're thinking, *Who's there?* And I say, It's Rachel. You answer back, *Rachel who?* Of course I answer, It's Rachel Kaplan and I'm here to say good-bye to *Domus Jefferson* and eat some lemon chiffon cake. Let me in!

"Even Putin's laughing at that one. Silly cat. . . . Call me, dear. . . . Good-bye."

CHAPTER 38

4 Days to the Celebration

Malcolm set down the sander, closed his eyes, and ran his fingers along the gazebo rail. It was so smooth it felt more like ivory than wood. He blew hard and brushed away the remaining bits of sawdust. He'd sanded and painted the rail once already, but when the paint dried, he'd not been satisfied with what he judged were imperfections. But they were blemishes Rain told him Bob Vila wouldn't have noticed.

The extensive and expensive project had become an escape from the drama of planning something that had traveled a universe beyond what anyone initially envisioned. He told Rain more than once that if it had been anyone but their generous neighbor driving the giant event, he would have pulled the plug long ago.

His creeping doubt about the entire transition made babysitting his pet project even more appealing. The details of the sale, the party, and the transition to their new life were overwhelming at times.

"Ladies and gentlemen," Noah said, holding a digital camcorder in his hand and surprising his father from behind. "We're here in the backyard spying on . . . What's the name of the guy from *Extreme Home Makeover*?"

"Ty Something."

"That's him." Noah turned the camera back on and pointed it at Malcolm. "Here we are with Ty Something, who is working hard on his secret project. How's it going, Ty?"

"Good," Malcolm said without looking up. "You hungry?"

"Why? You buying me lunch after the show?"

"Won't need to," Malcolm said, picking up a paintbrush to repaint the rail. "I'll feed that camera to you."

"And cut," Noah said. "Good stuff."

Malcolm tapped the edge of the paint can with his foot. "Stir that paint, Ed Wood."

Noah did as asked and the men enjoyed a rare conversation without the influence of Rain, A&P, or any of the other self-appointed party planners.

"What are they up to in there this morning?" Malcolm asked.

"Same stuff. Food, talking about getting another tent, finding a new DJ because the other one fell and broke his hand."

"Lucky guy," Malcolm said with a wry smile and he dipped his brush in the paint.

"You know, Dad, when Rachel called it off and left, and A&P convinced us to go ahead with this thing away, I thought it would be low-key, you know? But really? This is way more work and way bigger than a wedding would have been."

Malcolm moved the brush across the rail as if painting a masterpiece, leaning in close and eyeballing every millimeter. "I could have told you this is how it would end. Your mother, A&P, Samantha, plus your uncle Matt getting involved? It's some weird therapy I think. . . . Toss me that rag."

"Uncle Matt does seem really excited about the whole thing."

"Helping makes him feel better, I would imagine. But just between us? Your mom and Anna Belle are only letting him feel like he's making any real decisions here. He's just a pawn in their little game." Malcolm got on his knees and dabbed at a spot on the underside of the rail.

Noah sat on the top step of the elevated gazebo and looked back at *Domus Jefferson*. "It's really happening." He said the words more to the air between him and the Inn than to anyone else. "I wonder how many people in history have ever been raised at a B&B. You know? Basically my whole life here. I just wonder . . ."

Malcolm tapped the excess paint from the brush and set it on the paint can lid. "Not many," he said.

"Maybe none."

"Could be."

"I'm like a pioneer, Dad."

Malcolm joined him on the step. "You're something," he said and he loosened the straps on his kneepads and slid them off. "You're a different one, that's for sure."

"Yeah?"

"You don't need me to tell you what a good kid you are."

"Maybe I do." Noah turned the camera back on, turned it around, and held it out in front of them. "I better get this on tape."

Malcolm gave him *the look*.

"Maybe next time," Noah laughed and put the lens cap back on.

Malcolm noticed a spot of wet paint on his thumb and wiped it on Noah's arm. "You sure seem to be doing well, all things considered."

"Am I?" Noah said.

"Look at you. You seem at peace. I can't imagine coping with this so well at your age. I was a wreck in my twenties."

"I guess I hide it better than you." Noah's eyes went to the swing. "It stinks, every day still stinks. But what am I going to do? I just keep on going, you know. Working on my art, doing this thing for A&P, getting ready for the big day here, keeping busy. I think all that helps."

"Good for you. That's why you're a unique kid. This thing would eat a lot of people up."

"Thanks, but you had your heart broken a few times and you survived pretty well, right?"

"Survived, yes. Pretty well? That's up for debate."

"You're here, and the woman you love is right inside there, so I'd say that's doing pretty well."

Malcolm smiled and nodded slowly. "But it was close. I think back on how I almost lost your mother. What a fool I was. A few things go differently and I'm not here today. And neither is she. And neither are *you*."

"You don't think it was meant to be?"

"Meant to be? I don't believe in *meant to be*."

"Hold up now—you don't think you and Mom were meant to be together?"

Malcolm looked at his son. "I hate to rock your belief system right here and now, but no, I don't."

Noah playfully punched his dad in the leg. "Don't make me turn this thing back on."

Malcolm slid away from Noah and turned his hips to face him. "Let me ask you something. Was I meant to punch Nathan Crescimanno that night he disrespected your mother?"

"Like was it meant to happen?"

Malcolm nodded.

"I guess. He was a jerk and you flattened him. You did what anyone would do."

"But it put me in a world of trouble, didn't it?"

"I guess so."

"I'd say two years in Brazil avoiding the law and not being there for my parents is a world of trouble."

"I guess. But you were there in the right place to defend her. And I'm glad you did."

Malcolm thought a moment. "But I chose to hit him, yes?"

"For sure."

"What if I hadn't? What if I'd walked away, driven your mother home, and begged her not to marry that creep. What if I'd said, *I'll do anything to win you back.*"

"She might have had second thoughts about that loser. Especially after that night."

"Exactly. And we might have been married even sooner."

Noah sat confused before asking, "You have regrets then?"

"Of course I do. I wish things had gone differently. I love Brazil and the memories I made there. And I love your mother. But the choices I made gave me less time with her than I might have had. And it was all so close. Do you know how close she was to marrying that man? How lucky I am she didn't? I almost lost her, son."

"This is what I'm saying, that you guys are meant to be together."

"No, we were not *meant* to be together. It looks that way now, and I love her with all my heart—I am thankful every day she's mine—but we *made* it happen. We worked and worked and fought through tough times when other people might have given up."

Noah looked away again. "Huh, you're seriously killing romance for me, Dad."

Malcolm stood, stepped off the gazebo, and faced his son. "Listen to this, Noah. I know it's not what they say in the movies, and it's not terribly romantic or poetic. But it's the truth. We don't just fall in love through magic. We don't stay married because the stars align. Those things happen because we *make* them happen. Your mother probably could have found happiness with that guy, even if he was a loser. The truth? He was a decent guy mostly, he just didn't know how to deal with his fear. And I could have married someone else and probably been happy too."

"So why didn't you?"

"Because I *wanted* your mother. I *wanted* to love her. I *wanted* to stay married. I *wanted* to work at it. It wasn't meant to happen like the sun coming up every morning. I *made* it come up."

Noah studied his father's eyes but said nothing.

"May I ask you an honest question, son?"

"Mm-hmm."

"Do you think Rachel will just show up here one day and say *let's get married?*"

"She might."

"Might?"

"If we're *meant* to be, yeah. I think so."

Malcolm put one foot on the step next to Noah and leaned down. "She won't, son."

"You don't know that. When she's ready, she might. She's taking time to sort through everything. Come on, it's been a tough time for her and her mom. Giving her space is the least I can do, right?"

Malcolm leaned down even further. "Do you still love her?"

"Of course I do."

"Do you still want to marry her?"

"More than anything."

"Then go get her. Don't trust that she'll be led back out to the valley by some magic force. Life is a game of inches, Noah. If you blink, if you take too many breaths waiting for the universe to change her mind and deliver her to you on some shooting star, she'll be gone. . . . Trust me, son, I almost lost your mother, and I have luck—in part—to thank for giving me another chance with her. You might not be so lucky."

Noah stood and gazed off. Enough time passed for Malcolm to walk back up into the gazebo, put the lid on the paint, set the brush down, and return to his son's side.

Malcolm put his arm around Noah and said, "Do you want to read something, son?"

Malcolm invited Noah to make himself comfortable inside his office and wait for him.

Noah slouched on the couch and let the cool air dry the sweat beads on his sideburns. "Bring a drink, Corn Pops," he shouted into the hallway.

Malcolm found Rain and A&P sitting at the smaller table in the kitchen and poring over a list of RSVPs. Malcolm whispered something in Rain's ear and she met the words with a smile, then a kiss. Malcolm grabbed two bags of chips from the counter and two bottles of IBC Root Beer from the refrigerator.

Malcolm had returned to the office and shut the door behind him before Noah had time to wonder what his father was up to. Malcolm handed his son a drink and a bag of chips and retrieved a yellowed envelope from a small box in the bottom drawer of his desk. "Guess how many people have read this letter? Two. Two people. Your mother, who wrote it, and me." Malcolm handed the envelope to his son.

"Uh, I don't know. I shouldn't."

"Yes, you should. Your mother sent me this letter while I was in Brazil running from my life. I didn't open it then. I didn't open it until I came home for Grandma and Grandpa's funeral."

"No way, I can't read this. This is too private."

"It's all right, Noah. Your mother knows. She's always known one day I'd share it with you."

"I don't know." Noah extended the letter back toward his father.

"Noah Cooper, read the letter." Malcolm added *the look* for effect.

✉

September 1, 1987
Dear Malcolm,

It's been over a year since I've heard from you. Truthfully, I know the exact number of days since you left, but admitting that doesn't make me feel proud. If anything, it makes me feel guilty.

I'm writing because I want to thank you for defending me that night at Woody's. It was the most terrifying thing for me. Ever. I don't know what would have happened if you hadn't been there. No, we do know what would have happened, don't we?

Mostly I'm writing to tell you that I miss you.

I want you to know that Nathan and I are engaged and are planning to get married soon. I finally have a ring, even though we haven't set a date yet. Thinking about it, I bet you've heard the news by now from Sammie or your mother. It's really going to happen this time.

I know you don't care for Nathan. And I am aware that Nathan isn't perfect, but is he perfect for me? He might be. He's offering a safe life and a future without fear or uncertainty. That is what I like about him, that is what I've always liked about him.

He doesn't have secrets. No secret past or secret dreams. I know his thoughts and I know where he stands on everything.

But what about you? I have never known for sure. I've only known that we move at different speeds and have wanted different things at different times. You said once we were two ships passing in the night. That's not us at all. We're not passing in the night; we're in different oceans.

Malcolm, I wish I knew what you were doing at this very moment. Instead I can only imagine your days in Brazil writing and traveling. You're making friends with everyone because that's what you are so good at. You're speaking the language like a native by now. I imagine your hair is long because your sister isn't pestering you to cut it. Am I right?

I know where you are. But where is your heart? Do you think of me? Do you wonder about the "what if" questions that I think of every day? Are you afraid?

Or have you met someone who has given themselves to you in ways I would not yet. Are you in love?

Sometimes I look at the sky and wonder what time it is where you are. I like to imagine that you wake up wishing you hadn't run off.

Why? Why did you run off? Was it me? Was it Nathan? Was it the fight? Or was it just time to do something new and exciting and be somewhere exotic far from this boring life in the valley?

Are you ever coming home?

I am going to finish this letter and rush to seal it and send it with your mother's care package. Please use the phone she's sending. Call her, please. She worries about you constantly.

Am I being unfaithful by writing this letter? I'm not even going to reread it because I don't want to lose my nerve.

Malcolm, I still love you. I know that's wrong to say because I love Nathan, too. Truthfully I have no idea what will happen in the months ahead, but I know I will wonder every minute if you're coming back. If you don't come back I will marry Nathan and make a good life. I know I can.

But what would life be like with you? I won't know if you're in Brazil and I'm in Woodstock and in between us are miles and miles of questions and doubts.

I've seen you fight. I watched you fight in high school when you thought it was the only way to right a wrong. I've seen you fight because it was the only way you knew how to express yourself.

Come fight one more time, Malcolm. Not with your fists. Not with anger. Come fight with your heart. Walk to my door and tell me you and I can make a life, too, but a better one. A scary, amazing, unknown life. An adventurous life.

Maybe nothing changes. Maybe you stride back into town and our futures remain unchanged.

But maybe we make it work. Maybe your heart wins. Maybe my heart wins, too.

> *Waiting,*
> *Rain*

CHAPTER 39

3 Days to the Celebration

When Angela and Jake said they hoped to save money and avoid getting a rental car from Dulles Airport, A&P insisted on picking them up and loaning them a car to drive while in town. "The break away will do me good," she told Samantha and Shawn. "Please let me do this. I'll get them safely home." Then she snickered, "And I'll try not to eat that little granddaughter of yours."

They relented and Samantha used the unexpected downtime to kidnap Rain for some long-overdue fun with her sister-in-law. "No planning this morning. No phone calls. None of that. If you say the words *hors d'oeuvre* or *guest list* I'll arrest you and lock you in the county jail until Tuesday morning."

After the ladies disappeared from the Inn for a Saturday morning adventure, Shawn apologized for his hectic work schedule and volunteered to help Malcolm finish the gazebo. All that was left was the cupola, and Malcolm appreciated another set of hands. While the two men worked and shared stupid jokes their wives wouldn't appreciate, the Inn's new owners pulled up and surprised them with a visit to check on the property and the transition.

Mr. Van Dam took pictures of the gazebo and quizzed Malcolm about the value of the materials and potential uses. Across the grounds, his wife walked alone and enjoyed the comfortable fall valley air. They stayed an hour and left when Malcolm said he and his brother-in-law needed to run into town for supplies.

"You're coming Tuesday?" Malcolm said as he shook Mr. Van Dam's hand.

"We'll be here," Mr. Van Dam said. "It's a valuable opportunity to let people know the good-bye is for your family, not the Inn."

Malcolm bit his tongue, wished them well, and followed them down the driveway in his pickup truck.

"Supplies?" Shawn asked as Malcolm pulled onto Route 11.

"Slurpees."

Noah spent Saturday morning writing and rewriting his first letter to Rachel. Finding the right words was difficult when his mind was trained to think in colorful images, not verbs and nouns. When the words failed him, he took breaks to put finishing touches on the painting A&P was expecting to be presented on Tuesday.

In the early afternoon he walked with a notepad to the Giant Food on Braddock Road. He sat on the curb in the back of the lot near the fading white spray-painted *X* where he'd proposed to Rachel, his back brushing lightly against a boxwood bush. He wrote another draft, read it back silently, then read it back out loud. He walked into the grocery store for a Kit Kat and a Sierra Mist. He tossed the note in the trash as he left the store and returned to the curb to once again attempt to write what his mind so clearly saw.

Rachel wanted nothing out of her Saturday except to stay busy. She cleaned her apartment, did laundry, and answered half a dozen work e-mails, all before lunch. She checked her Facebook account, which she hadn't touched in weeks, and smiled that it still showed her relationship status as *Engaged* to Noah Cooper. She left it unchanged, wished one of her very first roommates a *Happy Birthday,* and logged off.

She ate a small sandwich and an apple and packed a snack for later in the afternoon. Then she set off for a long ride along the C&O Canal bike path. She rode all the way to Great Falls, soaking in the colors of the changing leaves along the trail, feeling the wind burn her cheeks and the hills burn her legs. She considered calling Noah and having him come to the rescue and save her the long ride home. But the idea of returning on her own and collapsing on her couch, completely spent, having given herself an entire day independent of the world and dependent on no one, was simply too appealing to ignore.

This is my day, she thought.

She sat on the river overlook and marveled at the view. Other bikers and hikers came and went. Some offered a friendly hello and Rachel returned the greeting with a warm smile that felt natural and genuine. The forced politeness and mandated professionalism of her daily routine didn't apply. She hadn't felt so at ease and powerful in a long time.

An old-fashioned telephone ring startled her. She pulled her Blackberry from her bike pack and checked the caller ID: Mom.

This is my day, she thought again. She pressed a button and watched the screen send the call to voice mail.

She continued watching the screen and waited for the voice mail alert. *This is my day.* But the alert never came. "What are you up to, Mother?"

A gaggle of joggers passed behind her and called out more hellos and good afternoons.

Rachel didn't answer them, and even though she held the phone in her hand with no one on the other end, she heard her mother's voice rushing in the white water below. *We're different; he's different.*

Rachel finished the familiar phrase, "We're better; he's better."

She toggled through her directory and stopped on her mother's name. *Am I ready?* she thought.

Rachel pressed CALL before allowing herself the time to talk herself out of it—again.

"Rachel?"

"Hi, Mom." Rachel could already tell her mother's voice was breaking like the water below in the Potomac.

"Thank you, Rachel."

Rachel took a few breaths as her mother sniffled. "For what?"

"For calling."

She sighed. "You don't need to thank me, Mother. I'm sorry it's taken me so long to talk."

"If I don't need to say thank you," she paused to blow her nose, "then you don't need to apologize."

Rachel stood up and brushed bits of gravel from the back of her Spandex bike shorts. "How have you been?"

"I've been all right," Stephanie said as she stood, stepping away from her recliner and standing in front of her thimble collection. "Daniel visited last week."

Rachel felt her peaceful day of empowerment floating past. "That's nice." She forced the words out as routine demanded.

"He wasn't alone, dear."

"Pardon me?"

"He wasn't alone. He brought someone. A woman."

Rachel moved the phone from one ear to another and moved away from the railing. "He did?"

"Her name is Isabella. She was very sweet."

"I know," Rachel said softly.

"I know you do."

Neither spoke and Rachel paced along the trail, struggling for words.

"Rachel, you might not care to hear this, maybe not, but I'm doing better."

"That's good, Mother."

"I'm getting help again." Stephanie put a hand on her heart, even though she knew Rachel couldn't see it. She gave her daughter a chance to respond, and when she didn't, Stephanie put a finger on the side of her head and continued. "I've needed help . . ."

Rachel remained quiet.

"Sweetheart, I've said I am sorry every day since I saw you last. I've said it as I watch television alone in my bedroom late at night. I've said it to Daniel. To your father. I've said I'm sorry to my friend, Arianna. I even said I'm sorry to the delivery boy from the bagel shop who meets me at the gate. I've said sorry over and over again hoping you'd hear one of them."

Rachel didn't know when it had started, but rain was beginning to drizzle and her shirt was stuck to her back. She protected the phone from the rain as best she could as she removed a poncho from her bike pack.

"You might not be ready to hear one of my sorrys. I know. And I also know you have a lot of other things besides me on your mind. Who knows, maybe I'm not on your mind at all. . . . Daniel told me about you and Noah. I'm sorry for that, too. I'll say it as many times as you need to hear it. If there is one thing I would wish for you, Rachel, it would be for you to have him and leave me. He's a good man from a good family. You don't need my opinion though, do you? You already know what kind of family you could have with them. If you can't hear me now, and if you never ever hear me again, I pray to God you hear that man and how much he loves you. You could have something in your soul forever that I only got to taste. . . . I want that for you."

Rachel sat on the overlook again and rested her forehead against the metal rail, the phone still pressed against her ear under the yellow poncho.

"Rachel, I hear you there. Please hear me: *I'm sorry.* Every day since we left Kansas City, I have been full of regret. I regret not staying and facing whatever would come. I regret not telling you. I regret letting Daniel send those postcards and leading you to believe your father was alive somewhere living out a better life while we did the same. I regret not being the mother you deserved on the day I held you in my arms for the first time and promised you the world. I have not given you the world. I am sorry for that, too."

Rachel's throat was tight and sore from fighting the chokes

and sobs that threatened to escape. She put her hand between the rail and her forehead and felt a raindrop drip down the end of her nose until gravity pulled it to the river below.

"I have asked Daniel to leave me be. He hugged me a final time and left me a final thimble. It has the seven bends of the Shenandoah River hand-painted around it. It's quite special. He has her now to care for, and I will care for myself. That's what I'm doing for myself. A small step . . ."

In her quiet condo two thousand miles away, Stephanie turned her back on her thimble display on the wall. "There isn't much I can give you that you don't already have. But I offer it anyway. You leave me be, too. Go find what I didn't. Go be what I wasn't."

CHAPTER 40

"Running out of nights like this one." Rain rolled over on her pillow and faced her husband. Malcolm was sitting up in bed with his laptop balanced on his knees; the light from the screen was the only thing keeping their bedroom at *Domus Jefferson* from being coal-mine black.

"Not many at all."

Rain put her hand up his T-shirt sleeve and lightly scratched his upper arm. "Isn't it nice, though?"

"Isn't what nice?" Malcolm said but didn't turn away from his work.

"It's a full house," she said. "The Inn is booked to the closets."

Malcolm gave a little snort. "If we had had more nights like this maybe we wouldn't have sold out in the first place."

Rain pushed herself up. "Where did *that* come from?"

Malcolm continued tapping away on his keyboard. "I'm just

frustrated. I've gotten four e-mails from the Van Dams today and I've only answered two. More questions, more ideas, more concerns, more lists, all in the name of due diligence. Well, I've got some due diligence for you, Captain Coast Guard—this place is still mine."

Rain put her hand on the top of Malcolm's laptop and began to shut it, pausing briefly for him to nod his approval. When he did, she closed it and put it to the side. "Wouldn't you rather work out your frustrations on my back instead?"

Malcolm couldn't have objected if he'd wanted to because Rain was already backing into him and pointing to her shoulders. He obliged and kneaded her shoulders with his knuckles before working down the spine.

"This is what we wanted," Rain said. "A fresh start. And we knew from the beginning the family moving in wouldn't be the same as the family moving out. It's like Alex said, we don't get a choice in a market like this."

"I know all that. But now that it's here and it's happening and they're so . . . so not like us, it's hard to get used to."

"Little lower," Rain said, reaching behind her and touching her lower back.

"We were so busy this afternoon I didn't even tell you they came by, did I?"

"Today?"

"When you and Sammie were gone. Shawn was helping

outside and they just pulled up like they own the place already. Walking around, taking pictures, asking questions he's now asking me *again* by e-mail. I know it's not right, or kind, but I'm at the point where I hope they don't show up Tuesday. Maybe they could have a car accident on the way—"

"Malcolm!"

"Nothing serious, just a fender bender, stuck on the road, maybe a broken arm or something."

"You. Are. Terrible." She turned and faced him. "Spin around." They switched places and Rain massaged Malcolm's shoulders. "Just think, in a few weeks we'll be in our new place with our new view of the river. No breakfast to make unless we want it. We could actually go to Candy's or Sun Rise, wouldn't that be nice?"

Malcolm made a sound that could have either been a signal he agreed or a moan that she'd found the right spot on his back.

"There's a lot to miss, but it's a little exciting, too, right? Just us for the first time in our entire marriage. We can travel without making arrangements. We can be gone for more than a night or two. A week in Brazil? Two weeks in Rome? You'll wake up whenever you want to and work on your novel. I'll wake up whenever I want—"

"Which will be an hour before me."

"True. But who cares? I'll read, I'll walk, I'll make a mess and *not* clean it up."

"You? Not clean up?"

"I know, rebellious, right?"

"Mmm, more like a big-time turn-on." He tried to turn and face her with his lips already puckered, but she stopped him with her index finger on his cheek.

"Easy big fella. There will be time for that, too, and without an audience in every room."

"When do we move out again?"

Rain wrapped her arms around him from behind and rested her head on his upper back. "I know it's been a lot—to put it mildly. Between the Inn and Noah, it feels like I haven't had a good night's sleep since spring. But this was right when we made the decision and it's still right."

Malcolm kissed her arm. "I know it is. It just needs to happen already. Sometimes I feel like we're losing someone, like it's Mom or Dad slowly dying and we're saying a long good-bye, you know what I mean? Makes me realize what a blessing it was that my folks went the way they did."

"I know," Rain said, nodding behind him.

"And A&P? I can barely be around her without feeling guilty."

Rain sat up again. "Speaking of A&P, did you see her after she dropped off Angie and Jake?"

Malcolm turned and once again they faced each other. "No,

she didn't even come in. I went to help them in and she was headed out in a hurry."

"Huh. Hope everything's all right," Rain said. "They took forever getting back here."

"I'm sure it's fine." Malcolm moved the laptop to his nightstand and lay down. "That little Taylor is a doll though. Makes me want a grandkid."

Rain slipped under the covers and snuggled up next to him. "Look at you, Mr. Softie."

In the September blackness, Rain mentally ticked through the final preparations for the last two days before the very public good-bye to *Domus Jefferson*. Aunt Allyson, Laurel's younger sister, was due to arrive from Las Vegas. Pastor Robinson, still saddened that the wedding was off, remained committed to attending the revised celebration anyway. He'd also agreed to share some remarks and offer the prayer at the luncheon. Matthew, still managing a divorce and a business-in-flux, would be the last to arrive. Though Monica wouldn't be attending, she had sent a thoughtful e-mail to Rain wishing them well in the new phase of their life.

As the final minutes of the day drained away, Malcolm and Rain snuggled silently in the bed that once belonged to Jack and Laurel Cooper, in the same room that held their final breaths, and in the Inn that since 1968 had held them all together.

CHAPTER 41

2 Days to the Celebration

The second he pulled into the parking lot, Malcolm was grateful he'd warned the pastor. Many of the guests who'd already arrived in town decided to attend Sunday afternoon services in the same Mount Jackson church that had held Jack and Laurel Cooper's funeral on April 17, 1988.

Malcolm sat next to Rain in their usual spot. He thought of the night they buried his parents and of the highly emotional service beforehand. He could still see Uncle Joe, a different man than he'd ever known, standing humbled and brokenhearted at the pulpit.

Rain remembered that night as well, but as the end of her long engagement with Nathan and the beginning of a life she cherished with Malcolm. In between the sweet reminders of all they'd survived together and all the adventures yet to take, she worried about the most minor of details for the celebration bearing down on them.

Noah skipped the service and made a trip to Reagan National Airport to pick up Rachel's mother, Stephanie. She'd agreed to come only the day before, and only on the condition he not tell Rachel she would be there. "If she comes," she'd told him on the phone, "I want her to come for her, or for you, and not because she feels obligated to me."

Noah agreed—reluctantly—to honor her request.

"Mostly," Stephanie added, "I'm coming as much to thank your family as anything. To thank them for bringing me out of the past."

Noah kept his promise. He did, however, tell his parents because he suspected they would want Stephanie to stay at the Inn. He was right, and they reserved one of the guest rooms for her stay. Though he didn't yet know whether Rachel would show, Noah worried that if she did she'd resent not being told in advance. Her unwillingness to commit one way or the other convinced him it was a chance worth taking in order to get Stephanie there. Staying connected to the woman he still prayed would be his mother-in-law, especially amid the uncertainty of his relationship and future with Rachel, was comforting.

On their drive to the valley, Stephanie and Noah talked about everything but the topic that most interested him. He longed to pry for details on Rachel, for any shred of insight into her personality, how she thought, and how those thoughts affected her decisions. Instead they spent mile after mile talking about the Virginia weather, Stephanie's new therapist, and Indian reservation casinos.

Noah was so excited when they stopped in the *Domus Jefferson* driveway that he didn't even think to open Stephanie's door or offer to carry her bags. He sprinted up the walk and took the porch steps two at a time. "Aunt Allyson!"

"Noah! How's my little prophet?" Allyson stood up from the rocking chair on the porch and wrapped her arms around him.

When they separated Noah examined her from head to toe. "You look exactly like you did the last time I saw you. Crazy rhinestone dress. Hat bigger than the sky. Same boots?"

"Same boots? Not even close. These are five hundred dollar Hornback American Gators. I'm a bestseller now; I have to keep up appearances." She hugged him again, even tighter. "I missed you, boy, and Jesus isn't happy about all this going on for you, all this drama, what that girl has done to you. He's not happy at all."

"He's not?"

"No. He told me the other night at bingo." Allyson noticed Stephanie approaching the porch. "Is this her? Is this Rachel?"

"No!" He hadn't meant to sound so offended. "No, this is Rachel's *mother,* Stephanie Kaplan."

Allyson reached out with both arms, oversized charm bracelets dangling from each wrist. She beckoned her in for a hug with a wriggle of the fingers. "Come on now."

As they hugged, something Stephanie was no more comfortable

with on this trip than her last, Allyson said, "You're too young to be a mother with a child that old. Look at you. You're just gorgeous. You're model gorgeous. You're Zsa Zsa gorgeous."

"Thank you. No one has said that in . . . I don't remember when."

"Then you, my new sister, are hanging around idiots." Allyson removed her hat and fussed with her hair. Stephanie's brow furrowed at the sight of the thick, bright pink stripes in Allyson's otherwise dark hair. "What are we going to do with that daughter of yours? I've heard so much about her. Does she know what she's got here? This boy is magic."

"Alrighty then," Noah said, raising a hand. "Why don't we head inside?"

"And," Allyson continued, "I've heard all about you, too."

"You have?" Worry frosted Stephanie's voice.

"Not *all* about you," Noah assured her as he quickly ushered them through the door.

Inside the Inn Malcolm, Rain, and the others greeted Stephanie warmly, as if no one knew the past or worried about the future. "Our home is your home for the next few days, all right, Stephanie?" Rain meant every word.

Over an early dinner, Allyson shared with her customary dramatic flair a round of stories about her campaign for president of the HOA in her planned retirement community. "I trampled the guy. Tripled his vote count."

Malcolm gestured at her with a fork full of country-fried steak. "How many votes were cast?"

"Couple hundred. Final tally was 129 to 39. Beat some retired baseball player—old guy never saw it coming. I printed campaign posters, hosted free breakfasts, did stand-up routines in the community center. I crushed Spencer. *Spencer, Spencer,*" she said, mocking his name. "What's worse than Spencer? And his goofy nicknames. They call him Deezer or Weezer or some nonsense like that. Who runs for HOA president with a name like that? Nice guy, but no match for all this." She extended her arms and shook her newly enhanced chest. The room erupted in laughter. "Yes, I've had some work done. Not bad, am I right or am I right?"

After dessert Noah excused himself for his return to the city.

"You sure you can't stay?" his mother asked.

"Wish I could. I've got to pick up A&P's painting tomorrow at the frame shop. I'll be back in time though. I wouldn't miss a second." He didn't add the much more pressing detail: he still had a letter he needed to deliver to Rachel.

Stephanie was the first to retire for the evening. She thanked everyone for welcoming her back and including her in their excitement. "I don't know how my story will end," she said, standing in the doorway, "but I'm thankful for you." There was more she'd wanted to say, but fatigue—emotional and physical—won the moment and she gracefully withdrew for the night.

Later, during a heated game of rummy in the living room, Allyson asked why she hadn't yet seen A&P.

"We haven't seen her much either," Rain said. "She's probably preoccupied with arrangements for the next few days. You wouldn't believe how much she's poured herself into this."

"Sure I would," Allyson said. "She's a Cooper at heart."

They exchanged stories and memories for another hour. Allyson learned for the first time about Matthew's troubles and promised half-in-jest to "beat him down" when he arrived for the festivities. Rain and Malcolm learned that interest in Allyson's stand-up act had skyrocketed with the success of her memoir. "I'm doing two nights a week at a club on Fremont Street."

More stories followed, then some laughs and a few tears from Allyson. When Malcolm couldn't keep his eyes open any longer, he bid a tired good night.

Alone as midnight neared, Rain retrieved one of Noah and Rachel's two books full of letters and shared it with Allyson.

They sat close on the couch and together read the notes of congratulations, poignant advice, and humorous accounts of honeymoons and anniversaries from some people they knew and many they didn't.

Allyson wished someone had done the same for her when she married her fourth and final husband.

Rain wished one day they'd become real Wedding Letters, not just thoughtful words on pretty stationery.

CHAPTER 42

1 Day to the Celebration

onday morning began with a flurry of activity on the grounds of *Domus Jefferson* unlike anything it had ever seen. Huge white reception tents were erected and flowers from two local flower shops began arriving. A&P had shipped in roses from Colombia and pounds of chocolate from Sweden. Both filled the air with smells that would intoxicate the crustiest of curmudgeons.

Rain made breakfast for those staying at the Inn and lingered over the cleanup longer than she ever had. The weight of the week and the emotional farewell was more bittersweet than anything she'd ever experienced. She told Malcolm she'd prayed and cried more than she had since she'd buried her own father in 1975.

A company from Winchester delivered two inflatable moon bounce castles and set them up on the side of the house opposite the tents and gazebo. Another company delivered two port-a-potties, and a sign maker strung a banner by the road that would have been visible from Rachel's apartment in Fairfax.

The caterer delivered boxed lunches for that afternoon and filled five wooden barrels with ice and hundreds of bottles of bottled water and soda. Another crew began setting up for a light dinner to be served that evening for those already in town for Tuesday's official good-bye.

The DJ set up a sound system and showed Malcolm how to operate it in case he wanted to use it before the celebration day. He also installed a portable all-weather dance floor and small platform stage. Malcolm almost choked when he signed the invoice and reminded himself A&P was covering many of the expenses.

Guests who'd been staying at the three local hotels began arriving and catching up with the Coopers. Some of the men carpooled to the river to fish; others, including some of their wives, formed foursomes and went to Shenvalee Country Club for a round of golf. Those remaining at the Inn fought for the chance to hold Baby Taylor.

Several of the visitors asked Rain what to do with their Wedding Letters. A&P had encouraged them to mail the letters or bring them to the party, but she was nowhere to be found. Rain tried her cell phone and again worried aloud to Malcolm that something was wrong.

"She's been a fixture here for weeks, but the last couple days I've seen her for maybe ten minutes—that doesn't worry you?"

Malcolm shook his head. "Stop worrying. She's up to her

eyeballs with stuff. I bet you anything she's just taking a deep breath before tomorrow."

"I hope so."

What Malcolm didn't mention was that he'd seen their family attorney, Alex Palmer, pulling out of A&P's driveway earlier that morning. He reminded himself he wasn't worried because she was also a longtime client of Alex's.

Besides, he thought, *she promised not to meddle.*

"Still on for a mid-afternoon date?" he asked Rain.

"You sure we have time?"

"We have all the time we want. It's our party."

"You're cute," Rain said, then she patted his cheek and kissed him. "It's not *our* party. It's A&P's and my party. You know how these things work."

"Yeah, yeah, so the date?"

"I suppose."

"Pick you up later? All right?"

"Right as Rain."

Malcolm put Angela in charge of the Inn at 3:00 P.M. "Back soon, keep everyone happy, OK?" Then he and Rain slipped out the back door, into his truck, and down the driveway. They rode through Woodstock and waved at a pack of old friends in town for the celebration who were on a walking tour of downtown. They waved back, and the couple continued down Main Street.

He took her exactly where she'd predicted he would: The Woodstock Tower. Malcolm stood behind her atop the metal platform and wrapped his arms around her waist.

"How many times have we been up here?" Malcolm asked.

"Oh, wow, I don't know—a lot. More than I could count."

"Exactly. More than we could count. They all blend together, don't they?"

"Uh-huh." She leaned into his chest and put her arms on top of his.

"But some stand out. The night you rescued me from myself after I found out about Mom and Dad. The time on Noah's birthday when I told it all to him for the first time. The day after you had your last miscarriage."

She nodded and he felt her exhale.

"I want you to remember this one, too."

"How could I not?" Rain said. "Everyone we know is back at the Inn wondering where we are." She pulled lightly on his arm hair.

"They're in good hands. Plus I want you to remember it for another reason." He spun her around. "May I see your ring?"

"Why?"

"May I?"

She twisted it from her finger and handed it to him. He dropped it in his pocket and then dropped to one knee. "Rain Cooper, will you remarry me?" As he said the words, he slipped a stunning diamond ring on her finger.

"What in the world?" She studied the ring and counted the tiny, individual diamonds.

"Let's renew our vows. We've talked about it; why not now?"

Rain was still counting the diamonds and admiring the weight of the broad band. "But we were going to wait until our thirty-year anniversary."

"I know." Malcolm stood and put his hands on her hips. "I know we were. But why? Why wait? We have everyone we know here, plus a lot we don't, all hanging around the Inn right now. Our family is here, the people we love most are all here to say good-bye to *Domus Jefferson.*"

"True."

"*And* there's food and seating for everyone in the county. *And* there's a DJ and a dance floor. *And* we'll even have a pastor tomorrow."

"Also true." Rain smiled.

"Plus I spent a fortune on that ring and built a stupid gazebo. So let's use it. What do you say?"

"When you put it like that," Rain giggled, "how could a girl say no?"

"So that's a yes?"

"Yes, Mr. Malcolm Cooper. I will most definitely remarry you."

"Whew." Malcolm swiped his forehead.

"But don't think for a second you're getting out of a big second honeymoon."

CHAPTER 43

Good-bye to *Domus Jefferson* Celebration

Noah went to bed Monday night praying for one thing: overcast skies. When he woke up in his apartment on the morning of September 27 and looked out the window, he wasn't disappointed. Threatening clouds, no sign of the sun, and a gloomy weather forecast.

He sent a text to Rachel before he'd even climbed out of bed.

Noah: morning!
Rachel: Hey you.
Noah: at work?
Rachel: Home.
Noah: :)
Rachel: What are you up to?
Noah: nothing, why?
Rachel: Team wouldn't let me come in today.
Noah: weird
Noah: everything ok?
Rachel: Boss says I need a day off.

Noah: :)
Noah: i have something for you
Noah: bring it by?
Noah: that ok?
Rachel: Sure. See you soon.

Noah showered, shaved, packed a bag with enough clothes for a few days, and reread his letter to Rachel, rewritten a final time the night before in a booth at IHOP. Before licking and sealing the envelope, he had included a napkin drawing, also created over pecan pancakes and chocolate milk.

With the painting A&P generously commissioned framed, doubled boxed, and loaded in his truck, Noah drove to Rachel's apartment and parked in the closest open visitors' space, almost two full buildings away. He looked in the rearview mirror and checked his hair and teeth. Then he picked up the envelope from the passenger's seat and stepped out of the truck.

The walk to her door felt like a mile hike with a fifty-pound pack. He said hello to a couple leaving their apartment and nodded at a woman getting in her Smart Car. He carried the letter in one hand, wishing he'd thought to bring flowers or another stuffed squirrel as well. At the bottom of the stairs he actually considered leaving again to visit the closest florist. The thought flew away and was replaced by fresh nerves.

He rang the bell and waited so long he wondered if Rachel had left. He rang it again.

Finally the door opened and there stood Rachel in jeans and a T-shirt that read, I TOOK THE PLEDGE.

Noah thrust the letter at her. "Don't say anything, not even hello. Just stand there for a second." He marveled at how beautiful she was even without makeup, even wearing something she'd yanked from the drier. He tried not to count how many times he'd missed seeing her in recent weeks.

"Read this. Not now, not until I'm gone. But read it. It's not long. It's my first Monday Letter. Whether I see you later today or not, I'm going to write you one next Monday, too. And the Monday after that. Writing is not as easy for me, and maybe it's silly and childish, but here it is. It's a start. It's *my* start."

She held the envelope in her hands and turned it over and over again.

Noah looked into her eyes and craved a moment like all those he'd seen in the romantic comedies she'd made him sit through or like a scene in one of her guilty-pleasure novels. He wanted to pull her into his arms and kiss her, or for her to do the same to him.

Neither did. Instead he pointed at the letter and said simply, "Read the letter. Check the weather." Then he spun on his heel and dashed down the stairs before his heart could win an argument with reason.

Rachel whispered a good-bye, shut the door, and sat at her kitchen table.

✉

September 26, 2011

Dear Rachel,

    I've lost count which draft this is. Let's just say there have been a lot. Some long. Some short. All of them lame. Until now, right? If you're reading this then I've decided it's finally worth giving to you.

    For a long time after you called us off, or called off the wedding, or postponed the wedding, or whatever it all was, I tried to put myself in your shoes. I thought I needed to understand what you were going through to know why it was happening. I went from hurt to angry to hurt to confused to depressed and to confused again.

    I know now how useless it all was. I will never know what you've been trying to deal with. I won't. How can I? I feel dumb for thinking I could at all.

    What I should have done is to tell you what my own experience is instead of trying to get inside yours. I told you back at my folks' place that my grandma Laurel had been attacked. Not just assaulted or beaten up. She was raped by a sick man high on drugs. It happened when my grandpa was out of town, and she didn't tell him right away. She was confused, too. And scared. She found out she was pregnant and she had the baby, but she didn't tell Grandpa about the attack for a year. I guess only she knows exactly why.

    I think you figured this, but that baby was my dad. Yes. My dad came of that. The man went to jail and became a pastor. He even came to my grandparents' funeral. But that's another story.

When my dad found all this out, he felt like he didn't know who he was anymore. He and my mom got married, but Dad had it tough for a while. Anyone would. He was depressed and felt guilty for not getting along better with my grandpa when he was alive.

It took time, a lot of time, but my mom and dad got through the worst of it. He started to understand that he didn't have to be anything he didn't want to be. He made his life. Not his history. He told me when I was a kid that history is dangerous if you pay too much attention to it, because tomorrow hasn't happened yet.

Tomorrow hasn't happened yet, Rachel. You decide what happens tomorrow—not your mother, not Daniel, not your biological father, not your boss. Not even me. Just you. You decide what tomorrow's history will look like.

When I set out to write this letter I wanted you to know how perfect we are for each other. I thought you would read this and think God meant for us to find each other in a world of ten billion people. But that's a lie.

You'll find someone else if you want to. Someone special who maybe will treat you better than I do. Someone smarter, someone richer, maybe even someone better looking. (Though I doubt that last one.)

I could do the same thing. I'll start looking at other girls again at some point in time. One of them will catch my eye and maybe *it'll be her, or maybe it'll be the next one, or maybe it'll be after ten more girls that I'll give someone a ring and we'll make a happy life. Just like you did with your life.*

But why? I don't want to settle, even though I could. I don't want you to settle either, even though guys will line up for the chance to be with you. Sure we could be happy with other people, but why?

You're my best friend, and I want to be married to my best friend. I want to argue about how cold the house should be in the summer. I want you to be there when I give my Caldecott acceptance speech. I want to sleep on the couch when you get mad at me for saying something stupid, because trust me, I will say something stupid.

Being together is going to be a lot of work. But it's a job I want. And it's a job I'm qualified for because I love you.

Love is a choice and I choose to love you.

Forgiveness is a choice, too, and we'll need to do a lot of it to make a life work.

How much do I love you?

If you asked me to never paint again, I'd stop.

If you asked me to move to the Arctic, I would.

If you asked me to walk to the ends of the earth for your favorite flavor of ice cream, I'd ask what time you needed me home.

Rachel, you are the same person today that you were the day I met you. Your mother is the same person today as the day she had you, as the day she left Kansas City with you, as the day she met Daniel, as the day she told you the truth. The soul doesn't change, just our understanding of it.

Rachel, nothing about yesterday matters. Even this letter, if I fail to honor it, means nothing down the road. All that matters right now is today. And today I want to marry you.

Go outside and look up. Then imagine where I am, where I'm going, and where I've always been. Whether you see me or not, I'm here.

I love you, Rachel Kaplan.

Noah

CHAPTER 44

A&P started her Tuesday with another meeting with Alex
Palmer and Angela's husband, Jake. She felt guilty that
she hadn't been around to help more during the final hours of
planning for the celebration, but it was obvious Jake and Angela
needed her help more. Still, she couldn't wait for the meeting to
end so she could get across the hill to *Domus Jefferson* and begin
making up for lost time.

She decided to check the mail a final time before taking Noah
and Rachel's third book of Wedding Letters to the Inn. She knew
without Rachel there, the letters wouldn't be celebrated or shared
with the other guests, but this was the day appointed for their
delivery, and she'd convinced Noah he needed to read them and
keep them, at least until it was clear they had no long-term meaning. She'd also committed to him that no matter who he married,
or when or where, she'd do the same thing all over again.

A&P and Putin walked to the mailbox on the edge of Route

11 below her home. She pulled open the creaky metal door and removed half a dozen last-minute additions to the collection. She opened and read them as she walked back up the hill. The first four were from people she'd nudged in the last week to get their letters in on time, just in case. The fifth made her drop the other four to the ground.

She gathered the letters, staggered to the porch, and sat on the steps. Then she read that last letter again to be sure she understood. Across the hill children ran around the Inn playing tag, and she heard their faint laughs and shrieks. Putin crawled onto her lap and licked the envelope.

A&P sat for five minutes, thinking hard. Then she got up, went inside her home, opened the book of letters, slipped the other four into plastic sheet protectors, and reread the fifth yet again.

She called Malcolm but hung up before he answered his cell. Then she called Rain and did the same.

"What do I do?" A&P asked, but Putin didn't answer.

She put the letter in her purse and picked up the book of letters. She ran her finger across the initials and began to walk.

No one with any history at the *Domus Jefferson* could ever recall seeing even half as many cars in the small parking lot. They were jammed in and tripled-parked. Others were parked alongside Route 11, and one of Samantha's deputies worked traffic control.

They came from all directions. Some came because they hoped a wedding might still occur, others came because they'd stayed at the Inn and had become family—a few actually were family—and still others came without any connection to the Inn at all. They came because someone knew someone who said a party was happening with free food, face painting, and dancing.

Malcolm and Rain spent much of the afternoon watching it all from two rockers on the porch. The rockers to their left and right exchanged visitors every now and then as friends wished them well or stopped by to share a favorite story.

Matthew and his son, LJ, arrived, a pleasant surprise not even Matthew had expected until the night before. In a quiet conversation in his office, Matthew confided to Malcolm that he wanted to turn his life around but didn't know where—or how—to start.

Malcolm comforted his brother and encouraged him to seek spiritual help from their longtime family pastor before returning home from the celebration.

Around lunchtime, Noah arrived alone. He gathered the immediate family in the living room of the Inn and presented A&P with her painting. She wept openly at the vivid depiction of her home and the two adults standing off to the side. What Noah hadn't told her was that he'd added Alan, her husband, to the painting at the very last minute. "He's been here all these years anyway," Noah told her. "Might as well be able to see him."

Later Noah and LJ snacked in a corner of the main reception tent and caught up on the news about Rachel, LJ's recent track success, and Monica's business. "Tell Aunt Mon I said hey, would you?" Noah asked him.

Allyson was beckoned to the swing for a long chat with A&P. Allyson shooed away some children who were trying to see how many people they could fit on the bench. The women talked for as long as they could about A&P's decision, and Allyson's opinion was exactly what she'd expected to hear. "Do it."

Malcolm kept watch for the Van Dams and was surprised they hadn't been among the first to arrive. Rain suggested calling to be sure they were all right, and Malcolm considered it for as long as it took him to realize they were low on ice.

Alex Palmer and his wife also came. Malcolm questioned why he'd been meeting with A&P and he responded with a smile, "Sorry, Malcolm. Attorney–client privilege."

While he'd chosen not to attend, Daniel still sent a large bouquet of fall flowers and a card to the Coopers thanking them for taking care of Rachel and Stephanie and wishing them well on their next phase of life. Malcolm made a mental note to write him back after the dust and drama settled and thank him for having done the same thing.

Stephanie mostly stayed away from the chaos, choosing

instead to sit in a camp chair in the distance watching people pose for photos, negotiate turns to hold Baby Taylor, and reconnect with the Coopers. Just like Noah, she checked the driveway more often than she needed to in hopes Rachel would appear.

She didn't. Rachel had received several urgent text messages from Tyler, her best friend at work, asking her to call him back. But with so much to process about the day she'd gone back and forth from dreaming about to dreading, she turned the phone off and buried it in her purse.

At 3:30 P.M. the crowd was called to assemble in front of the gazebo. The wooden padded chairs were filled in seconds and most people were left to stand along the sides and the back. Pastor Robinson took the microphone and asked for reverence.

"Friends of the Coopers. Friends of the church. Friends of the Inn. And friends of our God in Heaven. Welcome to this celebration and to this surprise renewal of wedding vows."

The crowd buzzed with excitement, and Pastor Robinson grinned until the noise fizzled into silence. "This day is special, not because of this family or because of this chance to say good-bye. It is special because like all days, it is a gift from God and we thank Him for it."

"Amen!" someone shouted from the crowd. Other voices echoed it.

"We would be remiss if we did not have a moment of silence to remember Jack and Laurel Cooper who revived and restored and resurrected this spot of land and this historic Inn. God be with them."

Only Baby Taylor could be heard cooing somewhere in the crowd.

"What was once a wedding, today becomes a renewal. Please stand and join me as I present to you Malcolm Cooper and Rain Jesperson Cooper."

From the speakers sitting high atop tripods, the wedding march began. The standing crowd parted and Rain and Malcolm appeared. Rain was dressed in a white blouse and a dark brown, knee-length skirt. Malcolm wore a gray suit, white shirt, and no tie. They walked arm in arm down the aisle and to the head of the gazebo. Malcolm smiled down at Noah who was sitting on the front row between Allyson and A&P. Noah tried but could not smile back.

Pastor Robinson stood on the top stair. "Do you come here today to renew your vows?"

"We do." They said the words exactly as they should have, in unison.

As Pastor Robinson began the ceremony, a car with DC tags pulled halfway up the driveway and onto the grass. Noah craned his neck, hoping to catch a better view, but saw only two men step from the car.

Just latecomers, Noah thought as the men mixed into the standing crowd.

The pastor read a special prayer he'd written and a verse from the New Testament. Then he invited Rain and Malcolm to say their vows. Neither had written any but both spoke eloquently from the heart. Only the first few rows heard them, but those that did knew they would likely never forget the words.

Pastor Robinson offered another short prayer and repeated the all-important question from their wedding over two decades earlier. The answer was the same, and he invited Malcolm to kiss his bride.

As the crowd cheered and the children raced away to resume their games, a sheriff's department SUV pulled into the driveway with its lights flashing. Stephanie felt her heart skip out of her chest.

The SUV didn't stop at the makeshift grass parking lot at the bottom of the hill. Instead it pulled up and parked directly behind the gazebo. One of Samantha's deputies got out of the SUV driver's side and disappeared into the crowd. A moment later another person got out of the other side and retrieved something from the backseat.

Noah rose from his seat. *Rachel.*

She approached the gazebo, carrying a long, black garment bag and an air of confidence.

Noah stayed planted in front of his chair. As Rachel passed in front of the newly remarried couple, Rain couldn't resist grabbing her by the arm and pulling her in for a hug. When they released one another, Rain took the garment bag from Rachel and held it in both arms.

Rachel stepped up and took the cordless microphone from Pastor Robinson.

"Hello everyone," she said.

The stunned crowd replied with a murmur of surprise.

Rachel walked toward Noah and stopped just inches away.

"Are you kidding me?" Noah said with a smile and enough butterflies in his belly they could have lifted him from the ground.

Rachel scanned the first few rows and immediately spotted her mother. "Hi, Mom."

Stephanie waved shyly with one hand and covered her mouth with the other.

Rachel's eyes went back to Noah. "There's no easy way to do this, is there?"

He shook his head.

"And this isn't some scene in a Nick Sparks' movie, is it?"

He smiled and shook his head again.

"I miss you and I love you and I miss you and I want to get married and I'm sorry." The words exploded out much faster and in an entirely different order than she'd rehearsed them on the long drive out.

Noah started to speak but she shushed him loudly into the microphone and the crowd laughed.

"I listened to you, now you listen to me. . . . You are right.

We can find other people. We can probably even find happiness with other people. But I don't want to. I don't want to be the Rachel Kaplan I can be with some other person. I want to be the Rachel Kaplan I can be with you. You hit me that day on my bike for a reason—"

"He's a terrible driver!" Matthew yelled from a few seats away and the crowd laughed again. Samantha, seated next to him, yanked on his ear.

"I don't dispute that." Rachel smiled. "What I do argue and what I will argue until we die—besides how cold we should keep the thermostat during the summer—is that it *was* meant to be. I might be happy somewhere else with someone else, but I don't want to be. I want to be happy with you."

"Are you sure?" Noah said.

"Actually, it's the only thing I'm sure of right now." The crowd began to cheer and Rachel shushed them, too. "Wait, I need to do this. Noah Cooper, will you—"

"No!" Noah took the microphone from her. "I asked you first. Will *you* marry *me?*"

Rachel shouted out a yes that didn't need a microphone to be heard across the grounds at *Domus Jefferson.*

The crowd cheered even louder as family members mobbed the couple. Rachel broke free and found her mother. "We'll need time," she whispered.

Stephanie whispered back, "I know."

Pastor Robinson descended the gazebo stairs and took his turn on the microphone. "I think we have a wedding to perform."

Rain and Stephanie hurried off with Rachel into the Inn to put on the dress and fix her hair. Samantha made a bouquet by pulling flowers from the arrangements scattered around the gazebo and the nearby dining tent. Matthew retrieved two cameras from inside and put Shawn in charge of one of them.

Malcolm dove deep into his upstairs closet and found his father's classic tuxedo that no one had worn in years. "This never fit me quite right," Malcolm told his son as he removed it from the hanger. "I have a feeling you'll be a different story."

Noah was different, indeed, and the tuxedo fit him perfectly. Even his grandfather's faded shoes looked like they'd been custom-made for Noah's feet. "You look just like your grandfather," Malcolm said, pride etched into every single word.

Malcolm, Matthew, and Noah were standing by Pastor Robinson at the bottom of the gazebo stairs when the crowd parted and Rachel floated through it with her mother and soon-to-be mother-in-law trailing.

Noah and Rachel's vows were as unique as the day.

"Rachel, I'm likely going to be a starving artist our entire marriage. I will create books for children that no one's children except for ours might read. I'll mess up more than I should, and I'll never want to live far from this valley. But I will love you more than you've ever been loved and I won't ever let you fall, because I'll be standing next to you."

"Noah, I'm still more broken than whole. My emotions are racing through me and changing directions more often than the wind. I don't know how this ends. I don't know how any of it ends, but I know it ends with you. And that's good enough for me."

Vows were followed by more cheers and a prayer. Then the pastor married them in as few words as possible. Stephanie stood on one side and Noah's parents stood on the other.

"I now pronounce you man and wife," the pastor said. "You may kiss the bride."

As Noah leaned in he whispered in Rachel's ear, "Don't you just love overcast days?"

CHAPTER 45

The crowd began to disperse for food and dancing and no one but Noah noticed another car arrive. This one was a rental and it pulled up onto the grass at the top of the hill, parking just behind the sheriff department's SUV.

A man climbed out of the vehicle and he lingered by the car, as though unsure where to go next.

Noah's attention was pulled from the newcomer when A&P called the family and those interested to gather up front so she could present the new couple with their two books of Wedding Letters and to make an important announcement. Quite a few people moved up to the front rows. Others remained standing but tuned in.

"First, an announcement, if I might," A&P began.

Family and friends nodded and went silent.

"I know that Malcolm and Rain are wondering where the

new owners of the Inn are. I'm sure most of you haven't met them yet and looked forward to meeting them today."

Rain surveyed the crowd for Mr. and Mrs. Van Dam, and Malcolm realized he'd completely forgotten about them.

"Allow me to introduce the *new* owners to you." She pointed at the first row. "Jake, Angie—come up here."

Samantha's eyes opened wide.

"Ladies and gentlemen, *Domus Jefferson* now belongs to Jake, Angie, and Baby Taylor."

Rain was nearly speechless.

Malcolm was not. "How? Anna Belle, you promised me. What did you do?"

"I had *almost* nothing to do with it. My personal attorney, Alex Palmer, presented the Van Dams with another business opportunity that was more attractive."

"More attractive?" Malcolm said. "The sale has already closed." He looked into the crowd for Alex and saw him smile, take his wife's hand, and blend into the crowd spilling out of the tent.

"You closed," A&P said. "You're right. But the Van Dams found something else and sold the Inn to these kids. Happens all the time."

"Happens all the time? How could they afford it?"

A&P fought a smile rather unsuccessfully. "They got a very good price."

"Angie?" Samantha spoke up. "What's going on?"

Angela handed the baby to Rain and put her arm around her husband. "Jake got laid off last month."

Jake nodded confirmation and blushed in embarrassment.

"A&P offered to help, but we couldn't take it. And she'd promised Uncle Malcolm not to get involved. So she—"

"Bent the rules," Malcolm offered.

"And she bought the Van Dams another place that Alex found. A place closer to the city. It was much more expensive, but it had a pool and trails—lots of things they were going to add here anyway. They jumped at it."

"Oh, I bet they did," Malcolm said.

"Mr. Palmer worked it all out. We don't really know all the details, just that we got it for a steal." Angela looked at her husband. "The Inn will be ours."

"But do you *want* it?" Rain asked.

"We do," Jake answered.

"So you're moving here?" Samantha said.

"Can't run it from the Midwest, Mom," Angela said.

"You're going to raise Taylor here?"

The baby cooed on cue and everyone laughed. "Yep. First steps, first words—all of it will happen right here."

Malcolm looked at A&P and shook his head. "You're in so much trouble, Anna Belle."

A&P's eyes were wet and she didn't speak for risk of

blubbering. Instead, she hugged him and listened to him whisper "Thank you" in her ear.

After everyone hugged everyone else, Allyson took a turn and called the group's attention. "You still have the letters, right, A&P?"

"Of course." She handed one book to Rachel and one to Noah. "It's the most letters I've ever seen come in." The couple flipped through the pages, capturing a few names here and there, but knowing there would be plenty of time later to read the letters.

"You'll laugh at these, and you'll certainly cry at these, I promise you. And kids, you will cherish every one forever, I know it."

Noah and Rachel hugged her from each side and after a minute Allyson poked her head into the mass of cheeks. "But isn't there one specific letter, A&P?"

A&P exhaled and pulled the final letter from her purse. "There is."

"Are you going to read it?" Allyson asked.

"My heavens, Ally, yes! Patience!" Normally the Coopers would have chuckled and teased their aunt for her meddling, but curiosity was running too high for anything other than holding their breaths. "If you're happy I'm reading this now instead of just handing it to you later, it was all my idea. If you're angry and wish I'd done it differently, blame your aunt."

Nods all around.

✉

September 21, 2011
Dear Rachel,

I can't believe I'm writing you. I have been looking for you lately. Then, just when I almost gave up, I found you. Was that God working?

I have been wondering how you have been. I have been wondering about your mother. I haven't seen you in so long. I wasn't sure at first if that was you on the web page about your wedding. Your name looked different, but I recognized you in the pictures. You look so beautiful. I am happy you are getting married to the boy on your web page. Noah? He looks like a good man. I hope he makes you happy. Hope he treats you good.

The web page said I could send a letter to the A&P, though it seems strange to send a letter to a store. Well, I can only hope this gets to you.

I have wondered a lot where you and your mother have been. I have also wondered what you did with your life. I am so happy to see what you are.

When your mother left, I was not very surprised. I wondered where you were and I looked for a while. But I gave up looking. I was angry, but I gave up on being angry too.

I bet you and your mother are more happy now than if you had stayed in Kansas City. I was mad you left. But not surprised.

I stayed there for a while and worked that same job. But they fired me. I did not work for a while and I got kicked out of the apartment. I lived in a shelter downtown for a while. But I got in a fight and they kicked me out. I lived in another shelter for a while after.

A while after that I got a job where I was a day worker. I got a job in St. Louis. Then Cleveland. All jobs with the same company. I slept in a trailer on the job site and they never kicked me out. I liked it there.

I am in Detroit now. There are not many jobs here, but I have one. And I like it. I work hard. I live in an apartment.

Rachel, I still get mad sometimes. But I don't get mad that I have not seen you or your mother. I get mad that I gave you a list of reasons to leave.

I am going to try to come to the wedding. I wrote down the date and the address from the web page. And I have some money saved up. I don't have very much. But I have enough, I hope.

If I do not come, will you write me back? If I do come, will you talk to me?

I am very proud of what you are.

> *Sincerely,*
> *Your father*

✉

The gazebo was quiet.

Rachel's eyes hadn't left A&P's since she'd begun to read. She felt as if she'd been swept up in a tornado and dropped back down in a different place and at a different time.

She turned around and faced those remaining within earshot of the post-ceremony drama. Her mother had retaken her seat and seemed to fumble her hands in her lap as though knitting some imaginary blanket. The color had drained from her face.

Rachel looked up and saw an aged man with cowhide-toned skin and tears catching in a thick black-and-gray beard. She made a step toward him.

"Dad?"

Stephanie stood and looked at the man for a flash. Then her eyes fell shut and she watched a slide show on a black wall. She saw a kitchen with peeling linoleum flooring. She saw a tool belt scatter. She saw a screwdriver, a list, a flashlight, Rachel's little face, veins popping, spit, a table leg breaking, another list, a man—her husband—rushing toward her with threatening eyes.

Then came sounds to accompany the images. The screams and curses, breaking glass, a thud, a thud she had heard in her sleep for years, a thud she still heard on too many nights.

She forced her eyes back open, but immediately the light at the edges crowded and pulsed toward the center. The scene shrank into a tiny white dot like an old television powering down. Then her mind powered down, too, and she collapsed to the ground.

A crowd converged, but Malcolm, Rain, and Rachel waved them off and someone soon arrived with a cold washcloth and a bottle of water. Stephanie wasn't out long, but later wouldn't have known whether it was sixty seconds or six hours. After being helped into a sitting position, she insisted on returning to her bedroom inside the Inn. She tried to walk on her own, but when she wobbled and nearly fell again, Malcolm carefully picked her up and carried her in his arms. Rain and Rachel ran ahead, opening and holding doors, and he placed Stephanie on her bed in her second-floor guest room.

Malcolm excused himself to find a doctor, Rain left to freshen the washcloth and to make some tea, and Rachel sat on the edge of the bed, brushing her mother's hair off her clammy forehead.

Her mother's first word after a long period of quiet calm was, "Go."

"What, Mother?"

"Go." Stephanie opened her eyes and patted Rachel's hand. "It's all right. Go."

Rachel kissed her cheek, whispered something so soft not even her mother heard, and turned to leave. She paused at the door and swiveled back to face her mother. "Are you sure?"

"Go, Rachel."

She found him in the crowd between the gazebo and the first row of chairs. She studied the man with the lines in his forehead and the deep, dark, tired eyes. His hair was still thick, though grayness threatened to overtake his temples. His eyebrows were a wiry mix of black and gray.

He took a step from the crowd and met her in the open. "Hi, Rachel."

CHAPTER 46

Y ou're very beautiful." He said the words so quietly they were
almost reverential.

She would have spoken if she could have.

"I hope it is all right that I came today."

Rachel opened her mouth, but closed it when no words came.

The remaining surrounding friends and family began to
withdraw, and soon only Rachel and the man remained. Noah
hovered nearby, unwilling to leave Rachel alone, but knowing she
needed privacy for this reunion.

She had so much to say and every possible combination
of questions and emotions blended in her mind. She offered a
simple, "You're here," but later wouldn't recall it.

"I am," her father said, taking a seat by her. "I'm here. . . .
Where do we start?"

Rachel said nothing.

He smiled at her and felt the sting of not having smiled more.

"I don't remember much about the time you left. I woke up in a hospital. I don't remember which one. I had an accident. During a fight. I went home after a day and you were gone. Both of you were gone. The man—the man next door? I don't remember his name—he said you left after the fight. He told me to leave you alone. He said you had gone away and were not coming back. He said you would not ever come back."

This is my father, she thought, and she couldn't fight the impression that his eyes looked as if life had been unfair and terribly unforgiving.

Rachel pushed out the words with all the air she could spare. "I thought you were dead."

"I guess I was," he said. "But I'm alive now. I am alive."

From the privacy of Malcolm's office inside the Inn, Samantha placed calls to police and legal contacts in Phoenix and Kansas City and shared the news. Later, she and Angela sat inside the gazebo and tried to put into words the colossal page that had turned in their family's history. Neither was successful.

Rachel excused herself and made a call to Daniel. He was both stunned and speechless. As the conversation ended, he made Rachel promise to relay his warmest feelings to Stephanie and to let him know if Rachel needed anything as her new life with Noah began. He also offered the use of any of his properties for a last-minute honeymoon.

Some guests left, but others arrived late for dinner and dancing and were oblivious to the drama of the afternoon. Rumors swirled, and soon not even the Coopers could have distinguished fact from fiction.

Dusk arrived and Rain, Angela, and Aunt Allyson sat scrunched in the swing. The tree branch bent to its limit and the women giggled and chortled. They wondered what Jack and Laurel would have made of the day and wished they'd been there to experience it. Rain was quick to comment that she didn't believe the Coopers had missed a single moment of the good-bye celebration.

Malcolm and a nervous Jake sat inside the Inn, and Malcolm gave Jake a crash course in his new life as the owner of *Domus Jefferson.* "I'll be as close as you want me to be, all right?"

Stephanie remained in her room inside the Inn processing memories and fighting the drift from reality to dreams and back again. A&P sat on the bed next to her doing what she did better than anyone. She listened.

Rachel's father spent much of the evening keeping his distance and wandering the grounds alone. He didn't know what September 28 would bring or whether he'd ever see his small family ever again. Still, he was quite content that if the reunion became nothing more than a moment in their history, another memory for generations to debate, it had been worth it.

Everyone, no matter their role in the latest chapter, wondered if the evening was happening right in front of them or in some blurry world they wouldn't remember when they awoke the next morning. But all were awake; all felt a sense of early resurrection.

As the evening's first cool wind gathered at the river and rolled up the hill and over *Domus Jefferson,* each actor looked up into the fall valley sky and saw exactly what they needed to. Nothing. Not a star to be seen and not a moon to show the way.

No matter—each knew exactly where their loved ones were. And why.

CHAPTER 47

Noah and Rachel spent the late evening in one another's arms in the small two-bedroom cottage Noah had grown up in. In whispers and between kisses they discussed whether to let the drama and weight of the day's events pass by and to share their first intimacy together the next night, in some far-off, exotic location. A place where the humidity wasn't stifling and the bed would be big enough for both of them. But as the minutes rolled by, the whispers fell too shallow and the kisses too deep for anything but what they'd long anticipated.

Soon after, the whispers returned and they wondered aloud whether they would be a king-size- or queen-size-bed couple. They imagined what their first home might look like. They discussed Noah's art, a doctorate for Rachel, and a baby for both.

The pace of conversation slowed and grew more serious. Rachel finally began to share with Noah the weight she'd been carrying alone. She apologized for leaving him on the swing weeks earlier and for processing the greatest emotional stress of her life alone when she didn't have to. Through warm, grateful tears, she promised never to leave him alone on any swing ever again.

Sleep won sometime after midnight and they drifted into dreams.

In the morning they ate a final breakfast with Malcolm, Rain, and the guests at *Domus Jefferson*'s generous dining room table. Angela followed Rain around the kitchen just as Rain had once followed Laurel two decades earlier.

After showers and with fresh clothes on their backs, Noah and Rachel said good-bye to the Coopers and the other guests. Samantha and Shawn stopped by to offer another round of congratulations and good-bye hugs. Neither had stopped smiling since learning Angela, Jake, and especially Baby Taylor would soon be much closer than they had ever dreamed.

Rachel shared a private moment with her mother on the swing. Stephanie remained uneasy and unsure about the days ahead, but promised that when she returned to Phoenix she would take some time for herself. Rachel also made her promise not to drive outside her neighborhood.

Later, as Malcolm loaded Stephanie's things into Rain's car for the long drive to the airport, they noticed A&P rolling and bouncing a wheeled suitcase across the grass from her home to theirs. She said on arrival, "I've always wanted to visit Phoenix. You have room for a friend? Maybe a week?"

Stephanie's mouth said nothing, but her eyes said *yes* and *thank you.*

Rachel and Noah made a stop at the Woodstock Hampton Inn on their way out of town for a short conversation with Rachel's father. Noah stayed in the car while father and daughter met in the lobby for no more than five minutes. When she returned, she carried a slip of paper with an address and phone number.

"What's next?" Noah asked.

"I have no idea."

Rachel knew exactly where they were headed when Noah bypassed the freeway and headed north up Route 11, Old Valley Pike. It didn't take long to snake up the switchbacks and pull off the gravel road at the trailhead to the Woodstock Tower.

The trail was empty on that Wednesday morning, the air thin and refreshing, the sun bright and warm. They climbed the stairs and stepped onto the metal platform. While Rachel leaned against the western railing and counted the seven bends of the Shenandoah River, Noah covertly pulled a black Sharpie from his front pocket and drew something on the floor in the corner.

"What are you doing, Noah Cooper?" Rachel faced him and wagged her finger.

"Just leaving something behind."

Rachel moved closer and crouched down to admire his work. She laughed at the cartoonishly obese squirrel. "Brilliant work," she said. "You're a shoo-in for the Graffiti Caldecott Award."

He put his initials next to the squirrel and tucked the Sharpie back in his pocket. "So where to?"

She put her hands in his jacket. "I don't have a care in the world about where in the world we go."

"Are you sure?"

"Positive."

"Rome? Brazil? Buffalo?"

"Anywhere we can sleep in, read some Wedding Letters, and, if you're lucky . . ."

Noah pretended to look embarrassed and covered his open mouth. "Oh my."

"I'm serious, Mr. Cooper. You pick. Let's go."

"Are you sure? Last chance to vote."

"Will you be wherever we end up?"

He nodded, smiled, and kissed her.

Then, with their lips still touching, she breathed the words, "That's all I need to know."

Tips for Assembling Your Own Wedding Letters Gift

Do you have a friend or family member getting married? Consider these suggestions as you prepare a gift they will cherish for a lifetime.

- A Wedding Letter is a personal note of love, encouragement, and congratulations to a bride, groom, or both as they celebrate their wedding. The letters can be typed, but a handwritten note adds a personal touch that many people prefer.

- Allow plenty of time before the wedding to gather letters. It's never too early to begin your project.

- Take special care to invite friends and family of both the bride and groom to submit their contributions to a Wedding Letters gift. If you only know one side well, consider finding a project partner to solicit and gather letters from the other side. The letters can be joined in the book at any point.

- Whether or not your Wedding Letters gift is a surprise, arrange for the letters to come directly to you, and not to the bride or groom or others who might be busy with other planning responsibilities.

- Suggest to the contributors they write uplifting and hopeful letters, not lengthy lists of do's and don'ts.

- Suggest a deadline for contributions, but be flexible and patient.

- If your budget allows, consider printing and providing custom stationery to those you invite to contribute letters.

- Gather the letters in a three-ring binder and consider safeguarding them with sheet protectors. A leather binder with the couple's names and wedding date engraved on the cover is a personalized and elegant option. Other options include presenting the letters professionally bound in a book or unbound in an attractive gift box.

Don't forget to contribute your own Wedding Letter!

isiting Woodstock and the Shenandoah Valley? Make your first stop the Woodstock Chamber of Commerce, located at 103 South Main Street, and ask for Jason's Special Trivia Question. Answer correctly and there could be a surprise in store for you. Also, be sure to ask for a map of places of interest in *The Wednesday Letters* and *The Wedding Letters*.

Before leaving town, take time to visit some of my favorite places:

Ben's Diner, Woodstock

Blue Canoe Crew, Woodstock

Community Theatre, Woodstock

Edinburg Village Shops

The Farmhouse, Woodstock

Four Star Printing, Woodstock

Historic Shenandoah Valley Courthouse, Woodstock

The Inn at Narrow Passage, Woodstock

Joe's Steakhouse, Woodstock

Katie's Custard, Woodstock

Meems Bottom Bridge, Mt. Jackson

Shenandoah Caverns and the Yellow Barn, New Market

Shenandoah County Fairgrounds, Woodstock

Three French Hens, Woodstock

W. O. Riley Park, Woodstock

Walton & Smoot Pharmacy, Woodstock

Woodstock Café

Woodstock Museum

Woodstock Tower

Woodstock River Bandits Baseball